Embassy Academy: Lethal Queen Bee

Emily Kazmierski

1

Alan Rook

Alan Rook's breath puffed as his feet pounded the sidewalk. Cold sweat coated his skin, making him wince against the frosted air surrounding him. He couldn't stop.

His late night runs had become the only way to control his fear, by shedding it in little droplets that traced the path of the sidewalk. Alan had been out every night for the past week, pushing his body along the same route. The familiarity of each street corner, each stretch between the ornate, ostentatious street lamps soothed his oversensitive nerves. His lungs ached as he wheezed. The muscles in his calves burned, but still he didn't slow.

The fear chased him onward.

Ever since that conversation with his goodie-two-shoes student Adrienne Lewis, he'd known his time at Embassy Academy was coming to an end.

Adrienne's stepsister, Charlotte, he understood. She was a manipulative social climber like him. But Adrienne was different. More honest. Alan had threatened her to keep her mouth shut, and it had worked, but only for a time. Eventually, she would tell someone about his dealings.

And now, with the death of another of his students, he knew it was time to move on.

It wasn't his fault that she had become addicted to amphetamines. That once they didn't give her the highs she craved, she'd pressed him for something more.

He'd denied her. Frankly, Alan deserved a medal for turning down the extra dough he could have gotten by peddling harder substances. It would have been easy, what with being surrounded by rich, entitled brats all day every day.

The dead girl's parents wouldn't see it that way.

They would be looking for justice for their daughter's death, and if they discovered it was him who'd sold her that first baggie of little white pills, well…

Alan would have to be more careful about who he sold to in the future. No more sniveling, snotty politicians' kids, that's for sure. He was sure he could find kids who were attending his next school on scholarship. The ones who were so bent on proving themselves that they'd take the help he offered them in the form of a chemical boost. Ones whose parents were less involved, or who at least held less sway in the current political climate.

He'd already begun looking for openings at other schools. His instinct was to get as far away from Washington, DC as possible, so he'd looked for job openings on the west coast. He'd never lived on that end of the continent, and the thought of waking up within running distance of the ocean was greatly appealing. He could picture himself on the beach in California, eating tacos and getting a suntan. Maybe he could take up skateboarding. Everyone out there skateboarded, didn't they?

An image of the ocean, deep blue and roiling, rose in his mind. Its expanse unfathomable. A reminder that ultimately his actions weren't enough to change the course of history. That his small-time dealings didn't matter in the grand scheme of life. He wasn't one of the villains. Merely an opportunist.

Even though he'd sold a teenage girl some drugs that had led to her downfall, it wasn't really his fault. Besides, she was the one who'd looked for something with "more kick," as she'd phrased it. And she'd gotten it elsewhere.

Blood roared in his ears, filling the silence of the night.

Less than a mile to the school, now. He'd be back in his tiny, stuffy room in less than ten minutes. The promise of a scalding hot shower was the only thing motivating him, making him push his wavering muscles further past the brink.

Far in the distance, lightning flashed. By the looks of it, there was a heavy storm coming.

The ache in Alan's shoulder was punishing, a result of the frigid temperature. His rotator cuff was almost fully healed, but it ached whenever the weather dipped. Anger flared in him. He'd never experienced pain like this before in his life, but one wrong swing in lacrosse practice and he had a debilitating injury. The only good thing about it was that it had made it so much easier to get his hands on product to sell, despite that one incident at physical therapy.

His lungs were burning. Screaming in protest of the punishing run.

He inhaled for a count of four and exhaled for eight. He was the master of his body, not his lungs.

Up ahead, the traffic light turned yellow, then red.

Alan groaned. He'd have to stop, jogging in place at the corner.

He hated that.

His shoe snagged on a raised step in the sidewalk, making him lurch forward toward the curb. Flailing his arms, he righted himself before he could face plant into the asphalt.

His shoe had come untied.

Heart straining loudly in his chest, Alan knelt down to tie

his laces, keeping the traffic lights in his peripheral vision. It was about to turn green. He stood just as the walk signal lit up. Perfect timing.

Alan didn't even bother to look as he jogged into the crosswalk. Rarely were there cars on this street this late at night, since it dead-ended into the academy.

He ignored his buzzing phone. Checking it now would disrupt his mental flow. Bending over, he untied his shoe, pulled the laces tight so they wouldn't come undone again.

A car's headlights slid over him as it sped around the corner.

Alan froze, hunched over in the street, his fight or flight instincts skittering in indecision. Rendering him inert.

The car sped closer. Did they not see him?

Fear crept up Alan's neck, whispering evil thoughts in his head.

It was ludicrous. The driver of that car wasn't aiming for him. Were they?

Blood bubbled in his veins as his heart pumped at double speed.

Yes. They were.

The car lurched toward him. Tires screeched. Burned rubber filled Alan's nostrils. Dropping the laces still gripped in his fingers, Alan lurched forward. His feet obeyed his commands, but it was not soon enough.

Metal met flesh in a crushing blow.

He felt nothing more.

2

Charlotte Cavendish-Holt

Fizzing lightness tingles through my arms and legs. Probably the wine I gulped down a few minutes ago. It's strange. I've never felt the need to break my own rule against drinking, especially in public, but tonight I just couldn't handle it.

Yet another night at a fundraiser for Daddy. Yet another disappointment.

Standing beside him during his speech, my lethal politician's smile firmly in place, would have been a triumph. The assurance that after the debacle that was last semester, Daddy finally sees me as worthy. But yet again he relegated me to the sidelines while Cal stood front and center with that asinine blank expression on his face.

You'd think that once Daddy realized Cal wanted to be an artist, not a politician, he'd look to his next oldest child. But no.

At my elbow, Adrienne stands with a goblet in hand, sipping at her sparkling cider. She's flanked by Mikhail, her shadow and protector, his eyes always alert for possible trouble. After all the drama last semester, Daddy assigned my bodyguard to Adrienne, leaving me free of the pesky tail.

My sister's nose crinkles in pleasure, making me want to burst into indecorous laughter, but I won't. Drawing attention to myself in such a state would not be beneficial for my future career as a politician. No, better to tamp down the bubbling sensation in my belly as best I can. It's not Adrienne's fault Daddy sees her as a potential heir. Adrienne is awesome. She's both incredibly naive and incredibly badass. She's sweet and knows how to bust her butt to get stuff done. Somehow, she managed to figure out who actually killed Na last semester. My stepsister may look like a doe-eyed Bambi with her wide set eyes, but she has guts. Substance. Still, would it kill her to get sick once or twice so she couldn't come to all of Daddy's campaign functions? Maybe then the press would stop gushing over her long enough to notice someone else.

I glance toward where my mom is standing next to Daddy as he talks to one of the senators from California. She meets my eyes, smiling. So she definitely didn't see me sneaking champagne inelegantly in the corner during the speeches.

Really, it was colossally stupid of me to swipe champagne at such a high profile event. The political scene in the U.S. is a battlefield of promising up-and-comers who've been gunned down by scandal before they could even reach the most prestigious offices the country had to offer.

That won't be my fate. I won't allow it.

Next time I feel like wallowing, I'll do it alone in my dorm room. Possibly with a mountain of those giant chocolate chip cookies Adrienne makes.

A giggle escapes me before I can stop it.

Adrienne shoots a concerned look my way, but I shrug her off.

I'm fine.

Still, maybe I should bow out and head back to the academy before someone sees me wobbling over the shiny wood floor of the great room we're in. After all, the speeches and rubbing elbows portions of the night are pretty much over.

All that's left is the dancing, and I don't have a partner.

Stupid, commitment-phobic Kenneth.

Mikhail strides toward us, having completed a perimeter check, and holds out a hand to Adrienne. Flushing from head to toe, she accepts it, and the two of them join the couples currently gliding over the center of the floor.

Across the room, Daddy is grinning as he talks to the Speaker of the House. He looks like the cat that ate the canary. Anger curdles in my stomach, like milk forming chunks once it's gone bad in Cal's mini fridge.

Screw it. I'm having another glass of bubbles.

Downing the last of the champagne in my glass, I lurch toward the nearest member of the wait staff, but my knees falter.

Adrienne spots it from the dance floor. "Are you okay?" she mouths to me.

"I'm fine," I mouth back. Fine, fine, fine. Honestly, that girl doesn't miss much when it comes to the people she cares about. She just wants us all to be okay. Too bad I don't want to be just okay. I want to be great.

The flute in my hand dings as I set it down somewhat sloppily on the nearest, white-cloth draped table, and meander toward Cal, who's slouching in his seat at our now-empty table.

"Hey, can I have your keys? I want some fresh air."

Cal's eyes move over me, and his hand stills over his pocket. "Are you okay?"

"I'm fine."

He leans closer. Sniffs. "Have you been drinking?"

I glare at him. "Don't go all big brother on me. I only had one glass. And I just want to sit in the car with the heat going. It's stifling in here."

"All right." He hands me the keys. "Bring them back in a

few minutes. I want to get out of here as soon as I get this over with."

I glance over my shoulder, wondering what Cal is gesturing at.

Daddy is making his way over to us, and he's got a supreme court justice in his wake. Oh. Judge Hastings. She illustrates children's books in her spare time. Daddy probably thinks she'll persuade Cal that he can be an artist *and* pursue another career.

Glancing between Daddy's practiced smile and Cal, whose slumping further down in the seat as if it'll make him invisible, I can't help but shake my head. Daddy's plan has about as much chance of working as the time Mom put the entire family on the keto diet for a month to curb my penchant for sneaking sweets. As in, zero.

Car keys in hand, I hurry outside before Daddy sees my hot, flushed face, and am blasted by the cold night air. Goosebumps rise on my skin, making me wish I didn't leave my faux fur jacket in the limo. Oh well.

The parking lot is well lit, and I feel powerful walking through the night by myself. No sister. No bodyguard. Only me. Sparks well up in my chest, making my entire being buoyant and invincible. I can handle anything. If this is what drinking does, I may have to break my rule again sometime.

Lightning flashes in the distance, catching my eye. The storm clouds are darker even than the night sky, and the scent of promised rain fills the air. "Hurry up, Char," I tell myself as I march toward Cal's car.

Climbing into the driver's seat is bliss. I haven't driven in so long. Not because I can't, but because it's simply easier to use our driver. Or Mikhail.

I strap in and adjust the mirrors so I can see everything.

Lightning cuts through the sky, much closer this time. The air hangs heavy with moisture. If it isn't raining by the time I get back to school, I'll be shocked.

I've only had one drink, but just in case, I touch one fingertip to my nose, then switch hands, like I've seen people do on television. I can do it perfectly, so I suppose I'm safe to drive.

The radio is blasting and I'm singing at the top of my lungs. It feels amazing, cruising through the clear city streets, alone. I'm almost to the school when something lowers right in front of my face, making me rear back against my seat.

Eeek! A huge, ugly spider hangs from my sun visor.

Biting back another shriek, I reach for the event program I threw down in the passenger seat. Clutching it in one hand, I roll down the window with the other. Icy air whooshes in the window, biting my skin.

With as much force as I can muster, I swipe at the leggy arachnid, hoping to throw it out of the car.

It clings to the paper in my hand, scuttling toward my fingers. I fling it out the window with a shriek. Gross. Ugh, I hate spiders.

The car jerks as it runs over something in the street, jostling me. My knuckles are white on the steering wheel. I swallow, trying to push my heart down from where it's lodged in my throat. What was that? I squint in the rearview mirror. It looks like a… rubber tire? What idiot would leave that in the road?

My heartbeat is erratic as I pull up to the school parking lot and roll to a stop next to the security booth. It acts like a beacon of light in the dark of the gathering storm. From inside the crisp, stone security booth, the night watchman fixes his eyes on me.

"Evening, Miss Cavendish-Holt," he drawls as he hits the button to raise the security arm. "Hurry inside, now. It's going to rain."

"Thank you," I say sweetly, turning on the charm.

I steer the car through the gate just as the clouds open up and start dumping. It's as if the clouds themselves have gathered over the academy to drench the grounds while leaving everything beyond the gate untouched by the winter gale.

"Geez, it's dark," I whisper, clutching the steering wheel. It IS dark. Quiet. Eerie.

I want to get inside pronto.

I step on the gas, making the car pitch toward the large stone steps leading up to the front entry. Yanking the steering wheel to the right, I pull into Cal's assigned parking space, thankful that it's close to the entrance to the dorm. I fumbled around in the darkened interior of the car for Cal's umbrella, but it's not where I told him to put it. "Ugh. Cal." I'm going to have to run for it.

Bracing myself, I fling the car door open and run around the hood, my high heels slipping and sliding over the slick, smooth stones. The rain pelts my bare head and shoulders, flattening my hair and catching in my falsies. Blinking rapidly, I try to clear my vision. A screech rends my lips as my feet threaten to slide out from under me. I have to get inside before Headmistress Morgan sees me. She'll take one look at me and know I've been drinking. Somehow. She's got killer instincts. Plus, that woman never liked me.

A thrill runs up my spine. There are few people who scare me, but Headmistress Morgan's beady eyes are unnerving, at best.

My crushed velvet frock is soaked and clinging to my skin as I slip and slide in an attempt to scurry up the steps and under the protection of the deep, columned entry and through the heavy, carved wooden doors into the dormitory. The foyer is lit by the warm glow of the ornate, brass chandelier.

My heels sink into the rug, and I start to relax. The coast is clear.

"You're back from the senator's fundraising event, I see. And dripping on our priceless Persian rug."

My blood runs cold as a drop of rainwater rolls down the back of my leg to the floor. My spine straightens of its own accord, and my shoulders push back. Swiveling on the balls of my feet, I meet Headmistress Morgan's observant eyes, putting on my politician's smile.

The woman is standing in the mouth of the hallway that leads to the academy building, her form illuminated so that it almost glows in the light of the sconces that line the space at her back.

"Good evening, Headmistress." My voice sounds smooth and carefree, but my legs wobble. No, my entire body. Whether it's from the champagne or the sheets of freezing rain, I don't know.

The older woman doesn't miss the movement. Her eyes scan my face as she frowns slightly. "Do you require assistance, Miss Cavendish-Holt?"

I almost recoil at the bite in her voice. Her words are sympathetic, but her tone is not even close.

The great wooden doors swing open and Cal clomps inside, sopping wet. "Good evening, Headmistress." His eyes meet mine.

"Good evening, Mr. Cavendish-Holt. I trust the event went well?"

"It did. Thanks." Crossing the room, my brother slings an arm over my shoulder. "We'll get out of your way."

We turn to go, but I stop when a firm, cool hand settles on my arm. The hairs on my skin stand on end.

"Miss Cavendish-Holt."

I steel myself and turn to face the headmistress. No doubt she smells the champagne on my breath. I'm dead.

Cal shifts, but doesn't drop his arm from my shoulders. He won't leave me alone. We may not be the closest siblings ever, but we've got each others' backs when it counts.

I will myself to exude the confidence and ease Daddy wears like a crisp suit. "Headmistress."

Headmistress Morgan's eyes glance over Cal before returning to me. "The next time you arrive at this school inebriated, your parents will hear about it." Her expression is haughty and piercing.

It takes everything in me not to squirm. "Yes, ma'am." My words are sure as I shrug off her hand. Taking off my Emily Allison heels, I swing them in my hand as I saunter up the stairs with as much gumption as I can muster. Cal's big feet leave wet shoe prints on the carpet.

Once we're out of sight, we lean back against the wall, awash in the glow of the sconces.

"Thanks for the assist, Cal."

"Any time." He shrugs, the charming facade he'd worn with Headmistress Morgan now discarded, revealing a boy who isn't always comfortable in his own skin. His sharp nose and hollow cheeks are wet from the downpour that continues to roar outside.

"Next time you want to leave an event early, find an excuse to take me with you. Especially if you've had some champagne. You shouldn't have driven home."

I smooth my wet skirt with both hands. "You know I don't drink."

My brother's eyebrow ticks upward.

"Fine. I'll bring you with me next time."

Cal's head bobs. "Go sleep it off, Char." He loafs up the stairs, pulling off his sodden jacket as he moves.

"See you for breakfast?" I call after him.

He lifts a hand without looking back.

I watch him go, once more wondering if Daddy prefers Cal because he's older, or because he's a guy. No, I know that isn't it. Daddy's never given me the impression that he's some anti-feminist meathead. So what is it? No matter the reason, there has to be a way for me to prove I'm deserving of his grooming, of his support after I earn my dual degree in Public Administration and International Relations. Then I can announce my intention to follow him into public service.

I unlock my door, and my eyes fall on the Georgetown University pennant that is tacked to the wall over my bed. It will be enough. It has to be.

Peeling off my bedraggled cocktail dress and underwear, I toss them into my hamper. Usually I would wash my face and brush my teeth, but I'm suddenly so tired it's all I can do to climb into bed.

No longer is the champagne frothing in my veins. Maybe my encounter with the headmistress was enough to sober me up. A deep sigh unfurls from my chest. Tomorrow begins the second semester of my junior year at the academy, and I have to make it count. It's probably the most important semester of high school. My future depends on it.

3

Bright red and blue lights shine behind my lids, waking me up. Groaning, I open my eyes. What is that?

The lights shine in through my wide open curtains, casting a glow in the early morning dawn. Apparently I forgot to close my curtains before I went to sleep.

I focus on the red and blue sheen of the light hitting my walls. Police lights. Oh no.

My chest tightens as if it's being gripped by a vise.

Cal is fine, I tell myself. I saw him last night right here in the dormitory.

The vise tightens.

What if something happened to Adrienne? Images of my sister, unconscious as her bodyguard, Mikhail, pulls Ambassador Sibale off her flicker through my vision. She'd been so pale, her neck criss-crossed with purpling bruises and reddening friction burns. Mikhail had scooped her up in his arms and laid her out on a bed in the next room, carefully brushing a sweaty red curl off her forehead.

I shake my head. Adrienne is fine. She's safe. Mikhail was with her last night.

But I can't shake off the clawed fingers of the unknown.

Pushing the covers off, I ignore my shivering as the cold air hits my bare skin. I get my fluffy white robe out of my armoire and tug it on as I totter to the window, careful to stay hidden behind my curtain. I do not want anyone to see me in this nubby, old thing. I've had it forever, but it's so comfortable I refuse to get rid of it.

Down in the courtyard, my eyes snag on Cal's car. It's parked crookedly in the middle of two spots. I facepalm. Clearly I was more drunk last night than I realized, parking like that. I'll have to move it sooner rather than later, once everyone comes inside for class.

Maybe then I'll be able to figure out why everyone is outside, despite the bone-chilling temperature this morning.

Interspersed between the rows of cars, people are gathered in clumps, whispering and casting wary glances toward the street. Several people in dark uniforms work in the road fifty yards away from the academy. First, a woman pauses near each of the small, numbered plastic markers to take photos. Another moves behind, taking swab samples and bagging them in individual containers.

My eyebrows furrow. Weird. They're working right about where I ran over that tire, their plastic markers a lot like the ones they use in police shows.

Nearby, two men load a large, black bag into the back of an official-looking vehicle. It looks kind of like a body bag, but that can't be right, can it?

I rub the sleep from my eyes and look again.

It's definitely a body bag.

Oh, no.

Dread pools low in my gut. Someone else is dead?

My fingers shake as I pick up my phone and call my stepsister, but I tell myself it's only because it's freezing in here.

No answer.

Another attempt. No response.

Cal's voicemail box is still full.

I dial my best friend, Genevieve, before remembering that

she doesn't get back from Belgium until this afternoon.

I clutch my robe around my throat, studying the crowd more closely. It's a mess of students and faculty, but I don't see my brother or my sister. Fear flickers in my chest. What if ...?

No, I can't think like that. They're safe. They have to be.

My eyes roam over the crowd again, and stall on Ricardo.

Something hot rankles in my belly, making my lips curl. I don't have enemies because if I did, it might affect Daddy's effectiveness as a politician. I won't do anything that jeopardizes his career, and my own by extension. But if I did have a hate list, Ricardo would be at the top.

He must feel my glare, because he glances up toward my window.

I duck behind the curtain, praying he didn't see me. I'd die if he thought I was checking him out. That arrogant playboy doesn't need any encouragement. Why Adrienne is still friends with him, I'll never understand. Yeah, he helped her out last semester, but he's still too much to take.

Hot annoyance gets the better of me, and I glance out again.

Ricardo is still looking in this direction. When he sees me, he gives a flirty finger wave.

I wish I was a snake-headed goddess who could turn him to stone. But unfortunately all my glare does is make him laugh.

Turning away, I stomp across my room and get dressed. That cocky, obnoxious flirt!

But before I do, I try calling Adrienne again. Pick up. Pick up. Pick up!

A knock on my door makes me jump clear out of my skin. "Who is it?" I snap.

"Charlotte, it's me. Adrienne. Can I come in?"

Relief floods through me as I hurry and fling open the

door. "You're all right," I say, throwing my arms around her.

A beat passes as she stands there, shocked. I'm honestly kind of shocked too. This might be the first time I've ever hugged her. I am *not* a hugger.

Adrienne's arms tighten around my back. "I'm fine," she whispers. "I came to check on you. Have you heard?"

I pull away, looking back toward the window, not even self-conscious that she's seen me in my ratty bathrobe. I must really like her, because nobody sees me in this thing. Not even Genevieve.

"Heard what?"

Adrienne closes the door gingerly, and crosses to the glass.

I don't miss the wary expression she sends my way.

"What's going on? Why are you treating my like a skittish animal?"

Adrienne bites her lip, and her face flushes. "It's just that, it's not good, and I don't know how you're going to react. I just want you to be okay." She swallows, and her gaze grows steady on mine. "You haven't been feeling the urge to… you know… buy any pills from Professor Rook recently, have you?"

My eyes widen in surprise. "Is that what this is about? You're worried I'll start taking uppers again? I told you. I'm done with that. Besides, it wasn't like I took them that often anyway."

Adrienne's eyes drop. "Okay, if you say so."

My brow furrows in annoyance. "What does that have to do with what's going on outside? I saw the body bag. Who died? You have to tell me."

Adrienne doesn't tear her eyes away from the scene down in the parking lot as she whispers, "He was hit by a car last night. He died almost instantly."

"He… he's dead?" Surprised sadness builds inside me.

Professor Rook may have been a terrible person, but he didn't deserve to die so abruptly. On its heels, relief seeps in. If Professor Rook is dead, my former bad habit is safe. Aside from the professor, my stepsister is the only one who knows, and she would never rat me out. A wave of guilt hits. What kind of monster am I that I feel relief at another person's demise?

Turning from Adrienne, I watch the scene playing out on the street. Two police officers are standing there, talking. Right where the accident happened.

Adrienne nods. "It was a hit and run. Whoever it was didn't stop. They left him in the middle of the road. He was out there when the storm hit." Her voice breaks, and she covers her mouth to hide the revulsion coursing over her features.

Indignation courses through me. What kind of selfish ignoramus would hit a person with their car and leave them there alone to die?

Wait.

He was killed before the storm hit?

Something in my gut clenches, hardening into dread. It creeps into my chest and curls its sharp, piercing fingers around my heart.

My eyes won't look away from the black car I now understand probably belongs to the morgue. Where they'll take the body to examine it for clues, to see if they can identify the driver who hit Professor Rook. His killer.

I try to gulp down the bile rising in my throat. Rub my fingers along my neck in an effort to slow my pulse. "Do they know what time he was hit?"

Adrienne's auburn curls brush her shoulders as she shakes her head. "I don't know. Before the storm, sometime? They haven't said anything official yet. The police."

But I already know what time it was when Professor Rook was hit. It was 11:17, right before the rain started.

My stomach heaves, but I force it to quell its rocking.

How do I know? Because that discarded tire? It had to be him.

I killed Professor Rook.

4

I am a murderer.

5

Blood roars in my ears, drowning out every sound but my pulsing heart. My stomach won't stop doing summersaults, and I must be turning green because Adrienne is watching me with a sympathetic expression.

"I'm so sorry about this," she says. "You must have been close to him, despite everything, and hearing that he's dead… It's hard."

I don't correct her. Better for her to believe I'm sad over Professor Rook's death than for her to find out I'm the one who killed him. If I tell her, she'll insist I come forward. Admit to what I've done. But if I do that, I'll be arrested. Charged with manslaughter, at least. It wouldn't take much for the police to discover I'd had a drink before I got behind the wheel, which would add another charge to the list.

If it came out that Professor Rook was selling drugs, it would lead to even more questions. If anyone found out I had bought from him, they'd never believe his death was an accident.

I've seen how public opinion can be swayed by journalists after something like this happens. It would only take one article with less-than-flattering wording, and everyone in the country would think I got rid of Professor Rook to cover my tracks. I'd be tried and condemned in the public eye by the end of the hour. Even if by some miracle I wasn't convicted of a crime in a court of law, in the eyes of the public, I'd be guilty. A cold-blooded murderer.

Something like that will follow me for the rest of my life. My privacy, gone. My future at Georgetown, gone. My career in politics, gone. Along with any hope I have of helping our country improve for everyone who lives here.

I can't let that happen.

A muffled buzzing hits the shell of my ear. My phone.

I'm tempted to ignore it, my frazzled nerves making me jittery.

The buzzing doesn't stop, and my sister bends over to retrieve the device from where I left it in my clutch purse last night. Her face blanches when she sees the screen. "It's your mom."

My heart freefalls with a clang into my feet. I cannot talk to my mom right now. She'll know the second she hears my voice that something is wrong. But if I don't answer… She'd be arriving at the school as quickly as it takes to dress and put on her makeup-free makeup look.

Squeezing my eyes shut, I take a deep breath. When I put out a hand, Adrienne drops the phone into my palm. My eyes snap open. "Here I go. Hi, Mom."

"Charlotte! How dare you keep me waiting when something so horrible has happened. I was afraid something had happened to you too. First Na, and now that cute young professor. Are you and your siblings all right? Want me to send a car for you?"

I wince at her words. If she only knew what Professor Rook was really like. Steeling myself, I go into damage control mode. "We're fine, Mom. Adrienne is right here with me. You don't have to send a car."

Adrienne's eyebrows wing upward.

"Honestly, I don't know what to think about that school.

When your father talked me into enrolling the both of you, he assured me that you'd get a first-rate education. That you'd be safe. What with his political aspirations on the horizon, I agreed. But now…" My mom goes on as if she didn't even hear me a minute ago. She's so wound up, it might be that my words aren't penetrating her scared mom adrenaline haze. "It's a good thing you three were still with us at dinner, far away from that mess. That reminds me. You didn't say goodbye before you left. What time was that, exactly?"

My throat goes dry. "Um, you're right. We were definitely still at the event when the professor was… hurt. I don't know what time exactly." Great. Now I'm a murderer and a liar.

Adrienne's eyes narrow. I can almost see the wheels turning in her brain, as if she's trying to figure out what time it was when I left the event. I'm banking on her preoccupation with Mikhail making it impossible. I do not want to have to explain to her what happened.

One look into those wide doe eyes of hers and I'd be marching my cute little butt into the police station to confess.

Mom's voice lowers an octave. "I missed you. Say goodbye next time. And be careful. I swear, if anyone else gets hurt I'm pulling all three of you out and hiring a private tutor. No amount of prestige is worth your safety. Are you sure you're all right? You're not just putting on a brave face?"

My teeth grind together. That's exactly what I'm doing.

"We're fine. Really. If we need anything, we'll call you. Okay?"

Her hesitation rings through the line. She's going to pull us out, right now.

I'm formulating arguments, gearing up for a battle of logic, when she relents. After five more minutes of reassurances, from me to her, she ends the call.

"She sounded pretty worried." Adrienne pulls her gaze away from the scene outside to meet my eyes.

"She'll calm down." I hope. But I can't worry about that now. I've got bigger fish to fry.

Swallowing, I choose a course of action. Professor Rook was not a nice guy. He sold drugs to a bunch of his students, and he was probably sleeping with some of them too. His death isn't a huge loss for our school, or our society at large. In fact, his death is kind of like accidental justice. An act of God, if you will. I didn't mean to kill him—didn't even see him, in fact— but I did everyone a favor. Now he won't be around to prey on more impressionable teenagers. Not that I'm impressionable. I'm definitely not. But still.

Yeah, that's it. It was justice. Inadvertent, but effective.

A slow exhale loosens the space in my chest. I flash my best smile at my sister. "Why don't you go on down to breakfast? I'll meet you there as soon as I'm dressed."

Adrienne watches me for a minute, clearly doubtful, but nods. "Okay, so I'll see you downstairs?"

"I'll be down in a bit."

I hide behind my door and peek around it as Adrienne swings it wide. I'm still not willing to risk anyone else seeing me in my pilly robe.

Mikhail is standing in the hallway waiting for my sister. She smiles up at him, and he does the same before his eyes flick to me. "Are you all right, Miss Cavendish-Holt?"

I pull my robe tighter around my neck. "Really? How many times do I have to ask you—" I cut myself off when I see the glint of amusement in his eyes. He's just calling me that to get a rise out of me. We've trod that ground enough that he knows I prefer to be called by my first name.

Mikhail's low chuckle confirms my suspicions.

"You're impossible."

Catching the slight upturn of my mouth, Mikhail's face flashes a hint of a smile. "It is not the first time you have said that to me."

"Probably won't be the last, either. Go on. I'll catch up."

Adrienne meets my determined look with a nod.

Seemingly satisfied, they leave, with Mikhail putting a hand on the small of Adrienne's back.

I close the door behind them, shaking my head. They are super cute together, but if they aren't careful, they'll be fodder for school gossip for weeks. Frankly, I was floored when Adrienne confessed they intended to date and Daddy actually agreed. Mikhail's military general father must be more important than I realized, or there's no way Daddy would allow it.

I peek out the window again, checking the progress of the investigation in the street. That section of pavement is roped off, but the markers have been removed. In the parking lot, several police officers are talking near their vehicles, but at the wave of a third officer, the crowd begins to disperse.

They thread through the lot, passing by Cal's car.

Cal's car.

My eyes nearly pop out of my head as I press my face to the window, trying in vain to get a look at the front of my brother's car.

If I hit Professor Rook, there's probably blood and guts on the front of it. My stomach lurches again, and I press my hand to my abdomen to will it to stop.

If anyone sees it...

Panic rises in my chest as I scramble to get dressed, checking out the window every few seconds. The police are standing two rows over from where Cal's car is parked, but if they decide to check the cars in the lot, they'll see it.

Crap.

I pull a thick, cable-knit sweater dress over my head, add fleece-lined leggings, and thick socks before shoving my feet into my chunky, vegan leather boots. Ordinarily I'd relish this last day of apparel freedom before I'm required to don my uniform, but I'm too rushed to enjoy the sensation of the soft fabric against my skin.

I slide one of my signature thin metallic headbands into my blond hair; the pressure behind my ears helps me focus. Grabbing my purse, I bolt toward the stairs. I pass another of my would-be nemeses, Gul Abidi, on the way down. Daughter of the Pakistani ambassador, she's talking to Grady Houser, the son of one of the senators from Texas.

"Hey, wait! Did you hear what happened?" Gul's eyes are glittering as she leans toward me to spill the dirt.

I literally cannot stop my eyes from rolling as I reply. "Adrienne told me. Keep it classy, Gul."

She narrows her eyes as I turn to Grady. "When did you get back? I haven't seen you around." He's wearing his usual casual attire—a navy tee emblazoned with a Dallas Cowboys star.

He taps the handle of the rolling suitcase at his side. "Just now. Freak snow storm grounded my plane for two days. Gul's filling me in on what y'all have been up to over the past couple of weeks."

"Great. See you guys later."

Gul's perceptive eyes are hot on my back as I descend past them.

As much as I'd love to dash down the stairs and outside, I can't. Not with Gul watching. I have to remain composed, serene. Ignoring the growing panic in my chest, I keep an even, slow pace. Inside, I'm screaming.

I have to get outside and inspect Cal's car before anyone else does.

The great wooden doors groan as I push them open. They're tight in their frame, swollen from the dampness in the air. They swing closed with a thud as I take the steps carefully, not wanting to slip on the rain-slicked stone.

The medical examiner's vehicle is gone, taking Professor Rook's body with it. But the police are still standing near the scene, talking.

Averting my eyes, I walk casually toward Cal's car, slipping my phone out of my purse. Maybe if they think I'm texting someone, no one will bother me.

I'm almost there. Only one more row of cars to go.

My heart is hammering in my throat as I approach the vehicle. I try not to picture the gruesome sight that likely awaits me, but it's almost impossible. What if there are clumps of hair stuck to the car's grille? What if there's a body-shaped dent in the bumper?

My stomach heaves. I should not have thought about that. Stop it, Char. Get a grip.

I round the nose of my brother's car and, taking a deep breath, I force my eyes to take in the car's front.

It's not as bad as I thought it would be. Maybe the rain washed some of the blood away?

It's not the worst, but it's not good, either. The car's bumper and license plate are dented in, and the hood is pushed in some too.

My jaw clenches. If anyone sees this, they'll know exactly what I did. It's obvious by the damage to the car. And what's worse? There's some kind of tissue in the wheel-wells. I plead with my brain not to think about what it is.

Too late.

I clamp my hand over my mouth to avoid throwing up. Closing my eyes tightly, I take several deep, grounding breaths. I have to do something about this. Right now.

Whirling around, I check the parking lot. There's no one too close by, but the police vehicles are still blocking the entrance gate.

I chew on my lip, thinking. I have to get the car out of the academy lot and to the nearest auto body shop. If I grease the right palms, I can have the car fixed in a couple of days. If Cal asks where his car is, I'll have to come up with something to tell him. He doesn't need to know anything, assuming the damage isn't enough to total the car. If it is, I'm screwed. Thanks to my parents, my allowance is ample, but it's not *that* sizable.

Okay. I have a plan. I can do this.

The crackle of the police radio cuts through the murmurs of the people still standing around in the parking lot. One of the officers ducks into his car, listening to the dispatcher. "Let's go," he calls to his comrades. They get into their cars and drive away, leaving the gate unguarded.

I slump against the side of Cal's car, relieved. I'm not going to have to sneak past them after all. Luck is on my side this morning. Unlike last night.

If I'm going to take Cal's car off campus to have it fixed, it has to be now.

The car unlocks as I step close to the driver's side door. The handle is ice cold when I wrap my fingers around it. Opening it, I toss my purse onto the passenger seat and step one foot inside.

"Well, well, well."

A shudder of distaste runs through me. Please, not now.

He has the absolute worst timing. I pull my foot out of the car. "Ricardo," I say, spinning to face him. "Go away."

His eyebrows rise into his curly auburn hair. "That's no way to treat a friend."

"We are *not* friends."

"Funny, I thought we were."

My fingers clutch the top of the door as my jaw clenches. "What do you want, bottom-dweller?"

The corner of his mouth pulls upward as he leans against the car next to mine, crossing his arms casually over his chest. "Nothing much. Just wanted to see if you've run over any professors lately."

6

My mouth drops open as I register what Ricardo has just said to me. He can't know what I've done. It's not possible. There is no earthly way he can have that information. He was nowhere near the accident last night, right? I snap my mouth shut and slip behind my politician's mask. Play it cool. "Kind of a cruel joke, don't you think? The man just died and you're already joking about his death? Go away, Ricardo. You're not funny."

Ricardo does not go away. He pushes off the vehicle and moves to the front of Cal's car, clucking his tongue as his eyes rove over the apparent damage. Then he doubles back toward me, stopping far too close.

My hair bristles, and firey ire builds in my chest, threatening to spill over. If Ricardo isn't careful, he's going to get burned.

His dark amber eyes flick to mine, his voice low, conspiratorial. "It's not a joke. You and I both know what you did."

My eyes slide over him, from his perfectly coiffed auburn curls to his clay brown skin to his hands slung in his pockets. So smug. So cocky. So not ready to spar with me. "I have no idea what you're talking about. I'm leaving. I suggest you move, unless you want to lose a foot."

Sighing, Ricardo leans even closer.

The urge to shove him away makes my fingers curl tightly against my palms, my perfectly buffed fingernails cutting into my skin.

"You're forgetting that after my latest window-breaking incident just before Christmas vacation, security decided to make me work it off. I've been moonlighting in the surveillance office, watching the feeds of the security cameras all around the academy's perimeter. It's been dull as tombs, until last night. That's when it got interesting." His eyes don't leave mine. Don't even blink.

Crap. I had completely forgotten he was serving in the security office, but I can't let him see his words have affected me. If I deny, deny, deny, he'll drop it. Won't he?

"It sounds to me like you're so bored in there watching those tiny video screens you're starting to hallucinate. Go take a nap."

Ricardo huffs, amused by my sharp, dismissive manner.

How did Genevieve put up with this guy? He irritates every cell in my body.

"Like I said, back up or lose a foot." I swing my car door open wider, forcing Ricardo to take a step away.

"I'll leave, if that's what you want, but before I do, care to tell me if this was an accident, or payback? I know about the drugs."

I can't help it. My eyes widen in shock. Adrienne told him? My jaw clenches as my lips purse. So much for sisterhood.

He must see the look of betrayal that crosses my face, because he shakes his head. "Adrienne didn't have to tell me anything, Char. I'm not a fool."

"Don't call me that. We are not friends, remember?" He knows about me buying drugs from Professor Rook? Double crap. I've been mean enough to him, there's no way he'll keep his mouth shut. It would be payback for all of the eye daggers I've shot in his direction over what he did to Genevieve. After he apologized to Adrienne at the end of last semester, I'd been almost ready to call a truce. But now? I don't think so.

Ricardo rolls his eyes. "Relax. I'm not here to get you in trouble, although I confess watching you squirm is immensely satisfying." The corner of his mouth ticks upward.

My lips bunch in disgust. "You're a pig. I don't know why Adrienne insists on being friends with you."

He shrugs. "I can be charming, if you'd stop looking at me like you'd enjoy slitting my throat. Seems you've got your hands full cleaning up another mess, anyway." He tilts his head toward the dented front of Cal's car.

"Would you shut up and go away? Actually, I take it back. Go tell Adrienne I'll be late for breakfast. I have to run a quick errand." I might as well make him useful if he's going to insist on being around.

Ricardo cants his head to one side. "Please?"

That does it. Ricardo is definitely going to lose a foot. No one would blame me. Even as I think it, I know it's not true. He knows what I did last night. I can't afford to piss him off, even if bending to his request galls me to no end.

"Please," I grind out.

Ricardo gives an exaggerated look of surprise and stumbles backward like I've shoved him. "You actually said it? You must be desperate."

"Ricardo, cher?"

Ricardo goes utterly rigid as the color drains from his face.

I look past him to see a beautiful black woman with hair in long locs, dotted with shimmering brass beads. Large, glossy brown eyes hover over sharp cheekbones and carved, hollow cheeks. I know those cheekbones. My eyes skim back and forth between the woman and my antagonist, who still hasn't moved.

This woman is Ricardo's mother.

I don't know the story, really. I just know that I've never seen her, and the rumor is that Ricardo himself hasn't seen her in years. But if that's true, what is she doing here?

Ricardo's Adam's apple bobs as he swallows, his eyes pleading with me not to leave him alone with her.

Oh, how the tables have turned.

I'm tempted to do exactly that, but something in the tense lines of his body stops me. I may hate Ricardo, but I hate bad parenting even more. I won't abandon him now. I can't.

Stepping up beside him, we present a united front against his mother.

He cuts a glance toward me, all arrogance siphoned from his expression.

"Ricardo, I knew that was you. When you were a baby, your hair came to a fine point at the nape of your neck. I used to trace it with my fingers. It's still there." She looks up at him with a shy smile.

Ricardo doesn't say anything at all. He simply stares at her, not blinking.

Mrs. LaGuerre shifts on her feet, waiting for her son to speak.

He licks his lips, glances at me out of the corner of his eye.

I can't peel my eyes away from this train wreck. I know a guy who needs rescuing when I see it. Smiling, I take charge of the situation. "Mrs. LaGuerre. It's nice to meet you. I'm Charlotte Cavendish-Holt." I hold out a hand, and she shakes it, turning her tentative smile on me.

"Ahh, I've heard a lot about your father. His stance on immigration reform gives me hope that your government isn't completely screwed."

My politician's smile falls into place. This I can handle. "My father would thank you for the compliment, but there is much work to be done. Is there something I can help you with? The administration office is in the building around the corner, if that's what you're looking for."

Mrs. LaGuerre's eyes flick to Ricardo, who hasn't moved. He's staring at her like a boy carved from stone. Waves of apprehension roll off him, buffeting my side like a sandy shore under a ragged tide.

"I was hoping to convince Ricardo to show me the academy's eatery, and maybe grab some breakfast. I'd like to catch up." The hope in her words hangs in the air as the seconds draw out.

When he still doesn't respond, I elbow Ricardo in the side.

Grunting, he seems to give himself a mental shake. "I can't now, Mother. My girlfriend and I are going off campus for breakfast. It's our last day of freedom, before classes start. Have to make the most of it." He wraps an arm around my waist and pulls me closer to him. His fingertips scald me even through my sweater dress.

Wait. What?

I start to splutter, but he gives my side a slight squeeze, as if pleading with me to go along with his ruse. So instead of stomping on his toes and running away, I clench my mouth shut.

Mrs. LaGuerre looks defeated, but she nods her head. "Are you sure? I'd really like to talk to you. I know it's been a long time."

"Like I said. I'm busy." Ricardo is ice cold as he dismisses her. It's kind of impressive, actually. Even I can't muster the courage to talk to Daddy like this.

The woman's eyes are sad as she looks at him, and then nods. "Enjoy your breakfast, but know this. I'll be back tomorrow. I'm not giving up so easily this time."

Ricardo lifts his chin in response, and his mother retreats toward the street, slipping into a black car parked at the curb.

Once it's gone, I peel Ricardo's fingers off me and shove him away. "Don't touch me. And your girlfriend? Dream on, playboy. That's never going to happen."

Ricardo licks his lips. "Thanks. For not saying anything."

His sincerity catches me off guard, and I'm not sure what to say in response. "You're welcome, I guess. But next time you see her, you have to set her straight."

His voice is so low I barely hear it. "If I ever see her again."

Despite my best efforts, I feel sorry for him. I know what it's like to want the attention of an unavailable parent. "You will. Now seriously, get moving. I have to go." I gesture toward the road with the car keys still clutched in my fingers.

"Here." Without asking, he takes my keys and slides into the driver's seat. "Let me help you out. It's the least I can do."

My mouth springs open to argue, but he gestures to the other side. "Just get in the car, Blondie."

Fuming, I walk around the crumpled hood, letting my eyes slide over the damage one more time. What must it have felt like for Professor Rook to be slammed by the wide swath of metal? There wasn't a scream, so he must have been surprised. It must have been so sudden, he had no time to react.

Sliding into the passenger seat, I buckle before clamping my eyes shut.

"Seat warmers? Nice." Ricardo puts the car in reverse and backs out of the space. In a couple of minutes my buns are toasty warm.

It's only a momentary distraction from the thought tornado that's threatening to shred my composure.

Did the professor feel anything? Or did he die instantly?

Would it help to know he didn't experience any pain? The questions burrow down deep inside me, and I know I'll never be able to dig them out and toss them away. I can lie to myself about the rightness of this thing I've done until I'm blue in the face, but I'll never get over it. I killed a man so easily, without even realizing what I'd done. I'll carry this truth with me for the rest of my life. Maybe longer.

Ricardo drives me a few minutes away to an auto body shop tucked into the back of an industrial park. The painted logo on the corrugated metal reads, "Mo's Auto Shop."

I appraise the grungy building before turning in my seat to face Ricardo. "This is your idea of helping? This place looks like it hasn't been cleaned ever."

Ricardo throws an elbow over the steering wheel and chuckles as he meets my eyes. "It's killing you that you're not in the driver's seat, isn't it? Always have to be in control. Do you ever just relax?"

I cross my arms roughly over my chest, and my sweater dress bunches up around my elbows. "None of your business."

He chuckles. "Thought so. Look. You stood by me back there, with my mom. Thanks for that, by the way. Let me help you out with this. Mo's a decent guy. He can fix your car, no questions asked."

I narrow my eyes in suspicion. "Why are you helping me? I've made it abundantly clear that I don't like you."

"No, you hate me, but so what?"

I look over the auto body shop again, and force my features out of a scowl. "Mo, huh?"

"Yeah."

Securing my purse on my shoulder, I nod. "All right. Let's go."

I walk quickly ahead of Ricardo into the building. He may have driven here, but I'm the one in charge. I'm careful as I walk to keep any part of my person from touching the greasy walls. If I get any of the unidentified gunk on my clothes, I'll have to burn them. And this is my favorite sweater dress.

Mo takes one look at my car before announcing that he can have the work done in three days. Two if I'm willing to pay extra.

"How much extra?" Ricardo asks, at the same time as I say, "Done."

Mo nods, wiping his hands with a dingy cloth and tossing it aside. "I'll go print out the work order. Have a seat in the waiting room."

My heart is pumping at top speed as I sit gingerly on the edge of one of the seats in what Mo generously called the waiting room. It's more like a glorified broom closet with faded art prints on the walls and two chairs shoved into not enough space.

I take deep breaths, feeling my diaphragm filling with air. I'm going to get lucky. This is going to be way easier than I thought. Once the car is fixed, I'll be fine. I glance at Ricardo. I still don't understand why he's helping me, but I'm not going to argue about it. At least not right now.

As if sensing my eyes on him, Ricardo lifts his gaze to me, his lashes catching the light from the filmy window.

He studies me for a second, quiet. It makes unease crawl up my spine.

He must decide something, because his lips part. "Can I ask you something? What was it like? You know."

My chest burns. He wants to know what it was like hitting a man with my car? The truth is, I don't really know what to say. It wasn't any worse than running over one of those obnoxious undulations some neighborhoods put in to keep people from driving too fast. My airbags didn't even deploy. Actually, maybe I should have those looked at. They might be faulty.

"I'm not talking about this with you, or anyone for that matter."

He simply shrugs. "Fine with me." He sits back in his chair, drumming his fingers on the armrests. His head lists to one side as his eyebrows rise. Then he leans toward me again. "I've been thinking, why don't we? Fake date, I mean. If my mom is going to be popping up at school and catching me off guard, I could use a buffer. You're so bent on being the center of attention, you'd be good at that."

I'm already shaking my head with displeasure. "First of all, that was rude. I am not that self-centered. And there is no way on earth I'm fake dating you, not even as a buffer for your mom. Adrienne would never believe I agreed to date you after all the crap I gave her last semester. Genevieve would never forgive me, even though she's currently preoccupied with Kita Ryou. Put that thought out of your tiny brain. It's not happening." My fingers pinch the air in front of me to emphasize my words.

Ricardo shrugs. "If you say so. Oh, I almost forgot." He fishes a thumb drive out of his pocket and holds it in the palm of his hand so I can get a good look at it.

"Is this supposed to mean something to me?" I ask, the annoyance clear in my voice.

"It will in a minute. I told you I was working the surveillance desk and saw you get back last night, right?"

I go still. I had completely forgotten about the surveillance video. Ricardo saw it. Who knows who else saw it. And if they put two and two together, which they will, I'll be screwed. My composure starts to crumble. Yanking my headband out of my hair, I smooth the strands down with the mini brush I keep in my purse before sliding the metallic band back into place.

Once I've set the lines of my expression, I level a glare at him. "Are you trying to blackmail me, Ricardo? Because that's low, even for you."

"What? No! Here." He drops it into my waiting fingers and holds both hands up. "I downloaded the video onto this thumb drive, and edited the file on the school's drive so it doesn't show your car getting back. I don't think the security guard will notice it, but the police were on campus this morning asking for the footage. They'll see the skip in the video. It's the best I could do."

I squeeze the thumb drive in my fingers and hold it over the floor, frozen in indecision. Part of me wants to crush the evidence before anyone else can get their hands on it. The other half wants to watch it over and over again, to give my mind more ammunition I can use to pummel myself whenever the guilt starts to fade, to keep the heavy, suffocating pressure in my chest.

Making up my mind, I tuck it into my purse. I'll watch it later. Then I'll destroy it.

Still, the doubt niggles in my mind. I have not been nice to Ricardo. It doesn't make sense that he's giving me this so freely. In my experience, no one at Brat Academy does a favor without expecting something in return. So what does Ricardo want?

If he decided to, he could turn me in to the authorities, and I'd be toast. I smooth down the lumps in my skirt. Maybe I should try to keep him happy. Placate him, somehow. Maybe I should have taken him up on his offer to fake date, just to keep an eye on him, but I can't seem to make myself open my mouth and tell him I'll do it.

Maybe now is the moment my hard-fought plans go up in flames.

7

The cold winter days are lengthening, but it's still dark early. The moon is an orange orb in the sky, caressing the pavement as I run laps around the academy track. I don't dare run outside the grounds, even though, unlike everyone else at school, I'm not worried about there being a repeat of the other night.

My knee is solid as my foot pushes off the sidewalk. Good thing my doctor okayed me to go start exercising over Christmas break. It would kill me if I didn't have a way to burn off some of the excess energy coursing through me.

Lights in the dormitory windows draw my attention. Adrienne invited me to watch a movie with her and Mikhail in the student lounge, but I couldn't sit still. Had to get out.

I've been avoiding Cal all day so I don't have to explain where his car went. It helps that I know him so well I know where he's likely to be at any given time of the day. From there it's simple to stay out of his path. My addiction to knowing the details has proven useful, for sure.

I've also been keeping tabs on Gul, who has spent nearly the entire day filling everyone in about Professor Rook's death as soon as they're in the door. She's single-handedly started a handful of rumors about the professor's death, beginning with the one about him purposely jumping in front of the car that killed him, to his death being a hit ordered by someone who didn't like that he'd been peddling drugs to their special little snowflake kid. So far I haven't heard anything even close to what really happened, but Gul does seem to hear about what goes on in the school before anyone else, and if she gets close to discovering the truth, I need to know about it.

I reach up to pull my knit headband forward over my ears, which are probably bright pink in the frigid air. Doesn't Gul have something better to do than broadcast the academy's seedy underpinnings to everyone? Anything?

Genevieve gave me a big hug when she got back this afternoon, her eyes asking me if I'm okay after what happened to Professor Rook. She knew about my arrangement with him, and her concern was sweet. Once I assured her I was fine, she dropped it. Hence why she's my best friend. She doesn't push when it's clear I don't want to talk about something.

Nervous ripples course through my body. Every minute I expect someone to tell me they know what I did last night. Accuse me of mowing Professor Rook down in revenge. Or maybe in the name of that most primal instinct: self-preservation.

My phone buzzes in my pocket. Probably another text from Cal, asking about his car.

The warmth of my breath puffs upward in amorphous wisps as I round the corner. One more lap will mean three miles. Then I can quit and go inside. It's Monday night, which means Cal has art class across town. He's not on campus, so I won't have to worry about ducking him. If he comes by after class, I'll pretend I'm not in my room. Then I won't have to come up with an explanation until tomorrow.

A paranoid feeling that I'm being watched creeps up my neck, making me look over my shoulder. There's no one outside, but a shadow moves away from one of the lit windows.

Chills run down my spine. It's getting too cold to be out.

The bare branches of the trees lining the track seem to

stretch and twist in the shadows, bending lower. Reaching for me. Their dry, brown stalks yearn to snag my shoulders and ponytail.

I shake myself. Get it together, Char.

Down the track, a car's headlights flare to life, and my eyes widen. Professor Rook gives a devilish grin behind the wheel. *Payback time.* His mouth doesn't move, but his words reverberate clearly in my ears.

The car's engine roars as he guns it. He's coming straight for me.

Blood rushes in my ears as panic rises in my chest. I try to run, pumping my legs, but each step feels like I'm muddling through a snowbank without making any progress.

I push off the rubber track as the car rounds the curve, its horn blaring.

I jolt and sit up in bed, my breath coming in short pants. Cold, sweaty strands of hair are glued to my cheeks and neck.

Exhaling, I try to rein in my breathing. It was just a dream.

I watched the surveillance video right before I fell asleep. Watched as Cal's car crept into the academy parking lot with its front bumper dented. That and the time stamp on it are damning, despite the fact that the accident isn't in the video. It was too far down the street. That fact didn't stop my subconscious from torturing me with that nightmare.

Closing my eyes, I flop back on my pillow, jabbing two fingers into the side of my throat to check my pulse. It's racing. I have to get a grip or I'll slip up, and someone will find out what I did.

Professor Rook was a drug dealer. He deserved justice. That's what I gave him.

But even as I think these words, I know they're not true. Justice and vigilantism are not the same. Even when it's unintended. What am I going to do?

On my desk, my phone is vibrating. Cal's persistence is surprising. He's not usually so driven.

The noise stops and my muscles relax. I stare at the ceiling, hoping that when I close my eyes again, that oncoming car will be gone, back to the pits of my subconscious where it belongs. Then my phone starts up again.

Swiping it into my hand, I peer at the screen. My stomach bottoms out. It's not Cal. It's my ex-boyfriend, Kenneth.

I rub my eyes with my free hand, debating whether or not to answer. Why is Kenneth calling me at two in the morning? The jerk broke up with me, after all. He wasn't looking for commitment, he said, and no matter how much I argued that I was fine with dating casually, he didn't believe me. His feigned sympathetic smile flits through my mind, like he knew I was full of it, but didn't want to call me on it.

I frown in the dark. He was right. I'm not about casual dating and hooking up. Despite my no-nonsense demeanor, I'm looking for something more. All those happily ever after Disney movies that spoon feed little girls crap about true love and lifelong commitment and happy little forest animals that do your cooking and cleaning? My mom and stepdad have it. They're super sweet together when they're not so stressed out about his work. I've even caught them making out in the kitchen, which was gross, but reassuring. If anyone asks, I'll deny it, but I want the fairytale. All of it. Maybe even the spontaneous singing.

Unlucky for me, finding a guy with the backbone to stand by my side while I conquer the world hasn't been easy. It's been basically impossible. High school guys aren't ready for my intensity or my drive, which is why I don't bother dating them.

With Kenneth, I thought I'd finally found a worthy

partner. Turns out he doesn't want a partner either. He just wanted someone to mess around with in the few hours he wasn't nose-deep in sick people and bodily fluids.

No thanks.

Which is why I'm inclined not to answer the phone. I don't care to hear what he has to say. No matter what it is, it won't change anything. It's not like he suddenly decided he misses me and he wants me back for a real relationship this time.

Did he?

A tiny seed of hope opens up in my chest, and I hate myself for it. "Hi," I say, my voice softer than usual. Husky, even.

"Charlotte? Are you okay?" Kenneth's voice is hushed, as if he's trying to avoid being overheard. But there's another quality there that is more unsettling. A crackle to the edges of his speech. Kenneth sounds like he's freaking out.

Unease slinks in, making me pull my covers tighter around me with my free hand. "I'm fine. Why wouldn't I be? Why are you calling me?"

His voice drops even lower. "Look, I can't talk long, but I had to talk to you. I'm finishing up my rotation in the city morgue, remember?"

I shiver. Dead bodies gross me out. "Yeah, I remember." So, not calling to get back together, then. I pinch my eyes shut. "I'm failing to see how your morgue rotation affects me. It's 2 AM, Kenneth. What's going on?"

He huffs, and I can almost see him shoving his hand through his hair. "They brought in a guy from your school. A professor? He was hit by a car. Killed instantly, they said."

I sag, relieved. Professor Rook didn't feel any pain, then. It's not absolution, but it's more than I ever thought I'd get. "I heard about it. The police were here this morning, taking photos of the scene. I saw the body bag."

There's murmuring on the other end of the line, as if Kenneth is covering his phone's speaker to talk to someone else. Then he continues into the phone. "Look, I have to ask. Did you see him last night? This Rook guy?"

My stomach clenches as alarm bells go off in the general vicinity of my gut. He can't know. It's not possible. "No, why do you ask?"

A beat passes before he speaks again. When he does, his voice is tighter. He doesn't believe me. "You didn't see him at all? At your stepdad's event? Afterward?"

My blood is gushing through my veins now, spiked with adrenaline. I push out of my bed and let the cold air sooth my flushed skin. Pacing to the window, I peek between my curtains at the spot where Professor Rook was killed. Take a deep breath. Kenneth doesn't know. He's got another reason for asking. He has to have. I can spin this.

I take the offensive, trying to throw him off guard. "Are you accusing me of lying? Seriously, Kenneth? After everything?"

He groans. "Charlotte, you might be in deep, here. I'm just trying to help you. You have to tell me the truth. Right now."

It's now or never. "I didn't see Professor Rook at all yesterday. That's the truth." Technically, it's true. I didn't *see* Professor Rook.

"Listen. When they brought in his body, there was a box of his stuff. One of his shoes came off in the impact, and his watch was smashed. They also brought in… God, I can't believe I'm saying this. You didn't kill him, did you?" His voice gets more strained, more strung out as he talks. The thread of incredulity through it is unmistakable.

"No." I'm a stone cold liar.

He groans. "Then explain this to me. Why was there a program from your dad's event found near the body? Charlotte, it had a lipstick print on it. It looked exactly like that red shade you wear when you're feeling feisty. You know the one I'm talking about."

My hand flies to my lips. My program. The one I tossed out my car window with that spider on it. The same one I used to blot a new coat of lipstick after I drank that glass of wine. Shit.

I swallow. "A program?"

"If they test it for DNA, it won't match you?"

My breath hitches. I didn't even think of that. Chaotic thoughts ricochet through my brain, and I fight to wrestle them under control. It's like wrangling a half a dozen small children who are bound and determined to be the first ones to the cotton candy booth. Don't ask how I know what that's like.

My stomach bottoms out.

If the police run the program for DNA, it won't lead them to me. I'm not in any system that I know of. And so far, the police don't appear to have made the mental leap that it might have been someone at the academy who hit the professor. But since his body was found so near the front gate, they will. Once they learn the DNA on that program is from a girl, that narrows down their suspects a lot. What are there, seventy girls here at the academy, not including teachers?

Kenneth is lecturing in my ear, but I can't focus on the words.

If the police start looking more closely at us students, it's only a matter of time before someone, even accidentally, tells them that I spent a fair amount of time in Professor Rook's classroom. If they request my DNA, I could refuse to comply, but that would only make me look more guilty.

"Char?"

I force myself to respond. "I didn't murder the professor." What happened would likely be considered manslaughter.

He exhales loudly. "I can't believe I had to ask you that. I never in a million years…"

"It's not something I imagined either. So, about the program. What happened to it?"

The line goes quiet.

"Kenneth?"

"You have to realize, I thought you did it. I tried to help, but…"

"Kenneth!"

"I tried to take it. Burn it, but I wasn't able to. The police took it. They have it. But that doesn't matter, right? Because it wasn't yours?" That vein of distrust is back in his voice. I don't like it, not one bit.

"Thanks for trying to help me, but like I said, I didn't murder the professor. I don't need your help."

"Okay, I'll see you to—"

I hang up before he can say anything else. My phone drops over the side of the bed, swinging on the end of the charger cord. Just like me, it dangles by a flimsy thread.

So that's it, then. My days of freedom are numbered, and then my identity will change. Charlotte Cavendish-Holt, promising daughter of Senator Terrance Holt, will be no more.

I have no doubt what they'll call me, and by then no manner of trying to explain my intentions will matter.

I'll always be Charlotte Cavendish-Holt, cold-blooded killer.

And Kenneth? He's suspicious.

8

I'm out of bed by 6 AM. It turns out, knowing that I've killed a man also kills my ability to sleep. Endorphins are supposed to make people happy, but even after using one of the treadmills in the fitness center off the gymnasium, I'm still dragging. It takes all of my tricks to look bright-eyed and bushy-tailed as I swing by Adrienne's room to pick her up for breakfast.

The broad-shouldered form of my stepsister's paramour/bodyguard is welcome.

"Morning, Mikhail."

He returns my greeting with a small nod from his position against the wall between my room and Adrienne's. A quick scan of my person pinches his eyebrows together. "Are you all right, Charlotte? You look fatigued."

I wave him off. "I'm fine, and here's a friendly tip. Never tell a girl she looks tired."

His eyes don't leave my face. "Noted."

When my stepsister opens the door, Genevieve is already there. "Hey, Char, I'm borrowing one of Adrienne's vintage brooches. Which one should I wear?"

I rush in to help her pick one, thankful for the distraction.

"How are you feeling this morning?" Genevieve asks from where she's standing in front of Adrienne's mirror, pinning a silver cat to the lapel of her uniform jacket. "You look tired."

Behind me, Mikhail smothers a bark of laughter.

Adrienne, too, looks concerned. She's coiling a red lock

around her finger absently as she watches me.

I put on my brightest smile. "I'm fine. Really. Let's get to breakfast. I need an omelet."

Adrienne smiles tentatively. "If you say so. I'm ready for some pastries, myself."

"When are you not?"

We laugh together as we walk down to the eatery, Mikhail a constant shadow. Their companionship buoys me. With my sister, my best friend, and even Mikhail with me, I'll be fine.

"So, Genevieve, how was Belgium?" Adrienne asks as she loops an arm through mine.

On my other side, Genevieve beams. On a happy sigh, she tells us all about her family's trip to Bruges, where her grandma lives. It sounds wonderful, and I let myself get distracted by it as the beguiling smell of breakfast grows. I've never been to Belgium, and I would love to go sometime. Maybe Adrienne and I could visit Genevieve there this summer.

Assuming I'm not in prison.

The thought douses my enthusiasm. I can't think like that. I have to focus.

Everyone has pulled out the stops for the first day of school. I catch glimpses of new, expensive jewelry, watches, shoes, and even some brightly colored socks as the four of us navigate the hallway.

We're in front of the health center when its door swings open, and Kenneth comes out.

I stop in my tracks as his eyes focus on me, like twin blue laser beams. I never noticed it before, but Adrienne's nickname for him is intensely accurate. He does look like a Ken Doll. An unwelcome one.

"Charlotte, nice to see you." He gives a polite smile.

My hands find my hips. "What are you doing here? We

broke up, remember?"

Mikhail's eyes move between Kenneth and me as he assesses the situation. Not missing anything.

Eyeing the guy at our side, Kenneth shakes his head. "Don't you remember? You set up a rotation for me here with Doctor Paloma last semester."

Icy remembrance hits me like a wall of frigid air. I did that, but I hadn't heard from him until last night, so I assumed it hadn't been approved. Doctor Paloma didn't sound convinced when I talked to her in early December, but she must have changed her mind.

"You couldn't get out of it?" Inside, mortification is burning me up, but I don't let it show. To think, at the time I was excited that I'd get to see him every day. Maybe I'd even fake another bee sting.

"It was already set. Will you come inside so we can talk?"

My jaw almost drops, but I stop it. Reigning in my composure, I give him a dismissive smile. "I can't now. I have to eat breakfast before class."

Kenneth steps closer. "Please. I have to talk to you. It'll only take a minute."

I feel the unwelcome burning of eyes on me.

Adrienne is gaping at Kenneth, clearly as surprised as I am that he's here. Genevieve is more composed, and puts a hand on my arm as a show of support. Standing at her full height of 5'8," she's not easy to dismiss. Kenneth's eyes rake over her, and then my stepsister, before returning to me.

"Charlotte?" He opens the door wider, beckoning for me to precede him.

Shaking my head, I glance up and down the hall. We have an audience, and it's growing. Those closest to us are watching with interest, and awareness is spreading down the corridor. A short girl at the end of the hall goes up on tiptoes trying to get a good view, her dark eyes all I can see above the shoulders of the crowd. Gul. Curse everyone at this school and their drama radar.

"Charlotte, maybe you should talk to Kenneth?" Genevieve prompts, questions in her eyes.

Making a snap decision, I plead with my eyes for her to understand. Then I hook my arm around the elbow of the nearest boy. It's pure coincidence that he's so close. I'll regret this later, I am sure, but for now, it's my best and only move. With a yank, I pull him around to face my ex.

"Kenneth, have you met my new boyfriend, Ricardo?"

Ricardo's eyes go wide as he looks down at me, but he smothers his surprise quickly. His signature cocky grin spreads over his features. Holding out a hand, he says, "Kenneth. I've heard a lot about you, none of it good, I'm afraid."

Kenneth starts to splutter, his eyes swinging from Ricardo to me and back. "You… He… You…"

Ricardo winks at me, and my insides rankle.

Cool it, Char. You can strangle him later.

With satisfaction I notice that Ricardo is taller than Kenneth. I don't know why, exactly, but I find it immensely gratifying that my ex has to look up to my current, admittedly fake, boyfriend.

"Yep. I have a new guy. I don't waste time when I find what I want, unlike someone I know." My pointed meaning is not lost on Kenneth, whose skin flushes angry red.

Immediately the whispers move down the hall, rippling outward like a shockwave from where I'm standing at ground zero. In less than ten minutes, everyone in this entire school will have heard about me and Ricardo. Oh, joy.

Raking a hand over the back of his neck, Kenneth retreats

into the health center, shutting the door behind him. He's put off for now. It's only temporary, but it'll give me time to formulate a plan to handle him.

Trepidation wells as I turn to focus on Adrienne and Genevieve. Adrienne looks like she's about to burst, and is the first to speak. "Is this why you were so vehemently against us getting to know each other last semester? Because you had a crush on him? That makes so much sense. I knew you seemed unreasonably mad at him! Wow, I'm so happy for you." She gushes, beaming at us. "My best friend and my sister. Eek!" She throws her arms around us and jumps up and down.

Laughing, Ricardo says, "You got us, chouchou."

I fight the urge to roll my eyes at his cutesy nickname for my stepsister.

Ricardo takes my hand, twining our fingers.

It's all I can do not to yank my hand away. The way he's looking at me, with feigned affection, is making me want to punch him in the face. Of course, I'd never do that. I would never lose control in public like that. Or ever, really. I force myself to smile back, sweetly.

Maybe I should take up Krav Maga again so I have an excuse to beat the crap out of my training partner, even if it's not Ricardo. My grin widens. Maybe I could get Ricardo to come too. Then I really could punch him in the face.

Genevieve stands apart from us, her blue eyes watery as she stares at us, lips parted in cruel surprise. Her aghast expression drowns my sudden craving for violence.

I reach for her hand. "Gen, let me explain. Please."

Shaking her head, she bolts toward the women's bathroom.

A bunch of people swivel to watch her go. One whistles, irking me.

Untangling my fingers from Ricardo's, I excuse myself. I have to go talk to my bestie.

A cacophony of vibrations and ringtones fills the hallway, making me pause.

"What's this?" Adrienne says, showing me her phone screen.

"An all-school alert?" I mutter out loud, digging my phone out of my bag. Opening it, I click on my messages. There's a new one—from Headmistress Morgan.

Embassy Academy Alert

Attention, students.

All students and faculty who have a car registered here at Embassy Academy are hereby requested to refrain from driving off campus for the next several days while the police conduct their investigation in the vicinity outside our campus. A personal shuttle will be made available to students who require a mode of transportation for off-site appointments.

The crowd parts as Cal lopes toward me, looking up from his phone. Asif is with him. "Hey, Char, have you seen this? Where's my car, anyway?" Cal shows me the screen as he stops in front of where I'm still standing with Adrienne and Ricardo. "Uh, why are you holding hands with Rico Suave, here?"

All three of them swivel to me, and my stomach dips into my toes.

I am so dead.

9

After giving Cal some bull excuse about having his car detailed as a thank you for letting me borrow it, I hurry into the restroom. Genevieve is standing in front of the mirror, bracing herself on the white marble counter with outstretched hands. Rings glitter on her long, slender fingers. Her gingerbread brown hair hangs in waves that have fallen forward over her shoulders.

I never lie to Genevieve, but today I must. I can't tell her about what happened with Professor Rook, because then she'll be complicit. It's bad enough that Ricardo knows, and Kenneth suspects what I've done. Not Genevieve too. And I can't tell her that I'm faking it, because that would be far too embarrassing.

I square my shoulders, hoping I'm a good enough liar to pull this off. Stepping up beside her, I push her hair back over her shoulder. "Gen? Please let me explain."

Genevieve takes a couple of deep breaths and turns to me, her arms crossing over her chest. "Explain, then, s'il vous plait." The pain in her eyes kills me. I thought she was over Ricardo, since she's been spending time with Kita Ryou, but maybe I was wrong.

Licking my lips, I start weaving my web of lies. "You know how adamant I was last semester that Adrienne should stay away from Ricardo. I really did hate him. Or I thought I did." I give a huff. "When he started hanging out with us, I realized he wasn't so bad, but I'd been so vocal about hating him that I didn't know how to tell you. Do you remember late last semester, when we were supposed to go to *Coco. Zelda. Gloria. Louise.* and Kenneth bailed on me? Well, Ricardo and I danced together some that night, and we started talking. It kind of progressed from there. If you still have feelings for him, I'll break up with him." Please tell me to break up with him.

It would be the shortest fake relationship in history. But then I wouldn't have a buffer between me and Kenneth. The agony of my situation makes my fingers curl inward against my palms.

Genevieve runs her fingers under her eyes, wiping away hints of moisture. "I can't believe you didn't tell me. You have no idea how much that hurts. We're best friends, Charlotte, and you're dating my ex-boyfriend? What's worse, I have to find out about it in front of the entire school? That's not right."

I bob my head, ignoring the fact that Genevieve hasn't denied having lingering feelings for Ricardo. "You're right, absolutely. I apologize for not telling you sooner. Next time something big happens, you'll be the first to know." Another lie.

She gives me half a smile. "Good."

Time to steer the conversation away from Ricardo. "So, how're things going with Ryou?"

She laughs at my half smile. "He's really sweet. I think I could like him, but I want to take it slow. After, you know."

I do know. Genevieve's whirlwind romance with Ricardo left her with whiplash, and probably some trust issues. I'm not at all surprised that she's taking it slow with her new guy.

Genevieve throws her arms around me and hugs me tight. "I know hugs aren't your favorite, but..."

I wrap my arms around her too. "It's okay. I needed this."

It's true. I don't often initiate physical affection with anyone, but having my best friend's arms around me right now feels so good. It's steadying. Encouraging. A reminder that even though I did something unforgivable, I'm still human. Lovable. Worthy.

When we step out of the bathroom, hallway traffic has recommenced. Everyone is streaming into the eatery for breakfast, which smells amazing. The warm, heady scent of sizzling bacon and eggs filters through the air, accompanied by whiffs of cinnamon and maple syrup. Gen and I rejoin our friends, and merge into the flow of bodies.

Ryou is standing in the entrance to the eatery, and falls into step beside Genevieve. "You look pretty today," he whispers in her ear.

Shyly, she smiles, thanking him.

Mikhail and Adrienne lead the way to our table, which is getting a little small for all of us. Mikhail nods to Ricardo, and they push two of the long tables together so we can all fit.

Cal ducks toward me. "You seriously took my car to be detailed?"

"Yep," I answer, too brightly.

He laughs. "That's cool. Thanks." He and Asif meander toward the French toast station.

Genevieve, Ryou, and Adrienne have also disappeared.

I wrap my fingers around Ricardo's arm and yank him toward me. "Do you think Mo could finish Cal's car today instead of tomorrow? If I can't get that car back here, I'll be in serious trouble."

Ricardo's eyes shine as he shakes his head. "And here I thought you were going to seal our newly minted relationship with a kiss." He puts his hands on my arms, searing my skin.

"There is no conceivable circumstance in which I'm

kissing you."

"That wasn't always the case."

A memory attempts to push to the forefront of my mind, but I shove it back. "We're not talking about that right now."

Ricardo's thumbs move in slow circles over my skin, riling me up. Is he *trying* to provoke me?

He's my fake boyfriend, I remind myself. Act like it. I smile up at him, speaking through my teeth. "You'll come with me over there after school, right?" I hit him with my most charming smile at full wattage. It almost always gets me what I want.

Ricardo blinks. "Of course. We'll go right after class, and we'll bring Cal's car back. Don't worry. Now, have a seat, mon coeur. Allow me to get you breakfast." He grins when I squirm at the nickname.

"Don't call me that," I whisper. "And I can get my own breakfast." I try to break away from him, but Ricardo's fingers put the slightest pressure on my upper arms, gently holding me back.

Leaning in, he presses a quick kiss to my cheek. "Sit down. How will it look if I don't help you get your food? You can't tell me you didn't make Kenneth wait on you hand and foot. We have to make this look good." He relinquishes my arms before pulling out my chair.

My eyes narrow, but I take the seat anyway. "I did not boss Kenneth around." I absolutely did. "Besides, what's in it for you?"

Ricardo's head cants to one side. "Be cool, okay? My mom is here. Don't look."

I go still, squelching the urge to whirl around in the direction of Ricardo's glance. Tension hums through him as he helps me slide my chair in. He gives my ponytail a light tug. "I'll be right back.”

Smoothing down my hair, I take out my phone for something to do, not at all enjoying the stares I’m getting from everyone around me. This is so awkward. It was a truly horrendous idea to pretend to date Ricardo. What was I thinking, agreeing to this?

The next chair scrapes as it’s dragged out from underneath the table, and Gul sits down. Her expression cannot be described as anything but predatory when she levels her dark brown eyes at me. “So, you and Ricardo, huh? Spill.” She rests her chin in her hands and stares at me intently.

Shaking my head, I say, “I am not spilling anything to you. Besides, aren’t you too preoccupied spreading rumors about Professor Rook’s death?”

Something flickers over Gul’s face before she shutters her expression. “I’m not interested in that anymore. It’s old news. But you and Ricardo? That fascinates me. How long have you been dating?”

“Unh unh unh,” Ricardo says, tapping the back of Gul’s chair. “You stole my seat. Plus, my girl doesn’t kiss and tell.” His fingers caress the back of my neck, and I want to vomit.

Gul’s lips purse to one side as she looks between us, realizing she’s been thwarted. She pushes away from the table. “Bye. We’ll catch up later.” Her shiny black heels tap as she retreats to her usual table.

My friends slide their trays onto the table and take their seats, until I’m surrounded by friends and family.

“What did Gul want?” Genevieve asks, her eyes avoiding Ricardo.

“Nothing important.”

“As usual,” Ricardo says. He sets an omelet in front of me, prepared just the way I like it, paired with a glass of ice water. A crisp lemon wedge graces the lip of the glass.

I gape at the plate as he sets it down in front of me. "How did you...?"

He slides into his chair, tabling his own plate of bacon and eggs fried over easy. "I pay attention. Enjoy."

As surprised as I am that Ricardo knows my breakfast order, I don't really taste my omelet. I'm too busy worrying about whether Mo will be able to finish the repairs to Cal's car by tomorrow. If he doesn't, will the headmistress notice that Cal's car is missing? Will the police notice? A horrendous thought makes my lips part in shock. What if the police get it into their heads to inspect all of the cars on campus? What if they spot something on Cal's car that tips them off to what I've done?

Taking a bite of my breakfast, I chew, choking down the disparate pieces like bits of rubber. If anyone notices that Cal's car is missing, they'll undoubtedly ask him about it. He'll truthfully tell them that I was the last person to drive the car, and that will be it. My time is running out.

10

All around me, people are speculating about what happened to Professor Rook, and what it might mean that we're not allowed to drive our vehicles off campus for the next few days. Was Rook's death an accident? Was it not? If it was, what kind of person would leave a dead man in the road? If it wasn't, why did they do it?

The whispers make me feel naked and vulnerable, which I hate. No one has any clue what actually happened, and yet I feel exposed. Raw. I pull my uniform jacket tighter around my torso as I walk down the hall between classes.

Gul passes in the other direction, and I stare her down. It's 100% her fault that everyone is talking about this. Okay, maybe it's not, but I'm choosing to blame her anyway. Her deep brown eyes meet mine before flicking to the floor. Then she starts chattering to her companion.

I'm positive they're talking about me, but neither of them turns to look. Instead, they round the corner out of sight.

I stand frozen in the hallway, watching the flow of people as they go about their day, unfazed by the shadow of death hovering in the street outside.

I'd love to continue to blame all of the scintillating theories on the queen of gossip herself, but something about pointing the finger at Gul gives me pause. When I asked her about the rumors at breakfast this morning, she shut down. Something in her expression made me wonder. Was Gul actually afraid to talk about Professor Rook's death?

Like I told him to, Ricardo meets me outside my last class of the day. Slinging his arm around my shoulders, we walk through the crowd toward the parking lot. Nobody is used to seeing us together yet, so there's a lot of staring, which makes me want to scowl. Instead, my muscles fall into my practiced politician's smile. A bland, easy expression that feels like default. I am not used to being the subject of such probing study, and I'm quickly deciding I don't like it. When I'm on a stage speaking, that's different. Comfortable. This feels like… involuntary dissection. As if I'm wearing the emperor's clothes, and everyone can see through them but me.

As soon as Ricardo and I are outside, relatively alone, I push his arm off me. "We need to set some ground rules if we're going to keep up this charade. You're far too touchy for me."

Ricardo laughs. "You know a lot of people at school call you the ice bitch behind your back?"

I shoot a look his way. I'm aware of the nickname. It doesn't matter to me. I'm not here to make friends. I'm here to excel. Get into Georgetown. Take over the world. "Who cares? Where's your car?"

Ricardo's eyebrows shoot up as he looks around the parking lot. "I don't have a car."

"Then how are we getting to the auto body shop?" I whisper-hiss the last part, just in case someone is listening. I can't be too careful when there could be spies everywhere, just waiting to get their hands on some juicy gossip to propel themselves up the academy popularity ladder.

Ricardo laughs. "You heard the headmistress's announcement. We're not allowed to drive off campus anyway. We'll take the subway. Like normal people."

I grimace at the thought of being jostled about in a warm, smelly metal tube with a bunch of strangers. "Isn't it dirty? And crowded?"

His hand goes up, a finger pointed at me. "Wait. Haven't you ever ridden the subway?"

Gritting my teeth, I give a slight shake of my head. Admitting my inexperience to Ricardo makes my skin burn with indignation. Here comes a "popping my subway cherry" joke in three, two...

Ricardo laughs. "You're priceless. Today's your lucky day, mon coeur. If you're nice, I'll even let you sit in my lap so you don't have to put your royal behind on the *dirty* plastic seats."

My eyebrows shoot up. Not a subway virgin joke, then. Color me surprised. But if he thinks I'm sitting in his lap… "Ugh. You wish. Let's just go. And you have to stop with that nickname. I am not your heart."

Laughing, he leads the way toward the gate. "Good thing they lowered the safety protocols for getting off campus, isn't it? I wonder how long that will last, if the police think someone at the academy killed Professor Rook." He gives me a pointed look.

"Shh. Not here." I practically shove him through the iron gate, waving to the security guard in the booth as we pass. "Just going to the drugstore," I say by way of explanation. It's weak, but it'll do.

Ricardo leans backward heavily against my hands, stalling our progress. "Hey, slow down. There's no fire. Nicknames are one of my terms. If I'm going to keep fake dating you, I want to use pet names."

I don't stop propelling him forward. There might not be a fire, but there sure as hell is a deadline. I don't even want to think about what will happen if I can't get Cal's car back to the school parking lot by tomorrow morning. "Pretending to date you was such a mistake."

His entire body goes limp and heavy under my palms. "If you'd rather go tell Kenneth you lied about us dating, I won't stop you." He's teasing me.

"NO. No. Fine. Use a pet name. I'll deal with it."

He shoots a gloating look over his shoulder. "Words I never thought I'd hear. You know, a lot of people like terms of endearment."

I give him a little shove. "You're being mushy again. Knock it off."

He stops dead on the sidewalk, and I run into his solid back. "I could call you sweetie pie. Honey bun. Baby."

Rolling my eyes, I shoot around him and speed walk up the sidewalk. "Those are all so generic."

He catches up with me in a few easy strides. "Hence why I started calling you mon coeur."

"And I'll call you…"

"Ricky."

Genevieve used to call him that. I don't know if I can make myself use it too. Especially in front of her. "Didn't you try to get Adrienne to call you that? No. Think of something else."

A car slows and pulls alongside the curb.

"Wait," Ricardo says, pushing me behind him.

"Hey—!" But I don't argue any more. If he wants to get shot or kidnapped instead of me, I'll let him. He can be unpredictably chivalrous, but I'm sticking with self-preservation.

Ricardo's mom climbs out of the car, and Ricardo's arms relax, dropping from my sides.

I step out from behind him and take his hand in mine. If

anyone finds out my relationship with Ricardo is fake, it won't be because I didn't put on a good enough show. "Mrs. LaGuerre. Nice to see you."

"Thanks, dear." She focuses on her son. "If you're going somewhere, I can give you a lift." Hope lightens her expression as she smiles at Ricardo.

Ricardo's fingers squeeze around mine. "No, thank you. We don't need a ride."

I open my mouth to argue, but he gives a slight shake of his head.

"Goodbye, Mother," he says before leading me away along the sidewalk.

Looking over my shoulder, I can see that Mrs. LaGuerre hasn't moved. She watches us as we leave her behind, her shoulders slumped.

"Why did you do that?" I ask as soon as we're out of earshot. "She just wants to help you and get to know you again. Why would you reject that chance?"

Ricardo looks at me out of the corner of his eye as we turn the corner. "You wouldn't understand."

I huff. "I wouldn't understand a distant parent making overtures to get to know me? Oh, really? You've met my stepfather, right?"

He stops walking and indicates a set of steps that go down into the sidewalk. "We're here."

A man brushes past us, muttering something about "ignorant kids" under his breath.

"Is it safe down there?" I ask, peering down into the subterranean space.

Ricardo's face settles into the cocky grin that almost makes me want to do something I'll regret. "Stay close. I'll protect you from the mole people."

"Shut up."

He laughs all the way down the stairs, and I have to admit, I'm being kind of ridiculous. This is probably going to be good for me. I've clearly been living in a safe, cushy bubble for far too long.

With some extra persuasion in the form of government recognized currency, Mo agreed to work late and finish Cal's car. There are not enough words in English to express my relief. I'm honestly shocked the police haven't checked all of the cars on campus yet, and even though the headmistress didn't mention that it was a possibility, I'm certain it's only a matter of time. Besides, if the police were going to come inspect our cars, they wouldn't give us a heads up, would they? It would give the perpetrator ample time to have their car detailed. Exactly like I'm having done.

Nothing prepared me for the sight of Cal's car.

When Ricardo and I got back to Mo's this morning, again via the subway, which I'm kind of starting to like, the car is spotless. Not a dent in sight. No one would ever be able to tell that it had been damaged, much less that I killed someone with it.

Mo might be my new favorite person.

"This is fantastic."

Unruffled by my enthusiasm, Mo takes my credit card and runs it through his reader. Glancing up, he eyes the crest on my uniform jacket. "I was wondering, how'd you damage the car?"

Even though I'm ready with an explanation, I don't like the way he's taking in my uniform. Professor Rook's death has been all over the news, so there's no question Mo has heard about it. What if he puts two and two together?

"I hit a deer. It jumped right in front of my car. Can you

believe that?" I am scary good at lying, and I don't know whether I should be proud of the story that I just spat out without any prep time, or ashamed.

"Deer, huh? Wow. Didn't know we had them around here." His disbelief is palpable in his voice.

"Oh, yeah. Lots."

Ricardo covers his mouth to hide his smile. If he doesn't cut it out, he's going to give me away. Some partner in crime he's turning out to be.

We thank Mo and hurry out to the car before he can ask any more questions.

I only have fifteen minutes before class starts, and I'm starting to freak out just the tiniest bit about getting Cal's car back into its assigned space before anyone notices it's missing. I navigate the roads carefully, but a little fast. Ricardo acts like I'm trying to kill him and holds onto the oh crap bar the entire time. Not gonna lie. I take the next corner a little fast just to see if I can make him tense.

It works.

I am evil.

As if killing a man and lying about it didn't make that painfully obvious.

The music on the radio fades out, and the talk show host comes on. "We've got some breaking news for you this morning, folks. By now, everyone has probably heard about the hit-and-run that occurred just outside the Embassy Academy Monday night. I got the impression the police thought it was an accident, but new evidence has surfaced that proves it wasn't."

My heart leaps into my throat and I grip the steering wheel. What new evidence? It's a hard line to swallow, since it *was* an accident.

The co-host adds, "Yeah, this morning, our local news

outlet released the 911 call that alerted authorities to the accident, and it sounds like it was deliberate."

"It certainly does," the first guy says. "To me, it sounds like someone mowed the guy down, then kept on going."

I don't realize I've stopped the car in the middle of the street until the driver of the car behind me honks long and loud.

Ripped out of my shock, I maneuver the vehicle forward. We're almost at school. But honestly? If there was a witness to the accident, I'm already caught.

I wouldn't be surprised if the police were waiting in the parking lot, handcuffs at the ready.

Knowing it's inevitable doesn't prepare me for the sight of the pair of police cars parked in the lot as I pull in. My skin is crawling as I pull even with the black and white vehicles. One of the officers steps forward as I draw closer, motioning for me to roll down my window.

My pulse skitters. This is it—the end of the road. The 911 caller probably described Cal's car to the emergency operator, and here I am driving it. Taking a breath, I prepare to surrender with dignity. My future may be over, but I won't let them see me crying. That won't come until later, when Daddy gets me alone and conveys the depth of his disappointment at discovering that his stepdaughter has killed a man, effectively ending his political career just as it's beginning to ascend.

Putting on my politician's smile, I roll down the window. "Good morning, officers. Would you like a donut?" I hold up the pink box Ricardo's been holding in his lap.

The officer smiles. "Don't mind if I do." He takes a chocolate bar. "Thank you, Miss."

"You're welcome."

The officer checks the license plate on our car and looks at his phone screen. He's probably checking to see if it matches the one given in the call transcript, which it will. At least he'll have the donut to remember me by.

My pulse pounds in my fingers as I cling to the wheel. I can't peel my eyes off the officer as he scans his device one more time before looking up at me. "Have a good day." He steps back and allows me to pass.

Wait, what?

He's motioning for me to move along.

I manage to keep my composure long enough to pull into Cal's designated parking spot and kill the engine.

Grabbing a donut out of the box, I take a big bite. Chew feverishly. "I don't get it. Why didn't they question me? If the person who called 911 saw this car running over the professor, and then driving away…" I trail off as I look at the officers in my rearview mirror.

Maybe they're waiting to see what I'll do? No, that can't be right. If they have evidence that this car is the one that killed Professor Rook, they'd have asked me to come in for questioning right away.

"My distraction worked, see? Who was right?" Ricardo grins as he takes the donut box back, selecting one for himself.

I shoot a glare at him. Daddy says the best defense is a good offense, so as soon as Ricardo suggested getting the donuts, I knew it was a good idea. I wish I'd thought of it first. Then he wouldn't be sitting next to me gloating.

I toss the half-eaten ring back into the box. I'm too wound up now for a donut. I can't make sense of the police letting me go free without a single question. I have to figure out why they would do that. I have to hear the 911 call.

11

As soon as I'm in the dormitory, I bolt up the stairs away from Ricardo.

"Wait!" he calls, but I ignore him.

Shoving my way past people going down to breakfast, I reach the third floor. Behind me, someone makes a disgruntled hiss as I duck through a group of chattering girls. I'm in too much of a hurry to apologize.

"There you are," Genevieve says, pushing off my dorm room door. Her eyes skirt past me toward the stairs, but I don't miss the hurt there. "Did you go to breakfast without us?"

"She already ate?" Adrienne asks as she steps out of her room, her door clicking shut.

"No! It's not that. I had an… errand to run. Just give me a couple minutes and I'll be ready." Unlocking my door, I slither inside, blocking Genevieve from following.

"Hey!" Her word is cut off when my door closes in her face.

Wincing, I back away from the door. Guilt cuts through me for treating her like that, but I do not want my best friend or my sister to hear the 911 call. Better to apologize for being rude later. If they're still talking to me, that is.

I exhale as I dart to my desk and flip open my laptop.

Based on the lack of buzzing in the dormitory, no one else has heard about this yet. It's kind of surprising that Gul isn't already crowing about it. She probably has internet alerts set to notify her when anything about the academy is in the news. Come to think of it, that's not a terrible idea.

"Charlotte, I'm coming in," Ricardo says through my door.

I open my mouth to protest, but he's already sliding through the door. "Sorry, girls. My lady and I need a minute or two. In private, if you feel me."

I clench my teeth at Ricardo's ruse. As if Genevieve wasn't hurt enough already, now she thinks I dismissed her so I could make out with my boyfriend. Ugh.

Ricardo steps up behind me and puts his hands on my shoulders. "Have you got it queued up? I want to hear this too."

"Did you have to tell them we were coming in here to make out?"

Ricardo chuckles. "That's not at all what I told them, but if that's what you thought, I'd be happy to—"

"Gross."

He doesn't respond, instead leaning over my shoulder to type on my keyboard. I get a whiff of his cologne, something spicy and warm. He smells kind of like gingerbread, which I don't hate. I bet if I leaned closer I could…

Nope. Shake it off, Charlotte. I force my focus back to my laptop.

It doesn't take Ricardo long to find the first headline. It's breaking news on the first news site he checks. He pulls back, withdrawing his arms so I'm no longer boxed in. It's a relief.

Professor's Death Apparently Not an Accident

My throat constricts. The call makes it sound purposeful? This is very, very bad.

My finger hovers over the play button, but I can't do it. When it comes down to it, I don't want to hear Professor Rook being hit and killed by a car. The one good thing about being in the accident the first time is that I didn't hear him. I don't remember the sound of a dying scream or crunching bones. If I listen to this recording…

"Here, let me." With a gentle hand, Ricardo nudges my shoulder, but I swat him away. I get out of my chair and cross to my bed to grab my pillow, hugging it tight against my chest.

Taking my earbuds from the desktop, Ricardo pops them into his ears as he takes my seat.

Out the window, the police are walking slowly up the first row of cars, checking license plates and bumpers. What little time I have is winding down with loud ticks that reverberate through my head.

My entire body is tense as he listens to the call, wondering what he's hearing. Tires screeching over pavement. The terrifying last scream from a dying man. Ricardo's reflection in the window shows him leaning close to the laptop and squinting his eyes. Then he sits back and meets my gaze in the glass.

"You should listen to this." He gestures toward the computer.

Realizing I've got my fingernail in my mouth, I frown. It took me ages to stop biting my nails, but all of this stress is going to make me start again. "Are you sure? It's not… bad?"

"Just come here." He takes out the earbuds and gestures for me to sit. In his lap.

"Not a chance."

"Worth a shot." He vacates my desk chair, standing to one side.

Once I'm seated, Ricardo starts the call again.

"911, what's your emergency and where are you located?"

"Uh, oh my God. They… they ran him over. Didn't even slow down. My God."

"Ma'am, can you tell me where you are located?"

"I'm, uh… on Academy Road, in front of Brat Academy."

"Thank you. Units are on their way to you. Can you describe your emergency?"

Heavy breathing

"Ma'am?"

"Someone just got run over. They're in the middle of the street. I think I'm going to be sick."

Sounds of heaving

The newscaster explains that the call was made anonymously, and the police are asking the person to come forward. Whoever it was, they apparently didn't want to be involved.

The news report stops, and I sit back in my chair, my pulse ratcheted up and my stomach in so many twists I don't know if it'll ever unravel. This is bad. I knew—KNEW—that I had run over Professor Rook once I heard that he'd been killed. There was even gunk in my tire wells. But how do I explain that it wasn't purposeful, in contradiction to this 911 call? It'll be my word against an anonymous woman, and I bet everyone accused of a crime like this pleads innocence. No one will believe me.

Outside, the police are walking past Cal's car. Stopping to examine its hood. One of them stares at the license plate number for a second before looking at his phone.

A tightening in my throat constricts my airway. Did Mo miss something? Did I?

Ricardo leans a hip against my desk. "Why would the caller want to remain anonymous? They aren't guilty of anything, are they?"

I look up at him, my mind latching onto that idea. "I have to listen to it again."

It goes by in a flash, but I listen another couple of times.

As I listen, the voice starts to sound familiar. The cadence and accent bounce around my synapses, trying to find purchase. I'm almost positive I've heard that voice before. It almost sounds like someone trying to disguise their voice by putting on an accent. But why would they do that? I push that question aside. I must be imagining it.

"It's weird that the caller hung up before describing the car or checking on the body, right? If she'd stayed on the line, wouldn't the emergency operator have asked her to do that stuff?"

Ricardo shrugs. "Probably. I don't know."

"Then why hang up?" I start pacing back and forth across my room, tapping my lips as I think it through. The only explanation I can come up with is one that's far-fetched, but not unheard of. "What if the caller didn't actually see the accident? What if she was taking a walk, saw the body, and decided to concoct a story?"

"What would someone gain from that?"

My eyes widen. "Attention?"

Ricardo's head lilts to one side. "Then she wouldn't have made the call anonymously."

I sag. I'm grasping at straws. "You're right."

"Twice in one day. That must be a record for you."

"Shut up."

If it IS a hoax, it's drawing the police away from the actual facts of the case. Someone has just saved my bacon without knowing it. Whoever it is, I owe them big time.

"While I've got you alone," Ricardo says, leaning forward

with his flirty smile sliding into place. "We should talk about these rules you mentioned, for our relationship."

"Fake relationship."

He laughs. "Whatever you want to tell yourself. You're the one who announced I was your boyfriend in front of the entire school."

"I was just trying to get away from Kenneth. I don't have to explain myself to you." Without knowing it, I've crossed the room to plant myself right in front of him, and my pointer finger pokes at the pocket on the front of his tee.

Ricardo's eyes go heavy. Did I just imagine it, or did he just glance at my mouth?

He leans closer. "So, these rules…"

I take a definitive step back. "Fine. No kissing. No bossing me around, and no playing grab-ass in public where I can't stop you."

His hand rises to his heart. "Hey, I am highly offended. I would never touch you inappropriately in front of anyone. Especially in a situation where you felt you couldn't stop me. You, on the other hand, have already proven you're willing to touch me without my permission. Maybe I should be the one setting the rules."

My hands find my hips. "By all means, do tell me how to conduct my fake relationship. You're clearly the expert." I regret the barb as soon as I've said it.

Hurt flashes over Ricardo's face, but he hides it well. "Your rules are acceptable."

"Good. Remember, this is for show only. It makes Kenneth jealous, and it keeps your mom at arms' length. Once they're both out of our hair, we can stage a breakup and go about our normal lives."

Ricardo nods, glancing down at his phone screen. "On

that note, I should go change for class, and so should you. I know how much you hate being late." Reaching up, he musses his curly hair with both hands. "Have to keep up appearances, mon coeur." Arranging his face into an arrogant expression, he leaves.

Getting through the day's classes is like running an educational marathon, only the obstacles are my brother, Kenneth, and potentially the police. Every time I hear footsteps in the hall I expect it to be the authorities coming to arrest me, but it doesn't happen.

I keep playing the 911 call over in my head, analyzing it for clues. Is it a joke? Is it not? But I can't reconcile my memory of that night with the 911 caller's assertion that the killing was deliberate. Is that what it looked like from the outside?

All of this introspection is making my head throb, so by the time my final class of the day is over, I'm ready for a nap.

"Are you okay?" Adrienne asks as we walk up the stairs to our rooms. "You've been quiet today."

"Yes. Should we be concerned about you?" Genevieve adds, her forehead wrinkling as she looks at me. The hesitation in her voice indicates there's more she'd like to ask, but doesn't.

I'm grateful. I don't want to lie to her any more than is necessary. "I'm fine. Just a headache. I think I'll rest for a little while, and meet you for dinner."

"Let me know if you need anything," my stepsister says, putting a hand on my arm. "Would some macarons help?"

I perk up at this. "Macarons always help."

"I'll see if I can whip some up tonight once I'm done with homework," Adrienne says. "It'll probably be pretty late. Plus, Mikhail will want to help. I'm teaching him some." Looking up at the bodyguard, she smiles, a gesture he returns, albeit briefly.

"That's so sweet," Genevieve coos.

"That would be amazing. Thanks," I add.

They move off down the hall, chatting about their piles of homework, Mikhail moving fluidly behind them. I'm glad my sister and Genevieve are becoming friends.

I duck into my room and close the door. It's really sweet that Adrienne and Genevieve care about how I'm feeling. Honestly, before I made friends with Genevieve last year, the only person who showed concern for me was my mom, and she's been so busy since Daddy found out he was being tapped as the party's VP candidate that we haven't found much time to chat. Now that Adrienne and Genevieve are in my life, it's making me feel all of these squishy feelings that I'm not sure how to deal with. Messy emotions are definitely not my thing.

A knock on my door snaps me out of my wallowing. Wallowing is exactly what I was doing, and I hadn't even realized it. Geez, I'm becoming such a sap.

I pinch my nose to ward off the headache growing behind my brows, listening to see if whoever's on the other side of the door knocks again.

"Char? Are you in there?"

It's Cal, and he sounds timid, unsure. "Can we talk about the car?"

I don't answer. Nope, we are not talking about that right now. I do not want to have to come up with an excuse as to why Cal's car looks spotlessly clean and tidy, instead of the dusty, bug-spattered mess it was before I took it to Mo. I have no doubt that he would see through any story I could come up with on the spot. It would be a stretch for him to guess the truth, but he'd be suspicious. That's just what I need; another person wondering what I'm hiding.

"Char? Come on, I know you're in there. Let me in so we

can talk."

I shake my head, even though he can't see me. I am not letting my brother in here. At the very least, if he doesn't know what happened, he can't be implicated in it later. I'm protecting him as much as myself. Someday, if this all gets out, he'll thank me. Probably.

He knocks again, but after a minute, the hall goes silent. Cal must have given up and left.

I should be relieved, so why do I feel so alone?

12

I am never getting used to this. It's been a week since I announced to everyone at Brat Academy that Ricardo and I were dating, and people still stare at us as we walk down the halls hand in hand. Holding hands with him is a lot different from when Kenneth and I used to hold hands. Kenneth had freakishly small hands, so it always felt like I was holding hands with a sweaty little kid. Ricardo, on the other hand, has long, sinuous fingers and arms. Like I said, it's different. Not that I'm enjoying it, or anything.

Ricardo loves the attention, and plays it up whenever we have an audience. He'll put an arm around my shoulders or twirl my ponytail in his fingers, especially when his mom is around.

Adrienne is a huge fan of this development, and I catch her watching us with a big goofy smile on her face way too often. Mikhail seems to have more sense, because whenever he's around I sense he's keeping tabs on Ricardo, trying to gauge his angle. Having seen Mikhail in action, I'm glad. If Ricardo ever does something stupid—which, let's face it, is more likely than not—I'm sure Mikhail will have my back.

There must not be a lot of teachers looking for work in the middle of January, because when I walked into calculus the second day of classes, Headmistress Morgan and Mrs. LaGuerre were standing at the front of the room, the latter with an uneasy smile on her face. She must have been in the right place at the right time, because the headmistress announced that she was installing Mrs. LaGuerre as our interim calculus teacher while she looks for a permanent replacement for Professor Rook.

Immediately the chatter started, but was quickly killed by a stern look from the headmistress.

I wonder how Ricardo will do in his mom's class without me as a buffer.

At lunch, Ricardo is quiet, focused on his food.

"What, no witty remarks about how irresistible you are, today? Finally got a mirror, huh?"

Genevieve snorts into her drinking glass.

Ricardo shakes his head, putting down his fork and leveling me with an intense gaze. "You missed me that bad this morning?"

My mouth drops open. That is *not* why I was needling him just now. I admit that I noticed the fact that he wasn't following me around like a puppy, but miss him? "Don't make me laugh," I say, doing my best Danny Zucko impression.

"No need to letter in track to get my attention, mon coeur. I had a visit from the police this morning, which is why I wasn't in class." He holds up a finger to stop me when I start to speak. "Everything is fine. They simply asked me if I had seen anything of note while I was in the surveillance room the past couple of weeks. I told them the truth: I haven't seen anything they need to know."

Adrienne's face crinkles at his words. "Was it Cahill and Gupta? Were they nice to you?"

Ricardo smiles at her. "Yes, it was your fine detectives. They were perfectly professional. No harm done."

I exhale loudly. "That's good."

"Yes, it is." I owe him for this, but I haven't the faintest idea how to thank him. Patting him on the back is insufficient, but he gives me a chin lift to let me know he understands my intention.

Swallowing, I attempt to eat the rest of my food, but it's lost its intrigue. Ricardo could have given me to the police this morning, but he didn't. How will I ever repay him for that? I don't think pretending to be his girlfriend to help him avoid his mother is going to cut it. Taking a sip of my coffee, I focus on things I can control.

Across the eatery, Grady is eating at a table with a few others. I stand. I've been meaning to talk to him since I found out about Rhiannon. They used to date, so I can't imagine how he's doing since she passed away in rehab. Guilt twinges in my chest. I probably should have spoken to him sooner, since I'm not blameless in the circumstances.

The walk between our tables is short, and I'm standing at his back wearing a sympathetic smile. I don't usually do this sort of thing. Being sympathetic is not one of my gifts. "Hey, Grady?"

He turns around, and his brow furrows. "Charlotte? What's up?"

The girl next to him turns around and places a hand on his shoulder.

I try to stifle the surprise of seeing Gul with her hand perched on Grady's bicep. She's marking her territory. I had no idea they were dating. How did I miss that?

Mentally refocusing, I push ahead. "I just wanted to tell you that I'm sorry about Rhiannon. That must be hard for you, especially with Professor Rook's death." I don't add the part about Rhiannon's family not getting justice against the man who got their daughter hooked on pills.

With effort, Grady shrugs. "Honestly, it's been rough. She

ghosted me after her parents refused to let her come back this year, and then once she went into rehab…" Grady looks weighed down, sad, eyes red-rimmed. It's not surprising. He and Rhiannon seemed to be in love. They were so cute together, always holding hands and whispering in the hallways. Despite the odds of meeting your match in high school, I actually thought they might be forever. How wrong I was.

He continues. "We hadn't talked in months. It sucked, you know? But Gul's been great." Grady gives her a half-hearted smile. Something in my stomach twists. It must be bothering me, deep down, to see someone acting like a caring boyfriend so soon after my breakup with Kenneth. Who, I might add, never seemed to care about me as much as I did for him.

Adrienne pointed it out after we broke up, and she was so right.

Now my ex gets to see Ricardo and me acting all cozy in the halls every day. Suck on that, Ken Doll. "I'm glad you have Gul to support you. When did you start dating?"

Gul smiles, her perfect cat eyeliner making her look even more feline. "Over winter break. We bonded over being stuck here while our parents were away for work."

Gul's been pretty quiet the past few days. She hasn't stuck her nose into my business at all, which is unusual. I had wondered if she'd finally gotten her fill of gossip, with Professor Rook's death giving her fodder for rumors for months, but maybe she's been busy with Grady instead. Plus, he hadn't arrived when the accident happened, so she's had plenty of time to fill him in on all of her theories and speculation.

I excuse myself, and reclaim my seat beside Ricardo. "How's Grady doing?" Genevieve asks, so I tell her. "Hey, Char. I need to talk to you."

I whirl around to find Kenneth standing right behind me, in the middle of the eatery.

Of course, we have an audience. Everyone at the tables nearest ours is watching, waiting to see what I'll do. By this time, everyone knows the hottie intern in the health center is my former boyfriend. It hasn't escaped my notice that whenever he's outside the health center, he's always surrounded by girls asking for "health advice."

Ricardo turns in his chair and twines his fingers in my ponytail, giving it a gentle pull. Tingles ripple across my scalp.

Ordinarily, I wouldn't put up with the territorial crap Ricardo is pulling, but the flicker of jealousy in Kenneth's eyes makes it worth it.

My fake relationship is actually working! But even as the warmth of victory settles in my chest, another thought occurs to me. Kenneth was never serious about me. So why do I want to make him jealous so badly?

Leaning into Ricardo, I give him my best flirty smile. "Be right back."

Grin widening, Ricardo boops my nose. "I'll miss you, mon coeur."

He's so overly saccharine, it makes me want to hurl. But I stuff that impulse down and level a withering gaze at Kenneth. "What do you want?"

"We need to talk, but not here."

"If you insist." I get up, making a show of how much of an imposition it is for me to leave lunch to talk to Kenneth. If anyone wonders, I want them to infer that I broke up with him and not the truth. That he ended it because I wasn't enough for him. He said it was because he didn't want to commit, but I didn't believe him even the first time he said it.

Why would I be enough for an attractive, intelligent future

doctor like Kenneth when I wasn't enough for my biological father, my stepfather, or increasingly, my own mother?

Kenneth leads me into one of the treatment rooms in the health center. It's freezing in here, as usual.

I draw my uniform jacket tight around me and button it clear up to the collar. Pulling myself up onto the hospital bed, I cross my legs. Kenneth always liked my legs, and they do look fantastic in my uniform skirt and skin-tone tights. I might as well use them to advantage. "You wanted to talk?"

Kenneth rakes a hand through his straight, sandy brown hair before turning to me. His eyes skim up my legs before settling on my face. Pink spots appear on his cheeks. "Um, yeah. I wasn't at the morgue when they finished the autopsy on the professor who died, but my buddy was. I asked him to let me know if they found anything interesting."

My eyebrow cocks in disdain. I can't let him know he's got my interest. "And you thought I'd be interested because?"

"He called me this morning. They found something."

It's suddenly hot in this exam room. Fidgeting with my shirt collar, I sit up straighter. Kenneth has my full attention now. Is it possible they found more evidence that implicates me in Professor Rook's death?

I take in a breath as my pulse speeds up. Maybe Cal's tires are unique and they traced the tread pattern to his car. Or maybe they did match the DNA on my discarded program to me somehow. What if the anonymous woman who called 911 knew more than they said in that recording, and it's now coming to bear?

Schooling my features, I play it cool. "And? What did he say that was so interesting?"

Kenneth eyes me for a minute, then speaks. "They found marks from two different types of tire treads on the guy's body."

My mouth opens, but I snap it shut. "Meaning?"

"They think he was run over twice, by two different vehicles."

13

My head is spinning even as my brain starts to rationalize what Kenneth has just said. "Are you kidding me right now? They think Professor Rook was run over twice? Like, by two totally different cars? Do they know what time this happened?"

Kenneth nods. "They think it happened pretty quickly, because of the damage to the body. They noticed that the guy's watch was smashed right at 11, and figured that was the time of the first impact. They're not sure when the second impact occurred, but they're guessing it happened maybe ten minutes later."

A towering sense of relief fills me, spreading warmth from the crown of my head to the tips of my toes. "You're saying that Professor Rook was killed at eleven, last Monday night, and then someone else ran over his body sometime shortly after that. So, whoever ran over him the first time killed him, and the second time wasn't fatal?"

His eyes lock with mine. "That's what I'm telling you, yes."

I can't help it; I grin. There is no way I killed Professor Rook if that time of death is accurate. I didn't even leave Daddy's event until 11. I didn't get back to the academy until closer to 11:20. I'm not a murderer after all.

Kenneth is watching my every move, measuring my reaction.

I tamp down the surge of relief coursing through me and

soften my smile. "Thanks for telling me."

Kenneth stares at me, his lean body almost looming over mine. "The second car, it was you, wasn't it?"

Relief sufficiently killed.

"No comment."

He reaches for my hand, but thinks better of it, dropping his hand against his side. "I'm not the press, Charlotte. I'm not going to sell you out to a journalist."

It hadn't occurred to me that he would do that, but now that he's mentioned it? I'm not positive that he wouldn't, if the opportunity presented itself. "Why would you say that? Has someone approached you for information?" I push off the table and stand tall, meeting his eyes in challenge. "You cannot talk to anyone. You know how crucial this time is for Daddy's campaign. I am not admitting to anything, but if a scandal like this got out, it would ruin him. Hell, it would ruin me. If you care about me at all, you won't talk to anyone else about this."

Kenneth frowns. "Of course I care about you."

I roll my eyes. "Yeah. So much that you broke up with me right before Christmas."

He shifts closer. "Your thing with that Ricardo guy, is it serious?" Kenneth doesn't meet my look, instead carefully avoiding my face. He puts both hands in the pockets of his scrubs, and then takes them out again. He's not usually this shifty. It's strange seeing him ruffled.

Sensing weakness, I move to deliver a fatal blow. "I think it could be. Ricardo wants the same things I want. He understands me, unlike some people."

Kenneth huffs. "He's what, seventeen? There's no way he gets you. Seventeen-year-old guys are complete morons."

"So are twenty-three-year-old med students who lead on their girlfriends and then break up with them as soon as there's a whiff of anything commitment related."

"That's not true. I wasn't afraid to commit—" His tone is rough with frustration.

"Save it for someone who believes you. See you around, Kenneth."

I push past him and through the door.

"Charlotte, please."

Despite the hint of pleading in his voice, I don't stop. I don't want to stand here fighting with him anymore. I need to cool off, and he needs time to steep in his jealousy of Ricardo. I had hoped he'd feel the sting of envy and want me back, but I hadn't expected it to work so well and so soon. I leave the health center, making sure he doesn't see even a hint of my satisfied expression.

Adrienne closes her tablet case and stands up, stretching her arms wide. "I'm so tired of studying. I need a break. Want to go upstairs and see if there's anyone to hang out with?"
I barely look up at her from where I'm sitting at my desk with my nose buried in my history e-textbook, taking notes on Nelson Mandela.

"I can't. Too busy. You go ahead."

Adrienne's lips purse, but she doesn't argue. She's finally learning that when I say I'm too busy, I really am, and no amount of begging on her part can pull me out of my study hole. This semester is far too important in my grand plan to fritter away on hanging out in the upstairs lounge, anyway.

"See you later, then," my stepsister says, slipping out of my room with her things.

I sink into my note taking, reveling in the hush of quiet that envelops me. Adrienne, I've noticed, prefers to study in the same room as someone else, even if they aren't talking, but I much prefer to be alone. I don't focus as well when there are other people around. The pen-clicking, page turning, and head scratching drive me up the wall.

I'm neck-deep in my notes when someone knocks on the door.

I don't even turn toward it. "I told you I can't hang out now, Adrienne. I'm studying."

The door opens, and someone steps inside. Maybe my sister doesn't know when to quit, after all.

Someone leans over my shoulder to look at my tablet. "Apartheid, huh? Riveting stuff, isn't it?" Ricardo says with a low rumble at the shell of my ear.

I jump nearly out of my skin as I rear away from him. "What are you doing in here? Can't you see I'm busy? I thought you were supposed to be in the security office tonight."

"I have eyes, mon coeur. I can see that you're studying, but I got a night off, and it'll look suspicious if I don't spend this rare free evening with my fake girlfriend."

Disappointment pulls my shoulders down from around my ears. The evenings when Ricardo is stuck in the security office have been a welcome break from performing as his girlfriend for everyone at the academy. But from the determined look on his face, I'm not getting out of it tonight. Glancing at the time on my tablet, I note that I've put in a productive three hours of studying today. It wouldn't *kill* me to take a break. Still, I try one more thing. "You're a junior. You know how important this year is for college. Don't you think you should do some homework too?"

Ricardo nods. "I do know how important this year is, but I also know it's good to take a break. Relax a little." Gently, he pries the tablet out of my clenched fingers. Shutting it off, he sets it on my desk. "Your sister has everyone upstairs in the lounge for a game of truth or dare, and she'd like you to come. I told her I'd use my irresistible charm to fetch you, and how will it look if I can't get my girlfriend to come up for a scintillating game of sharing our deepest, darkest secrets?"

"I don't have any deep, dark secrets," I insist, crossing my arms. We both know that's a whopper of a lie.

Ricardo merely arches an eyebrow. "Then maybe you'd prefer a dare? I know you're dying to spend some time alone with me in a closet."

My eyes widen in horror. "You wouldn't dare."

He grins. "Wouldn't I? Imagine it. You and me alone in the dark. Of course, I'll have to mess up your hair to keep my reputation intact. Can't have people thinking I've lost my touch. It could be fun, you and me."

"You aren't touching my hair."

Ricardo draws toward me. "You think I haven't noticed the shivers you get whenever I do? I think you actually like it when I play with your hair."

I press my lips in a tight line. He's got me there. I've always loved it when people play with my hair. Especially guys. "Ugh. Fine. I'll come. But no seven minutes in heaven crap, got it?"

"Deal." Taking my hands, he pulls me out of my chair.

I don't bother to let go, because he'll want to hold hands as soon as we're in the hallway. Appearances, and all that.

When we get up to the lounge, it's packed. A roar goes up from a group of guys huddled around one of the two pool tables. A couple of girls stand at the stove, frying something on a griddle. Not only are Adrienne, Mikhail, Genevieve, Ryou, Cal, and Asif there, so are Gul and Grady.

I shouldn't be surprised. Gul probably picked up the scent of a game of truth or dare like my mom on the scent of a forbidden carbohydrate. Gul could sniff out dirt in a snow storm. Appropriate, given that there are snowflakes falling outside the lounge window.

I tremble, wishing I'd brought a sweater. It's chilly up here.

Ricardo must see it, because he pulls his gray hoodie over his head and offers it to me.

I want to decline, but Adrienne is looking at us like we're the cutest thing since that video of baby chipmunks she showed me last week, so I take the hoodie and pull it on. The inside smells of Ricardo—a musty earthy scent that, when combined with the warmth lingering from his body, makes me feel so cozy I could take a nap in it. I may detest Ricardo, but this hoodie is nice. I just might leverage my fake girlfriend privilege into keeping it.

I sit primly on the last free couch, and Ricardo plops down way too close to me, pulling me nearer until I'm leaning back against his shoulder and his arm is around me. The familiarity of it isn't terrible, but as soon as I think that thought I reject it. Of course it's terrible. This is Ricardo. A guy I've sworn to hate for his treatment of my best friend and my stepsister. He gives me a little attention—fake attention, at that—and suddenly I'm letting him snuggle with me on a couch?

Adrienne pipes up, explaining her rules for the game. We roll dice to see who goes first, and it falls to Genevieve. She asks for a dare.

"I've got one," Gul says. "Sing that song that's always on the radio. The one about east coast girls. Loudly enough to bring the rest of the boys out of their rooms."

It's a good dare. Genevieve is a terrible singer.

She blushes, and everyone laughs. Standing up, she clears her throat and starts to sing.

I can't help but crack up when she gets to the bridge,

which is a rap. Genevieve attempts to look cool as she moves through the upbeat words, but with her lithe figure and cinnamon brown waves, she just ends up looking silly. By the time she's done, we're all busting up laughing.

Genevieve bows deeply and plops down in her chair, sitting sideways so her legs drape over the rolled arm.

"Nice one," Ryou says, giving her a high five. His cheeks are pink from laughter.

"Thanks," she smiles back, looking pleased.

"My turn. I choose dare," Adrienne says.

"I dare you to go ten minutes without holding Mikhail's hand," Cal says.

Adrienne's face flushes magenta as the rest of us crack up. Even Mikhail looks sheepish under his beard.

We've all noticed that Adrienne can't seem to stop holding Mikhail's hand now that they're dating. It's actually really sweet.

"I can go ten minutes," Adrienne mumbles, but she's already twitching as she lets go of her boyfriend's hand where they're sitting on adjoining plush chairs, across from Ricardo and me.

"Ricardo, it's your turn," my stepsister says, taking the attention off herself.

"Thanks, chouchou. I pick dare."

I snort. "Of course."

His eyes peruse my face. "You know it."

Adrienne glances between us before focusing on Ricardo. "I dare you to look into Charlotte eyes and tell her two things you like about her—"

"And one you can't stand!" Gul cuts in.

"Gross," Cal grumbles.

Genevieve busies herself with putting on a new layer of lip gloss.

I'm not entirely surprised at Adrienne's dare. My sister is a hopeless romantic who wants all of us to be as blissfully happy as she is. I should have predicted she'd come up with mushy dares.

Ricardo laughs. "Are you trying to get me killed?" But he turns and locks eyes with me.

I have no idea why, but my heart is picking up speed as I look into his eyes. They're amber brown with darker rims. Who knew making eye contact with the guy I hate could be so intense?

Taking my hand, Ricardo speaks. "Charlotte, I like how, when you care about something, you throw yourself into it with everything you've got." His eyes flick over me. "And you're so—

"Watch it," I warn.

"I was going to say graceful," he laughs.

A curl of pleasure unfurls in my chest. I stamp it down with vehemence.

"Now something you hate," Gul says, prodding him.

Ricardo rubs his jaw, trying to hide his smile. He's loving this.

I, on the other hand, have never felt so exposed. I can't tell if he's being honest, or screwing with me, and it's throwing me off balance.

"Don't take this personally, but you're always wound so tight. You never relax. I always feel like I have to be on my game around you. I wish you'd let your guard down once in a while."

Genevieve winces, and Adrienne only just stops herself from nodding in agreement.

Does everyone think I'm a tight-ass? It's not a bad thing to be at peak performance all the time. I have expectations to meet. My parents' and my own. I don't have time for laziness. The idea that everyone thinks I'm wound so tight irks me, making me feel defensive. "I can't let my guard down, especially so you can feel better about yourself. I don't compromise. You have no idea how much pressure I'm under from my parents, and with my goals for myself. If I *relax*, that gives someone else the opportunity to do something better than me, get there before I do, and that's not acceptable."

I scoot away from him and cross my arms. Annoyance at his honesty flares hot in my chest, even as guilt enters the equation. Just because I was feeling attacked doesn't mean I should poke at Ricardo. Even if I do hate him. I huff out the steam that has gathered in my head. It's just a game, but I have a feeling I've just played into Gul's hands. If she wanted to rile me up, or provoke me into giving her something to gossip about, she succeeded. Stifling my frustration at Ricardo, I uncoil my muscles. If I stay clenched like this, my neck and shoulders will pay for it tomorrow.

"I'm not asking you to dim your light to stroke my ego, chère. I just want to have a little fun with my girlfriend. With you."

Now I feel guilty for blasting Ricardo, but I refuse to look him in the eye, even if what he just said was kind of sweet.

When I glance up, everyone is staring at me.

"What?" I ask.

Genevieve clears her throat. "It's your turn, Char."

"Oh. Right. I pick dare." I'm in the mood to run yodeling down the hall, or doorbell ditch Ms. Poppin, or something like that. That is not the dare I get.

When Gul leans forward to level my dare, she's got a sly look in her eyes. "We've never seen you and Ricardo kiss. We want you to kiss right here, right now."

"Yeah, kiss!" Adrienne exclaims, clapping her hands gleefully.

Cal wrinkles his nose. "I'm gonna go make popcorn. Let me know when it's over." He pulls himself out of his plush chair and shuffles across the room to the student kitchen. I look longingly after him, wishing I could excuse myself to make popcorn, but I can't. If I balk, they'll know something's up. When Kenneth and I were together, I was a lot more engaged with him than I am with Ricardo, and I'm sure they've picked up on it. I do not want them to find out I'm faking this relationship to make Kenneth jealous. Surely giving Ricardo one tiny peck won't be as bad as losing face, right?

Even worse, Genevieve is chewing on her lip anxiously. Turning to Ryou, she whispers something about needing a cup of tea, and follows Cal toward the kitchen. I stare after her, willing her to be okay with all of the shenanigans I'm putting her through by continuing my charade with Ricardo.

"We're waiting," Gul needles me.

I manage not to glare at her. Instead, I lean toward Ricardo and give him the quickest peck on the lips known to man. "There, we kissed. Ta da. Now you've seen it."

It's so fast that Ricardo doesn't even have a chance to kiss me back.

"Boo, that was terrible," Gul says, shaking her head in displeasure.

"Yeah, come on, Charlotte. This is truth or dare. It's only fun if you actually do it, not just halfway." Adrienne waves me back toward Ricardo.

I am going to kill her for this later.

My eyes narrow. Even though the thought of laying a real kiss on Ricardo has my body flushed with irritation, I never back down from a challenge. And Adrienne? She's just thrown down a gauntlet. "You want a real kiss? Okay. Here, take a picture so you can look at it later." I toss my phone into my stepsister's lap, face Ricardo, and pull him toward me by the collar of his t-shirt.

"Whoa, you—"

I put my lips to his and kiss him for all I'm worth. My competitive streak rears its ugly head. No one is going to say I can't kiss, especially when I'm put on the spot like this. I'm going to be the best at this, just like everything else.

It takes Ricardo a second to recover from the shock of my abrupt action, which makes me want to laugh, but I stifle it. Laughing while kissing would feel too intimate, somehow, like we were sharing in a secret. Which we're absolutely not.

Then he's matching me move for move, his lithe hand rising to my neck. After all this time, I half expected him to be a terrible kisser. You know, all that bravado as a front for lack of skill, but it's not. Ricardo can *kiss*. Still.

Adrienne and Gul start hooting, so I cut the kiss off with one last peck. My signature move.

When I pull away, Ricardo's got a dazed look in his eyes that he tries to hide by clearing his throat and looking away, but I catch it. I've gotten under his skin. Satisfaction courses through me. I have definitely won this round of whatever game we're playing. Yeah, it's definitely satisfaction. Not chemistry. That would be absurd.

"Wow," is all Adrienne says. "I never saw you kissing Kenneth like that."

"To be fair, we never really saw Kenneth," Genevieve says, offering Ryou a steaming mug matching the one in her hand, and retaking her seat. She takes a sip, not looking at me.

Gathering himself, Ricardo smiles, pulling me against his side. "Kenneth's got nothing on me, right, mon coeur?"

"Kenneth, who?" I reply, playing along. Rationalizations as to why I jumped into that kiss like I did skim over the surface of my thoughts. Never mind that I've just sprinted past one of the lines we drew in the sand. I couldn't very well refuse to kiss my apparent boyfriend, could I? I have to make it look realistic, which I did. And then some.

Deep down, I sift past the bull I'm trying to sell everyone else, and myself. Kenneth never kissed me with that amount of fire. Apparently, the antagonism Ricardo and I share makes for some steamy lip-locking. It absolutely cannot happen again.

The scent of piping hot, buttery popcorn wafts through the lounge. The microwave beeps.

"Is it safe to turn around?" Cal calls over his shoulder.

"It is safe," Mikhail replies.

Without thinking, Adrienne tries to take Mikhail's hand. "Oh shoot," she exclaims, turning red. "I forgot about my dare."

Stifling a chuckle, Mikhail wraps his hand around hers. A trace of a smile lingers. It's the most I've ever seen him smile, except for when we went swing dancing last semester.

"You made it six minutes," Genevieve says, holding up her phone to show us the timer. "That's not bad."

Adrienne ducks her head, biting her lip.

"Okay, okay. It's my turn," Gul says, standing up. "I choose dare, so make it good."

This one, I've got. "Since we all know how well you love to gossip…"

Everyone groans in agreement, and Gul shrugs, unapologetic.

People are gathering in the lounge to watch our game of truth or dare. The circle of bodies around us makes me feel like I'm in a fish bowl. Good thing all these people weren't around for my kiss with Ricardo. That would have been so embarrassing.

"I want you to go over to the window and narrate the weather to us. And make it boring." I draw out the last word in emphasis.

"That's easy," Gul says, but tromps over to the window anyway.

"Do it in a phony English accent," Cal puts in, plopping down in his armchair and munching on hot popcorn right out of the bag. "To make it harder."

Gul smiles and looks out the window. "That I can do." Clearing her throat, she begins "We're here in downtown District of Columbia, and I'm Gul Abidi with the weather. We've got a cold front moving in that will result in lots of snow overnight, but don't expect it to linger. We're calling for a warm, sunny day tomorrow that will melt the snow into ice…"

Recognition dawns like a flare in the dark as Gul speaks. She grows more animated as everyone jeers at her butchering of a London accent.

I've heard that accent before. In a recording of a 911 call.

Gul was the one who called emergency services after the accident that killed the professor. She must have seen what happened. She knows who killed Professor Rook.

14

Grady is still laughing as Gul sits down beside him. "That was funnier than sending someone on a snipe hunt," he says, holding up his hand for a high five.

She slaps her palm against his. "Thanks."

My instincts are humming. I'm right about the anonymous caller being her; I'm 99% sure of it.

"What's a snipe?" Adrienne asks, twirling a red curl around a finger.

Grady's smile is sly as he wraps an arm around Gul's shoulders. "Come on down to Austin sometime and I'll show you."

"Is it some kind of lizard or something?" Adrienne presses, disgust written on her features.

"They don't exist," Cal says between bites of popcorn. "What they do is send some dummy out into the woods with a sack and tell him snipes are easy to catch. It's a joke. Saw it on MyStream once."

"That doesn't sound very nice," Adrienne murmurs.

"It's hilarious," Grady says. "You never sent someone on a wild goose chase?" His eyes cut to me before he turns to whisper something in Gul's ear, making her smile.

Adrienne shakes her head vehemently. I'm not surprised. She's way too sweet to send someone on a fool's errand simply for a laugh. I wish I could send Kenneth on a snipe hunt.

I must be staring at Gul, because Ricardo nudges my leg

105

with his knee. "Hey," he whispers. "You okay?"

I nod. "Yeah."

Leaning closer, he whispers in my ear. "It looked like you'd seen a ghost back there. I've never seen you go so white, even when you sprained your ankle last semester."

"Later," I whisper back.

Cal munches loudly on his popcorn. "Who's next?"

Genevieve and Adrienne look around the circle, looking for the next person for the hot seat.

Gul's phone vibrates, and when she checks it, she sneaks a glance toward Grady, but he's not paying attention, instead running a hand over the seam of the couch's arm. Shoving it into the pocket of her designer jeans, Gul stands up, tucking her black hair behind her ears. "I'll be right back."

I shoot out of my seat. "I'm coming too."

"Suit yourself." She shrugs, tossing her hair over her shoulder and traipsing down the staircase.

I follow her until we're out of earshot of everyone, and then I swivel around in front of her. "We need to talk."

"About what?" Gul takes another step down, unbothered, but I keep pace with her.

"You were the one who called 911 to report Professor Rook's accident, weren't you?"

Gul's foot hovers over the next step, my words seemingly arresting her in place. Surprise flashes over her features before her expression closes off.

A group of guys come loping up the stairs, interrupting us. They greet Gul and me with casual head nods as they flow around us on both sides.

I'm quiet until the tide of bodies recedes up the stairs.

Gul picks up speed as she descends. "I don't know what you're talking about."

I jab my thumb over my shoulder. "I heard you up there. You used that horrendous accent when you talked to the emergency operator. I recognized your voice. Don't even bother denying it."

She shakes her head. "You must have misheard. I've never called 911 in my life. It wasn't me. Here. Check my phone." She unlocks it and holds it out in her palm.

I snatch the device out of her hand and scroll through the call log. My confidence drops for a second as I look, finding nothing. There's no trace of a call to 911. Could I have been mistaken? Huffing, I give it back. "You probably deleted it, for some reason."

"I don't know what to tell you." Gul tucks it into her pocket and walks down the hall toward one of the shared bathrooms on our floor.

I start to follow her, to push her further, but she waves me off over her shoulder. "I'll be back in a minute. I don't need company."

Grady passes me as I jog up the stairs. "Need a snack," he says. "See you in a few."

Ten minutes later, after Cal has doorbell ditched Professor Bins's private rooms, and Mikhail has tried to recite the alphabet backwards, with hilarious results, I realize Grady hasn't returned, and neither has Gul.

Over the next few days, Gul avoids me. When I try to confront her in the hall, she disappears. She's freakishly adept at vanishing in a crowd. Probably the reason she's so good at collecting dirt on the student body at large.

Finally, on Friday, I corner her outside our last class of the day. She fidgets with her hair, pulling it forward before pushing it back over her shoulder, pointedly staring at me.

I'll give her this: she doesn't back down.

The corridor is full of students and professors talking, stowing books and tablets, and messing around on their phones. I'll have to be careful if I want to avoid being overheard. Normally, I would choose a more private place for a talk like this, but she's given me no choice. At least here she can't deny it too vehemently without drawing attention, which I'm guessing she'd like to avoid.

"Why are you pretending it wasn't you who made that call?" I've listened to it a bunch of times since our game of truth or dare, and I'm absolutely positive the caller is Gul. Why would she deny it? That, I'm not sure about.

There are lots of possibilities.

She didn't see the accident, only the body, and lied about it to the emergency technician because she loves drama.

She saw the accident, but didn't see or recognize the driver, and thus doesn't think she has any reason to talk to the police further.

She did see the driver and doesn't want anyone to know because she's scared of them, for obvious reasons.

The last possibility is the one that has me the most intrigued, although, yeah, it's a little farfetched: Gul was outside at the time of the accident because she was in on it. The hit and run wasn't an accident, and Gul was in league with the killer.

"This again? I'm not the one who called, okay? I didn't see anything. Will you just drop it already?"

I cross my arms. "Not a chance."

Gul rolls her eyes. "Ricardo's right. You're like a rabid dog with a bone."

I stop. *Ricardo said that?*

"Yeah, he did, and I see his point."

I clamp my mouth shut. I hadn't been aware I'd said that

out loud. Plus, it's not very nice of Ricardo to say things like that about his fake girlfriend. "Well, Ricardo's a huge flake, so he wouldn't know."

Gul's eyes glint and a sly smile splays over her face.

I've let her goad me into saying something negative about Ricardo. Fake relationship or not, I know that's against the rules. Still, he broke them first. It serves him right. But if it gets around… "Look, don't tell anyone I said that."

"You know," Gul says, leaning in. "I find it really odd that you and Ricardo started dating over Christmas break, since I couldn't find a trace of conversation between you on social media. You two don't even follow each other, and the last personal photo you shared was of you and Kenneth. If I had to speculate, I'd say you were faking it." Her words are loud enough that if someone were listening to us, they would have heard it.

I glance around, checking to see if anyone's close enough to be listening. There are students dotted along the hall talking and goofing off, but no one seems to be paying any attention to Gul and me.

I swallow. Once again Gul's nose for news has led her true. She's got me dead to rights. It didn't even occur to me to doctor my online presence to reflect my new relationship status. I can't believe I overlooked it. Rookie mistake. One that I won't make again.

My eyes narrow in defiance. "Just to be clear, Ricardo and I ARE dating, but I'll stop hounding you about the call," I concede.

Gul cocks her head to one side, weighing my words.

If I've guessed incorrectly and she didn't make that call, there's nothing to keep her from floating her theory about Ricardo and me all over school. She'd love nothing more than to spread rumors about us, especially if I've been barking up her tree by mistake. It wouldn't be her first time savaging a new couple.

I unclench my jaw when she nods.

"Okay, I'll keep it to myself, but if you mention that stupid call again…" Her implication is clear.

"I won't."

Grady appears at her side, face drawn. He looks exhausted. "Ready?"

"I'm starving," Gul purrs. "Let's go off campus." She twines her fingers with his and saunters away, confident that she's won our match just now.

It galls me to no end that she got the upper hand. If I hadn't taken her bait, hadn't shot off my mouth, it may have ended differently.

I stomp up the hall toward the dormitory, my glower cutting a path for me through the crowd. Everyone is pumped that it's finally the weekend, and I was too, until a few minutes ago. I thought I'd have more clues as to what happened to Professor Rook, but Gul didn't give me anything but threats and warnings.

My fingers tap along the bannister as I ascend the dormitory stairs. I'll have to come up with another way to prove that Gul was outside the academy during that call. If I'm going to talk to her again, I'll need some leverage.

Which means I'll have to build some goodwill with my classmates so if Gul does spread rumors about Ricardo and me, they won't have long legs.

It looks like Ricardo and I will have to make another public appearance this weekend, and a cute one too.

My mind returns to all of the possible reasons Gul might want to keep people from finding out she made that anonymous call. Is she capable of participating in a hit and run that ended a man's life?

I don't know, and I can't think of a motive.

As far as I know, Gul doesn't have any reason to want Professor Rook dead. They didn't have much interaction that I saw, and I don't have any reason to suspect she bought drugs from him even once, let alone habitually.

So why would she protect the killer?

15

With Gul's threat hanging over my head, I have to go about my investigation into Professor Rook's death another way. And I need to play up my relationship with Ricardo so our classmates start rooting for us. That way if Gul decides to let her suspicions slip, people will be less likely to believe her. I hope.

I read the same paragraph of my textbook for the fifth time, rubbing at the back of my neck. I've been sitting in my desk chair for what feels like hours. Rolling my shoulders, I turn to where Adrienne and Genevieve are sitting on floor poufs, leaning against the side of my bed.

A quiet stream of classical music filters from the speakers on my laptop.

"I don't understand why my phyllo dough won't cooperate," Adrienne says, flicking her finger over the screen of her tablet. "It falls apart, every time. And Mikhail's birthday is next week."

Genevieve pats Adrienne's arm. "You'll get it. I know it. Just like you did with that calculus test last week."

Adrienne smiles in reply.

Since my concentration is shattered, I snap my tablet closed. Standing, I arch my back in a much needed stretch. "I need a break. I'm going downstairs for a bit."

Adrienne and Genevieve look up at me, one with a knowing smile and one with a carefully blank face. After truth or dare, Adrienne was definitely Team Ricardo and Charlotte, but Genevieve hasn't moved from her position of studied indifference. The fact that I'm lying to them only makes me feel worse.

"Can't seem to stay away from him, can you?" Genevieve asks, startling me out of my self-flagellation. "Just be careful, okay?"

I nod, thankful that she doesn't seem to be mad at me for supposedly dating the guy who broke her heart last year. I'm dying to tell both of them it's all a sham, but Ricardo and I promised each other we wouldn't tell anyone. We both have a lot to lose if people find out we're faking it.

"They're so cute," Adrienne gushes, coming to my defense. Of course, she would. She and Ricardo are close friends after spending so much time together last semester.

Genevieve's expression falters, but she doesn't say whatever's on the tip of her tongue.

I leave before she changes her mind. I'll explain it all to her, someday.

First, I go up to the student lounge and make some popcorn. Grabbing Ricardo's favorite hot sauce out of the cabinet, I trot down the stairs. "Going to see my boyfriend," I tell the first group of people I meet. Inwardly, I cringe. It's really none of their business where I'm going, but I have to make this look good.

Whispers feather into the air behind me. By the end of the night, everyone will know where I was tonight. For once, the grapevine is working for me instead of against me.

My fingers brush along the smooth, cold surface of the glass walkway between the dormitory and the academy building. On the other side of the crystal clear panes, the courtyard is mostly dark. In a far corner, something moves in the shadows. A couple availing themselves of the privacy of the courtyard at night. It's probably freezing out there, but they don't seem to mind.

I shiver and hurry to the far door. It's way too cold to be out.

Ricardo's jaw drops in surprise when I saunter into the security office wearing a cozy sweater dress and bearing hot buttered popcorn and chili sauce. "Popcorn? You shouldn't have. What do you want?" He hits me with a skeptical smirk.

I look around, never having been in this room before. It's a small space with a corner desk. On top of it sit three large flat screens showing various angles of the school's perimeter. Parking lot. Front gate. A narrow shot of the street outside.

The security guard wouldn't have been able to see the accident from here, but hopefully the cameras caught Gul walking outside. Or even the car that hit Professor Rook. Whoever was driving would have had to make a u-turn near the front gate.

Ricardo is sitting in a black desk chair, hunched in front of the screens, but leans back in his chair as he waits on me, expectant.

I smile sweetly. "What makes you think I want something?"

Ricardo cocks an eyebrow. "You've never willingly done anything nice for me in your life. Fess up. What is it?"

I plop down in the vacant chair beside him. "So… I'm pretty sure Gul was the one who made that anonymous 911 call, but when I asked her about it, she threatened to tell everyone you and I are pretending to date."

Ricardo's eyebrows fly upward, and an emotion I can't identify flies across his face. "So all of this, you visiting me tonight, is a show. Got it."

For some reason, this vexes me. "What else would it be?

We *are* faking it, remember?" As I say it, I realize how harsh it sounds. I should try doing something nice for Ricardo sometime, without strings. Maybe. I'll think about it.

Footsteps approach down the hall. Someone is about to catch us fighting. Great.

I have to do something. Heart skittering, I fling myself into Ricardo's lap and wrap my arms around his neck.

Ricardo's arm comes instinctively around my back, holding me safely in place.

It's... surprisingly not repulsive.

Officer Morris, the security guard, pops his head in, and his eyes widen when he spots me. Then his gaze flicks to Ricardo. "Using my office to pick up girls, eh? Can't say I'm surprised. I've seen you around, flirting with everything that moves." He says it like it's funny.

Ricardo's mouth flattens.

I tighten my arm around his neck and shoot the security guard a chilly look. "He's not picking up girls. Just me. We're dating." Ricardo may be a cad, but for now, he's my cad.

"Whatever you say, Miss Cavendish-Holt. Just make sure you're actually watching the security feed. No canoodling in here." The guard clomps off down the corridor, leaving us alone.

"Canoodling? Who says that anymore?" I laugh, catching Ricardo's eye. It occurs to me that I'm sitting in his lap, and that it's an intimate and precarious position. He must realize it too, because his arm around my back loosens.

"Ahem, sorry." I jump up, smoothing down my dress. "About that—breaking one of our rules, I mean. I won't do it again."

"If that's what you have to tell yourself." Ricardo scoops the popcorn bag into his lap and sprinkles it liberally with hot sauce. The hot kernels crunch when he bites down on a handful, his focus on the screens on the desk.

Clasping my hands, I frown. "I really am sorry. About everything. But the fact is, I need your help. I was hoping you'd show me the security feed from the night of the accident? I want to see if I can spot Gul outside around eleven. When Rook was killed. If you want, I'll fawn all over you in front of your mom tomorrow. Make her realize what she's missing."

"You think she's missing out?" Ricardo's tone is teasing, but there's an undercurrent I'm all too familiar with.

"Definitely."

He grins. "Deal. Come here." He pats the vacant chair next to his.

I take it, sitting primly on the edge.

Snaking his hand under my seat, he pulls my chair closer to his.

I yip in surprise, my attention snagging on the vein snaking up his corded arm.

"Just give me a second." With a few finger swipes, Ricardo pulls up a video file.

"Go to 10:30, and start it there," I command.

"Start it there…" He prompts me with one hand.

"Ugh. Please."

Ricardo hits me with his wide smile. "That's better. Here it is. What are we looking for, again? Right. Gul."

We skim through the footage. At first, I don't see anything. Maybe this was pointless.

"Stop. Go back. There she is." I clamp my hand over my mouth to stifle my enthusiasm.

Ricardo chuckles, and slows the replay.

Gul slips out the front door and slinks through the parking lot toward the front gate. When the guard in the security booth turns his back, she ducks under the window and slithers through the opening.

I look down to the time stamp on the bottom of the video. 10:53 PM

"Got her."

Ricardo backs up the video and takes a screenshot of her, including the time stamp. Then he turns to me. "What next?"

"Now we wait."

The minutes pass by on double speed, approaching 11.

Ricardo's arm stretches over the back of my chair, and his fingers coil into my ponytail, wrapping my blond hair in his fist.

My eyes start to droop at the pressure on my scalp, but I force them open. "Stop that. I'm trying to focus." Batting his hand away, I stare at the screen.

Leaning one elbow on the desk, Ricardo locks eyes with me. "So you're saying I'm distracting you?" His shit-eating grin is probably visible from space.

I roll my eyes. "Absolutely not. It's annoying. Knock it off."

"Whatever you say, mon coeur." He's still grinning. So smug.

I try to focus on the video, but my skin warms at the thought of Ricardo's fingers in my hair. It felt so good, I didn't want him to stop.

I hate Ricardo, I tell myself. But do I really?

The security guard puts in headphones and starts bobbing to whatever music is filtering into his ears.

Wait. "Stop the video. Play it back."

Ricardo complies, going back a few seconds.

Out of frame, headlights flash in the street.

Several minutes pass without movement, and then a dark figure dashes in through the gate and up to the dormitory door.

The security guard misses it, looking at his computer screen.

So, that guard should be fired.

And that was definitely Gul fleeing inside. She saw the accident, and lied about it. She looked freaked out when she snuck back inside, her movements jerky and her head held low.

Her mannerisms make me doubt she was involved, or even knew about it. Someone cold-blooded enough to arrange to have someone killed by being run over wouldn't be that skittish afterward.

So why was Gul outside school grounds that night?

16

It gives me so much pleasure to see Kenneth's envious face when Ricardo and I strut past the health center into the eatery for lunch. Eat your heart out, Kenneth. I'm so focused on watching Kenneth out of the corner of my eye that it catches me by surprise when Ricardo leans down and brushes his lips over my cheek.

"I'll meet you inside," he whispers in my ear. "Can you blush on command? Act like I'm saying something naughty."

"No way," I titter, but throw in a playful swat for good measure. "Where are you going?"

"Wouldn't you like to know." He winks as he walks backward away from me, then disappears into the crowded hallway.

I huff in amusement. If I didn't dislike Ricardo, I'd think he was funny.

"There you are. We need to talk," Cal says, snagging my arm and propelling me into the eatery and toward the pizza station.

I allow him to pull me along by the elbow. I've managed to avoid answering questions about his car for an impressive amount of time, but now that I know it wasn't me who killed Rook with Cal's car, I should probably explain what happened.

We join the back of the line, and Cal looks around to make sure we've got some privacy.

Honestly, he's less subtle than a fog horn.

"What's up?" I ask, feigning ignorance. Even if I'm going to be honest with my brother about everything that's going on, I can still have a little fun with him first.

Cal's head cocks to one side. "You know. My car? It disappeared the day they found Rook's body, and then it was mysteriously back two days later, and it was spotless. You had it repaired. You're lucky I'm the only one who noticed, or it would have looked bad."

I open my mouth to speak, but change tacks. My hands find my hips. "How did you know I'd had it repaired?" He must have seen it on his way into the dormitory that night. Otherwise, when would he have? It was gone early the next morning.

Cal glances around again.

Over his shoulder, I see Adrienne, Genevieve, Mikhail, and Asif at our table. Adrienne waves at us, so I give her a small finger-wave back.

"You swear you won't tell Mom and Dad?" Cal mutters, scooting forward in the line.

I'm doubly confused now. "Swear I won't tell them what?"

"I might have hit one of those concrete poles with my car. You know the ones in parking lots? Don't tell Dad, okay?"

My jaw drops. "You have got to be kidding me. You did that? I thought I'd killed Professor Rook. I had the car fixed to hide my tracks. I mean, it turns out I did run over him, but he was already dead when it happened. So, yeah." The words come in a rush, and I have to fight to remain quiet

It's Cal's turn to gape. Shaking his head, he brings his face down to mine. "You… you thought you'd killed Professor Rook with my car? And you didn't confess?" The unmistakable undertone of admonishment in the question cuts me to the quick.

I stare at the floor, my brother's rebuke ringing in my ears. "It was an accident, and it's not like the professor was an innocent lamb, or anything. He was a drug dealer, for goodness sakes!"

"How do you… You know what? I don't want to know. Still, killing a man by accident is wrong. I can't believe you weren't going to tell the police." He combs a hand through his icy blond hair, hair the same color as mine. "Unbelievable, Charlotte."

I start to spout all of my reasons for keeping quiet, but they're suddenly, obviously inadequate. I glance over my shoulder, and am brought up short by the dirty look the girl in line behind me is giving me. Did she hear what I just said? Crap.

"Are you going to move forward, or what?" she says, gesturing ahead of us.

Relief floods through me as I glance beyond Cal. The line has moved considerably, and we're holding it up. "Oh, sorry."

Catching on, Cal scoots forward toward the pizza station. He scans the row of available pizza toppings, not looking at me. Out of the corner of his mouth, he says, "How did you find out it wasn't you who killed him?"

Sighing, I tell him about that night. The "tire" I ran over. Kenneth calling me about it, and showing up at school. His buddy telling him that Rook was run over twice, and the timeline that exonerates me of manslaughter.

Cal's eyes meet mine. "You got lucky."

Straightening my headband, I nod. "You're telling me."

I should tell my brother the rest, but something holds me back from confiding in him about my fake relationship with Ricardo. I want to keep that to myself for a little while longer. Probably to make Kenneth even more jealous. Or something.

"So, are you going to tell the police you were the second driver?" My brother's wide eyes make it clear that he thinks I should.

"Maybe. Probably."

Cal shakes his head. "Shame, shame, I know your name."

"Shut up and grab some pizza."

The girl behind us bumps into me with her tray, and her apology is phonier than a politician who flip flops on issues every election cycle.

We get our food and walk toward our table. As I slide into the chair beside Ricardo, I realize that I feel lighter than I have in the two weeks since the accident. Confiding in Cal has loosened the knots in my chest. And so has knowing that he was the one who dented the car, not me.

Having a guy in my dorm room is weird. Ricardo wanted me to hang out in his room, but there was no way I was subjecting myself to the trolling that would happen if anyone saw me going into a guy's room on the fifth floor and shutting the door, so here we are, in my room instead.

Ricardo circles the carpet, running his fingers over the faux fur blanket thrown over the end of my bed. "This is *nice*. I'm going to come down here more often. What's that smell?"

"I don't smell anything." I shrug, feeling awkward, so I plop down into my desk chair.

Coming up behind me, Ricardo leans over and takes a whiff of my neck. "Are you wearing perfume? I like it."

"I am, but not for you." I can't stop the flush of warmth that moves through me. He thinks I smell good? I wipe the smile off my face. I've been spending too much time with Adrienne, and she's turning me into a sap. "Let's just do homework, okay? Help me practice my conversational French for the test on Friday."

"No problem, mon coeur."

I shoot him a disapproving look, which he totally ignores.

Taking a large, fluffy pillow off my bed, he tosses it on the floor and stretches out on his back with his hands behind his head. "Ahh, that's better. Now, what's on the test on Friday?"

I goggle at him. "You don't know? You're in that class."

He laughs. "I'm already fluent. I took it because it's a bird course for me."

"Yeah, yeah, well you may *fly* right through it, but I have to study." I slide into the floor and arrange myself on one of my velvety floor poufs.

We go back and forth, reading passages to each other from our e-books and quizzing each other on word meanings and verb conjugations. I'll never tell, but I'm actually enjoying speaking French with Ricardo. He's good at it, like Genevieve, so we fall into an easy rhythm. It's kind of nice having a peer to study with, even if he is exasperating half the time.

Outside my window, a car pulls into the parking lot. Grady gets out and circles around the hood to open the passenger door for Gul. Pressing her against the car, he kisses her breathless before taking her hand and walking her inside, where I can't see.

A sharp pain in my chest grabs my focus. Not too long ago, he was doing the same thing, only with Rhiannon instead. If only she hadn't gone to Professor Rook that first time. If only I had kept my mouth shut.

"Char? Hello?" Ricardo says, waving a hand in front of my face.

I start to shove him away, but my mind is already whirling. "What if the hit and run wasn't an accident? What if someone had it out for Professor Rook, waited outside, and killed him?"

"What makes you say that?"

I chew my lip, not sure I want to divulge what I'm thinking. He might think I'm off my rocker. Actually, who cares what he thinks? I don't. "I saw Grady and Gul outside, and it got me thinking. Professor Rook had to have made enemies. Hell, I wasn't a fan of his, and I bought from him a few times. Someone like Grady, he might be pretty mad at Rook, especially after Rhiannon's death. What if he, or someone else, decided to take matters into their own hands?"

Ricardo nods slowly, taking in everything I've said. "Okay, so who else might have it out for Rook? You, Grady…"

"Anyone who bought from him, maybe. Any parents, if they found out. I don't know who else." My eyes are pulled toward the window, where Grady's car is parked under one of the wrought-iron lamps in the lot.

"Wait," Ricardo says, bumping my shoulder with his. "It couldn't have been Grady. He didn't even get back to school until the afternoon after the accident. They had that snowstorm in Austin, remember?"

My eyes narrow. "That's what he said…" Typing on my tablet with rapid fingers, I pull up the news for Austin. Sure enough, they had a giant snow storm the first week of January that downed all of the planes near there for three days, just like Grady said. There's no way he could have caught a flight out of Austin in time.

Down the hall, a door slams.

A tingle of awareness runs up my spine. A warning. I go still, listening.

Ricardo opens his mouth to speak, but I put a hand on his shoulder, stopping him.

There's a faint shuffling in the hallway. Is someone listening in on our conversation?

Patting Ricardo's shoulder again, I gesture toward my door. Creeping across the floor, I fling it open, making the knob smack against the wall. The hallway is empty.

I could have sworn I sensed someone out here, eavesdropping on me and Ricardo talking, but the hallway is deserted. Some of the doors along the girls' hallway are open, so someone in one of the nearby rooms could have been the one doing it, but I'm not sure why they would. Unless someone was just being nosy.

Stepping up to the bannister, I peer over the edge into the foyer. Other than the security guard at the front door, there's no one there.

But as I return to my room, I can't shake the feeling that someone overheard Ricardo and me talking.

Adrienne's door opens. "What's going on out here?" she asks, looking past me down the hall. "Who's slamming doors?"

"I don't know. I thought—"

A blood-chilling scream interrupts me.

17

Trepidation thickens the air. Where did that scream come from?

Adrienne steps out of her room, eyes wide in horror. Her gaze rises to Mikhail, who tucks her into his side protectively.

I'm peering down the hallway as more girls peek out of their rooms. Girls spill out into the corridor, looking around for the person who let loose that shriek. A couple of guys follow their girlfriends out of their rooms too. "Where's the fire?" someone calls from somewhere behind me.

My mind is crystal clear and focused as I wait for another scream to slice through the growing buzz in the dormitory. Guys are clomping down the stairs toward our floor, calling out questions to those below.

No one seems to know what's happening, or who screamed.

A single question keeps revolving in my head. What if someone is being attacked, just like Professor Rook was? I make a split-second decision.

Mikhail throws out an arm to stop me, but I dodge past him and bolt down the hallway.

"Char!" Adrienne calls as Mikhail takes off after me.

Feet pound at my heels, making me shoot a glance over my shoulder. Despite my smaller, more fluid frame, the bodyguard is gaining on me.

I scan the faces peeking out of each door I pass, rounding

the corner.

Instead of tackling me, Mikhail passes on the inside and keeps an easy jogging pace a stride ahead of me. He's scanning the dormitory too, looking every bit the muscle in his gray tee and black athletic pants.

Adrienne and Ricardo come up on either side of me, looking as stricken as I feel.

That scream. It sounded primal. Afraid.

I've never heard such a terrified, excruciating cry, and the mental images it calls up make my heart skitter in my ribcage. Dali with tears streaming down her cheeks. Adrienne unconscious as Mikhail pried her attacker off her neck.

I don't know what's happening, but I'm going to find out. Nobody else is going to be hurt on my watch, if I can help it.

The sound of sobbing gets louder as the four of us jog along the hall, doing a quick visual check of each room as we pass.

Ms. Poppin comes running up the stairs, out of breath. "I was in the kitchen. What's going on? Do you know who that was?" she asks between pants.

I shake my head.

It's only been a few seconds, but there's a crowd of people behind me, each of them wondering what's going on. If something else has happened. If someone else has been killed.

We reach the end of the hall, and stop. The scream I heard brought everyone within hearing distance out of their rooms.

And yet, I'm staring at a closed door. This door is the only one on our hall that hasn't been flung open in the past minute, which captures my attention. The person behind this door has somehow managed to ignore the agonizing screech. Or she's the victim. It's Gul's door.

Something must be going on in there. Something Gul, or

someone else, doesn't want us to see. If it's the latter, the attacker must still be cornered inside.

I'm going to find out who it is.

I take another step toward the closed door and reach for the knob.

"Charlotte, let me," Mikhail commands, putting a heavy hand on my shoulder. "It is my job."

"Be my guest."

Mikhail advances toward the door, his body taut with energy, with Ms. Poppin on his heels.

I watch with baited breath.

Beside me, Adrienne braces herself with her arms wrapped across her chest.

Ricardo nudges me with his elbow and lifts his chin toward my sister. She's watching after Mikhail with wide, frightened eyes. Ricardo starts to chuckle, but I shoot him an admonishing look. "This is not the time."

Sobering immediately, he slings an arm around my shoulders and squeezes gently. "Just trying to cut the tension."

Together, we creep up behind Mikhail and Ms. Poppin while Adrienne hangs back with the rest of the crowd.

Mikhail opens the door a slit and pokes his head inside. After a moment, he retreats, gesturing for Ms. Poppin to enter.

I follow.

Gul is curled up in a ball on the floor, sobbing into her scraggly hair, which hangs over her face in sweaty strings. She doesn't look up when we enter.

On a gasp, Ms. Poppin kneels down and tries to pull Gul to a sitting position, with not much success.

My gaze swings past them, moving over the rest of the room. On the desk, Gul's phone is playing a video on a loop. I snatch it up and watch the screen.

The footage was shot at night, from a car's dashboard. I squint as the car passes under several street lamps, its headlights off. Bright white light flashes as the headlights spring to life, illuminating a man standing a few feet ahead in the middle of a crosswalk. The driver doesn't hesitate. With a screech, the car accelerates, ramming into the man and hurtling down the street away from the academy. The body is flung along the street and lands with a crunch. It's apparent from the video that it IS a body, not a living person any longer.

It's Professor Rook's death, playing in an unending loop.

Words flash along the bottom of the screen: "You're next." Then the video begins again.

Ms. Poppin asked Mikhail to herd everyone back to their rooms before she ran downstairs to rouse the headmistress. She left Adrienne, and I alone with Gul, tasking us with watching over her until she could get help.

In the hallway, the security guard has been called up from the front door and is patrolling the corridor. Ms. Poppin is obviously taking this threat to Gul very seriously, especially after last semester.

I shut off the video and manage to get Gul off the floor and onto her bed, where she's sitting encased in a large, fluffy, floral-patterned blanket she's brought with her every year since she started at the academy our sophomore year.

Saying she would be right back, Adrienne left at a near run.

Ricardo wanted to stay too, but I made him leave, thinking Gul would be more likely to speak candidly if he wasn't around. He's probably hovering outside hoping to hear our conversation. The idea of him being nearby is, curiously, comforting.

I give Gul an awkward pat on the back, and glance toward the door. What is taking Adrienne so long? She's the one who's good at sympathizing with and consoling people. Not me. I'm more the type to avoid situations like this because I simply don't know what to say.

Finally.

Adrienne re-enters bearing a tray of brownies and a mug of hot chocolate, which she hands to Gul.

Gul holds the warm cup in both hands but doesn't drink.

I help myself to one of Adrienne's fudgy brownies and take a nibble. They're chocolate heaven. I'm going to have to run a mile before tennis practice tomorrow to work off the calories, but it's worth it.

"Thank you," Gul whispers, her voice cracking. She won't meet our eyes, I notice. "Is Headmistress Morgan coming?"

I look at Adrienne, who gives a shake of her head. "I didn't see them on my way back from the student kitchen." She sits on the bed beside Gul and tilts her head toward the teary girl. It's a simple gesture, meant to give Gul comfort. How does Adrienne think of stuff like that?

I give myself a mental shake. I have to focus.

"Can you tell me about the video?" I ask, trying to imbue sympathy into my voice.

Adrienne frowns, but I push on.

"It would be helpful to know how it was sent to you, and by whom."

Gul nods, finally looking me in the eye. "I don't know who sent it. The message said it was from a makeup company I follow, but the email address must have been spoofed, because it wasn't from them. I started watching it because I was curious. I thought maybe it was a fan-made video, you know, but once I realized what it was… And then the message at the bottom popped up. I couldn't help it. I screamed."

I look between Gul and the spot where her phone is lying on her desk, screen darkened. "The video looked real to me, but I wasn't there when Professor Rook was killed. It's too bad we can't figure out who called 911, and ask them about it."

Gul doesn't miss my pointed look.

Adrienne takes a brownie and starts eating it quietly.

A ragged sigh comes from Gul's throat. "Fine, if you really want to know, it was me."

I refrain from pumping my fist, but it's a challenge. "I knew it. Why did you deny it?" I can't hide the exasperation that edges my words.

"Charlotte…" Adrienne says, her tone a warning.

"Sorry. Sorry. Let me try again. Gul, why didn't you come forward and speak to the police after the accident?" Pot, meet kettle.

Gul chews on her lower lip. "I didn't see anything, really, except a car hitting Professor Rook and then driving off. It was too dark to make out the car's color, or type. The license plate. Anything. So I figured once I reported it, that was enough."

"You're sure you didn't see the driver?" I press, my eyes locked on hers.

She shakes her head. "Even if I did, I would never tell, especially not after this."

I exhale. "What were you doing outside that night?"

Gul pulls the blanket tighter around her shoulders, her black hair tumbling down her back in disarray. "None of your business."

I put a hand on her arm. "I see your point. This video is clearly a threat. Whoever sent it to you probably also killed Professor Rook, and they think you know something about it. You should really talk to the police."

Gul's head shake is more vehement this time. "No way. I'm keeping my mouth shut this time."

I snort. It takes everything in me not to retort, "For once," but that wouldn't be helpful.

Gul must know what I'm thinking, because her expression hardens. "Look. I already admitted that I made the call. I don't know anything else. Please leave."

Popping the final bite of her brownie into her mouth, Adrienne slides off Gul's bed. "You won't reconsider talking to the police? I really think you should. They could keep you safe."

"After everything they put you through last semester?" Gul is practically spitting. "No effing way."

Adrienne shrugs. "I'm not going to say it wasn't scary, but they were just doing their job."

My sister. Always ready to forgive and forget when someone does her wrong. Even when it's the police trying to prove she murdered someone.

Clearly, whoever killed the professor does not have the same forgiving nature.

Adrienne leaves a brownie on a napkin on Gul's desk, and follows me to the door. "For later," she whispers.

Gul thanks her before turning back to me. "You're going to keep looking into this, aren't you? Since you're dating Ricardo, and he has access to the security footage?"

I square my shoulders. "Yes, I am."

Quieter, she asks, "Will you let me know if you find anything?"

I hesitate. She's presented me with an opportunity. Do I take the self-preserving route, or the right one? "Sure, if you keep your mouth shut about Ricardo and me." I'll probably let her know what I find, even if she doesn't agree, but she doesn't need to know that. I'm not perfect, obviously.

Adrienne's confused face turns toward mine. "What does she—"

"Nothing. Do we have a deal?"

Gul nods.

"I'll let you know what I find out."

Ricardo and Mikhail are waiting outside when we leave Gul's room.

They fall into step with us back to my room.

Mikhail stops in the hallway, reverting to his stance against the wall.

Closing the door behind my sister, I fill Ricardo in on our conversation with Gul.

"It's clear that the attack on Professor Rook wasn't an isolated incident. Whoever killed him sent the footage to Gul to scare her. What I'm wondering is this: is the killer simply trying to keep Gul from talking? Or do they actually intend to kill her?"

Adrienne, who seemed so outwardly calm during our talk with Gul, has gone white. "This school is way scarier than my old one."

Ricardo gives her a teasing smile. "Don't worry, chouchou. Your bodyguard won't let anything happen to you."

Perking up, Adrienne glances toward the door. "I think I'll go talk to him for a while."

Ricardo makes a kissy face, and Adrienne flushes.

I giggle. My sister turns red faster than our dad when Mom asks him to pick up personal hygiene products at the store.

Once she's gone, Ricardo saunters over to me and gives a saucy grin. "Want me to stay here with you tonight, to keep you safe?"

My eyes roll almost clear out of my head. "No, thank you.

Plus, it's against dorm rules."

He plops down on my faux fur rug and gets comfortable, despite my rebuff. "Had to try. So, what's our next move?"

"We go through the footage of that night again. All of it. Maybe we missed something."

<h1 style="text-align:center">18</h1>

Of course, the one time I actually want to spend all night in the security office alone with Ricardo, one of the security guards decides to do a butt load of overtime before his pregnant wife pops out their first kid. It takes us a week to get access to the security footage again, and that's only because said wife finally calls with the news that her water broke (gross), making Officer Bob run to his car in a panic, only remembering to call Ricardo down to the office as he speeds out of the parking gate.

I'm in my room studying, trying to block out Adrienne and Genevieve's chatter about vintage clothing when my door cracks open.

I whirl around to glare at whoever has the gall to interrupt us, but when I spot Ricardo's raised eyebrows, I fly out of my chair. "Are you heading downstairs?" I ask, sounding breathless with anticipation.

Adrienne and Genevieve's heads swivel between us. Adrienne is practically beaming, and Genevieve is shaking her head, not unkindly. I'd be thrilled that my best friend is adjusting to my boyfriend if it wasn't all a charade. I'm honestly a little scared to explain the whole deal to Adrienne. She'll be crushed. And Genevieve? Yikes.

"Yep. Want to be alone with me, mon coeur?" Ricardo wiggles his eyebrows and I can't help it. I laugh.

"You're such a dork."

"A sexy dork," he shoots back, leaning on the doorframe.

The hem of his shirt rides up just enough to give me a glimpse of taut brown skin over abs fit from running up and down a soccer field. I don't think I'd go as far as sexy, but…

Wait. Where did that come from?

Adrienne starts giggling, which jars me out of staring at my fake boyfriend. Fake. Boyfriend. I can't let myself forget that, despite how… diverting being in a pretend relationship has become.

"See you girls later," I say as I push Ricardo out of my room, closing the door behind us. "You're such a flirt. Don't you ever stop?"

Ricardo's eyes shine as he takes my hand, sliding his fingers between mine. "And miss your face when I say something suggestive in front of your friends? Never."

"You're impossible," I rasp, biting my lip to prevent a smile from blooming on my face.

Ricardo chuckles as he lets me steer him down the staircase.

The security guard at the front door nods as we pass, and I smile back. I don't envy his job of keeping all of us embassy brats safe all the time. We're not always the most polite, low-key bunch. And despite the fact that he was probably expecting a cushy job with little real danger, it's not turning out to be like that at all.

Ricardo updates me on Officer Bob's quick getaway as we settle ourselves into the chairs in front of the surveillance desk. I don't bother to keep space between us because Ricardo will pull my chair right up against his anyway. He has an almost non-existent personal space bubble and regularly situates himself well within my personal space. Usually when people do that it's a strong repellant, but I don't hate it when he does it. I must be getting used to having him around. Or something.

"Your sister is going to be crushed when we break up," Ricardo says, locking eyes with me.

"Any suggestions?"

"We could just not."

"Not break up? Who are you, and what have you done with Ricardo LaGuerre, Brat Academy lothario?"

"Kidding," he says, but his smile isn't completely genuine as he locks eyes with me. "Anyway, maybe we should kiss for a while in case anyone walks by." He winks. Actually winks!

"Gross. No. Plus, we agreed, remember? No kissing."

Ricardo's voice dips as he leans toward me, eyes heavy-lidded. "You already broke that rule, mon coeur."

My eyes narrow in my best impression of a scowl. "Stop calling me that. Our arrangement has nothing to do with your heart region."

Putting a palm to his chest, he mock frowns. "You wound me, Charlotte."

"You're fine," I shoot back. "And I don't want to stage a break up yet, because all of our flitting about is starting to make Kenneth jealous. Oh, and your mom too, I'm guessing."

It's as if the energy in the room was just doused with cold water, smothering it instantly.

I open my mouth to continue, but Ricardo shakes his head.

"Let's not talk about them right now." He hunches forward and pulls up the footage we're interested in. "Let's just watch this, okay?"

"Whatever." I scoot closer so I can see the screen better, sneaking a glance at Ricardo's profile. What just happened? One minute we were bantering, but now it feels like someone turned down the temperature in here to below freezing. Weird.

We go through the footage from the night Professor Rook

was killed, starting from early in the evening when Cal, Adrienne, Mikhail, and I leave campus for Daddy's event. Because it was the night before everyone was supposed to return to campus for the semester, there isn't a ton of activity. Most people don't come back on campus until they absolutely have to, preferring to remain at home or in whatever residence they use when they're in the country, but not at school.

There are only a few cars in the lot. Most of the students who have permits to park on campus took their cars with them over break. I pick out Gul's black sedan, and Grady's white SUV. Neither of their cars moves at all for the duration of the video, which makes sense since Grady was still in Texas, and I already know Gul comes outside on foot at some point.

Several other cars come and go. Professors and security guards, mostly.

Gul sneaks outside the gate right before 11 and flees inside shortly after, just like last time we watched the footage.

A dark car pulls into the lot, the driver pausing long enough to talk to the security guard at the booth while the man check's his credentials. Everyone who visits campus in an unregistered vehicle is required to present identification.

The car parks and its lights go off, but the driver doesn't get out.

I stare at it, a frisson of familiarity going through me, but I shake it off. It's probably someone's dad or older brother, coming to drop something off.

There's an uneven spot in the video, which is probably a result of Ricardo taking out the footage of me driving Cal's car on campus with the front dented in.

I turn toward him for the first time since we've been sitting here watching video. "Thanks for doing that. Taking me out of the footage. I don't know if I really thanked you for that, before."

Ricardo shrugs. "It was no problem. I did it for Adrienne." He emphasizes my sister's name in a way that makes me bite the inside of my cheek. It's a reminder that none of this is for me. Not really. I may not hate Ricardo anymore, but as far as he's concerned, this is all a huge favor to his good friend. It has nothing to do with me.

Cal shuffles through the gate and into the parking lot, scanning the inside of his car before climbing the stairs to the dormitory door. I smile. He was probably checking to make sure I didn't fall asleep in the car. I was kind of buzzed when I drove that night, which was obviously a mistake. I mean, I ran over a body without realizing it.

Never again.

Almost beyond my control, my eyes are drawn to the familiar dark car. I can't escape the hum in my instincts that indicates I've seen it somewhere before. Whoever's inside it has been sitting there for twenty minutes, not moving.

The driver's side door swings open, and my hand flies to Ricardo's arm, gripping it tightly.

"Ouch. That hurts."

"Shh," I hiss at him, unable to pry my attention from the video.

The driver of the car steps out, and my jaw drops. My fingers tighten around Ricardo's arm, making him cover my hand with his own and gently prying at my fingers.

He stops at the sight of the driver. Leaning toward the screen, he says, "Isn't that—"

"Yes." I'd know the back of that head anywhere. Have actually ridden in that car, though only once or twice.

It's Kenneth's.

He was on campus that night, mere minutes after

Professor Rook was killed.

19

Kenneth is ducking my calls, and he hasn't been on campus in days. According to Doctor Paloma, he's not scheduled to do any intern hours at the academy for a week, but there is no way I can wait that long to question him about why he was on campus that night.

There's no reason for him to be here, is there? It's not like he and I were going to meet up. Neither would he be here to see Cal, Adrienne, or Genevieve. Now that I don't feel so raw over the breakup, Adrienne's been more forthcoming about how she felt about Kenneth. Genevieve too, for that matter.

They both like Ricardo a lot more, and I refuse to analyze why their words sizzle all the way down my throat.

My lack of patience is the reason I convince Ricardo to go across town to Kenneth's apartment today after classes are over. If Kenneth won't take my calls, I'll show up at his apartment. Just like an obsessed ex-girlfriend. The irony doesn't escape me as Ricardo swings our arms back and forth, looking for all the world like a boy ecstatic about being with me.

People move aside for us as we walk up the sidewalk toward the nearest subway station. Several old grannies give us simpering smiles, and it's all down to Ricardo's apparent bliss. He's an excellent actor. Way better than me.

Even though I'm 100% committed to our plan of action, there's a ripple of unease in the surface of my mental lake. A prickle caresses my spine, as if someone's eyes are on me. I spin around to look behind us.

There's no one there I recognize. Just people shopping and getting coffee and commuting home from work.

Still, my instincts are trying to tell me something, and I always listen to my gut.

I scan the sidewalk one more time, mostly satisfied that there's no one following us.

Sighing, I take a deep breath as Ricardo pulls me down the stairs into the subway station. I tried to convince him to let me call a rideshare, but he said it was good for me to be among regular people, and if I'm deeply honest, he's right. I never realized how sheltered my life has been until we rode the subway that first time.

But last time, there was plenty of room on the platform, and the cars were fairly empty.

This time, there is no room anywhere. Crowds of people huddle near the yellow line, waiting for the next train to arrive. It's a high traffic time of day, and it's going to be an ungraceful race to see who gets seats in the next train car. Body odors mix with perfumes in an unappealing smell that makes me wrinkle my nose and focus on the dingy wall on the opposite side of the tracks. There's not near enough air in this concrete tube. I stuff down the nervous energy building inside me and focus on my breathing.

Our train arrives and we scramble inside, along with about a hundred other people. The car is absolutely packed. There are no vacant seats, and barely any empty space for standing. I grab one of the center poles with both hands and hunch my shoulders inward in an attempt to avoid coming into contact with anyone else. My personal space bubble is shot in a place like this. Closing my eyes, I try not to focus on the stench of body odor wafting off the grubby guy standing next to me. He smells like sweat and moldy concrete. It's not pleasant.

The ceiling of the train is far too close. Even though I'm not short at 5'6", I'm surrounded by taller bodies that block the windows so I can't see out. Conscious of my speeding pulse, I clamp my eyes shut and take several slow inhales, letting the air out slowly through my mouth.

Someone presses close to my back, making me shrink inward closer to the pole.

"Are you okay?" Ricardo whispers in my ear, his breath tickling my sensitive skin.

Wrestling myself back under control, I open my eyes and find that Ricardo's got his arms circled around me, his brown hands next to my fair ones on the support pole. The only one encroaching on my personal space bubble is him. My entire body relaxes as I realize I'm cocooned within his arms. Not expecting this reaction at all, I assess my physical response to his nearness. After a second, I realize there's no discomfort weaving through my muscles. Ricardo's presence at my back doesn't feel like an invasion. It must be because his closeness is much preferable to anyone else's, especially stinky concrete guy. Swallowing, I whisper, "I might be a little bit claustrophobic."

Ricardo scans the car before meeting my eyes over my shoulder. Concern is evident in his face. "It's pretty tight in here, but we've only got two more stops to go." His pinky strokes my finger in a gentle gesture that sends warmth through me.

I nod quickly.

For a fake boyfriend, Ricardo is remarkably sweet when no one's watching us.

The train car comes to a stop at the next station, stealing my balance and throwing me into Ricardo. The press of his front against my back sends an electric jolt along my skin. My breath hitches as the scent of his cologne occupies my attention. Cardamom and vetiver.

"You smell good." My eyes widen as I clamp my mouth shut. Great. Hanging out with Adrienne has infected me with an embarrassing case of word vomit.

Ricardo's arms tighten around me. "It's all part of my evil plan to make you fall in love with me." The note of teasing in his voice cuts through the cloying scents of the train car and gives me something else toward which I can channel my focus.

"Good luck with that. It's never going to work."

A shiver runs through me as he leans even closer, his lips grazing the shell of my ear. "Don't be so sure, mon coeur."

My face goes hot.

Our stop can't come soon enough. And not just because being this close to so many people is squeezing the air out of my lungs.

The train comes to a smoother stop at our station, and I don't hesitate. I scramble out of the train, elbowing people left and right in an attempt to put some distance between Ricardo and me. I'm pumping the breaks on our whole fake relationship thing, starting right now. We're not on academy grounds, so there is no earthly reason we have to have any physical contact whatsoever. No point in flirting, either.

The underground station is overly warm and suffocating. I can't stay here.

I bolt up the stairs and stand on the sidewalk, taking in great gulps of the crisp winter air.

Ricardo comes bursting out of the station, swiveling as he looks for me. Relief cuts across his features when he spots me and heads my way. "Are you okay? You ran out of there so fast."

I shrug his hands off my shoulders. "I'm fine. Let's go.

Kenneth's place is only a block away." I speed walk, ready to get to our destination and focus on something other than Ricardo. Or that packed subway station. I am not taking a train back to campus. If Ricardo doesn't want to rideshare with me, he can walk.

When we arrive at the apartment building, I'm surprised to discover it's not as upscale as I expected. Kenneth's family is well off, but you'd never know it from looking at this block of apartments. They're non-descript gray with dingy white trim. The cars in the lot are not all that nice, either, ranging from neon colored sedans to older model trucks.

Kenneth's dark sedan would easily be the nicest in the lot, but it's not here. I frown, hoping we haven't come all this way for nothing.

When we knock on his apartment door, a guy I've never seen before answers. This guy, who is apparently Kenneth's roommate, tells us he isn't home. "Hey," he says, eyeing me. "Aren't you that high schooler Ken was dating? The high maintenance one?" His eyes rove curiously over Ricardo before cutting back to me.

I glare at the guy's audacity as I tap my foot. "I'm turning eighteen in two months, and I am not high maintenance."

Ricardo opens his mouth to speak, but wisely shuts it again when he sees my laser-like glare.

The guy shrugs. "Like I said. Ken's not here. Don't know when he'll be back." He shuts the door in our faces before I can get a word in edgewise.

Frustration bubbles up in me. Yanking my phone out of my purse, I call my ex. It goes straight to voicemail. That little jerk just declined my call. "I know you're there, Kenneth, so you can stop avoiding me. We need to talk. I saw you on the surveillance video of that night. Why were you on campus? Call me back." If that lovely message doesn't prompt him to call me back, I'm not above showing up at the hospital where he's interning and making a scene. Normally I'd scoff at the idea of using feminine stereotypes to get information, but I'll make an exception in this case.

Hanging up, I turn to Ricardo. "This was a bust. Stupid Kenneth. The first time in weeks I actually want to talk to him, he won't answer. I'm calling a car. Let's go."

"Whatever you say, mon coeur."

I don't deign to respond, still fuming about not catching Kenneth at home.

My foot taps against the sidewalk as we wait for our ride to arrive. Something smells amazing, but I told the rideshare driver where I'd be, and I'm not budging.

There's a food truck across the street, a lobster roll emblazoned on one side.

Oh my great giddy aunt, that sounds tantalizing right now.

"Want me to get you something?" Ricardo asks, gesturing toward the truck.

Yes. "No, thanks. I can wait until we get back to school."

"Suit yourself." He jogs across the street, buys a lobster roll from the food truck, and comes back with it. Up close, the smell of fresh, toasted bread and melted butter is intoxicating.

My feet take an involuntary step closer toward that mouth-watering sandwich.

Ricardo must notice his food has my complete attention, because he holds it under my nose, smiling like a fool "This looks delicious. Want a bite?"

I'm way past tempted, but sharing food is far too… intimate. "Share food with you? No thanks. There's no telling where that mouth has been."

His grin widens. "This mouth hasn't been anywhere recently, but we could change that." He puckers up and makes a smacking noise.

"Gross. No thanks," I shove him away, laughing.

The uncomfortable energy between us breaks, and Ricardo's mouth relaxes. "Whatever you say." He dives into his sandwich, making exaggerated moans of pleasure as he eats. It's kind of obnoxious, but now I'm starving.

"Okay, I'll be right back. I'm getting one of those. Don't move, in case our ride shows up."

"Mmph," Ricardo says, mouth full. He plops down onto a sidewalk bench and works on his sandwich as I wait for the crosswalk sign to light up, indicating my turn to cross the street. Looking up and down, I march across, not lingering. I'll never take a crosswalk slowly again after what happened to Professor Rook. Not that I'm a leisure walker to begin with.

I order a sandwich and wait in line, trying to ignore the discomfort in the back of my mind. My proximity alert is going haywire. Glancing around, I make eye contact with Ricardo. Other than him, I don't see anyone I know. So why do I feel like I'm being watched?

20

Expectant energy hums through the classroom as our professor walks into class. I look up from my tablet and am arrested by the clear excitement she's holding in check with a pleasant smile, her lips twitching to expand into a full beam. She looks way too thrilled to be thinking about World Governments. Immediately, suspicion makes my instincts hum. Usually when the teachers around here look excited about something, it's a back-breaking project or a mind-strippingly difficult exam, or something else that will result in late nights of studying while chugging coffee and cursing the pallbearers of education.

One by one, the other students in my class catch sight of our professor, and freeze. Nervous apprehension coats the room, almost strong enough to taste.

The professor leans against her desk, waiting until she has the attention of everyone in the room, before speaking.

"Now that I have all of your eyes, I have a special announcement. I hope all of you are making progress on your service project research, and I have something that should motivate you to do your best. I have the privilege of announcing that at the end of the semester, when the time comes to present your ideas, Senator Terrance Holt has agreed to be here. The student who most impresses him will secure an internship in his office for two weeks over the summer. I'm sure I don't have to emphasize how fantastic an internship will look on your transcripts, especially for those of you who wish to study political science in college."

My mouth drops in surprise, even as everyone swivels to look at me. I pull my features into a serene mask, not letting them see that I had no idea Daddy was doing this. No one told me anything about it, but now the professor's buzzing makes sense. A two-week internship in Daddy's office would be a killer addition to anyone's resume, and everyone in my class starts twitching like sharks when there's blood in the water.

I glance around the room, sizing up my rivals. Where before the other students in this class were mere annoyances, now they're my direct competition.

A good number of the students in my class intend to go into politics, so the competition is going to be fierce. Sylvia's dad is gearing up for a gubernatorial run, and Rahul's dad is in the British Cabinet. Still, I'm pretty sure I can best both of them.

The biggest surprise? The focused look on Ricardo's face as our professor gives us a few minutes to work on our projects. My sister told me he wants to be a teacher back in Haiti, so why would he be interested in an internship with a U.S. Senator? Being a teacher is noble, but it doesn't exactly require government experience. And really, it doesn't matter if Ricardo tries for the internship or not. He's a good student, but I'm better. I can beat him handily.

This internship? I'd be perfect for it. Plus, it would be a great way to show Daddy that I could be his heir apparent. It's a good thing Cal isn't in this class, or there's no way I'd ever win the internship. Frowning, I shun the thought as soon as it rises. It's not Cal's fault Daddy is so blinded by oldest son syndrome that he inadvertently ignores me. At least, I'm pretty sure that's what it is. None of that is on Cal.

This is definitely going to require a lot of late nights, but it's going to be worth it. Having Daddy to myself for two weeks? Priceless. Bucking up, I take my tablet out and pull up my project research.

Despite the dead silence outside my door, I can't sleep. I'm way too keyed up about the internship announcement in class this afternoon. And my resulting conversation (re: argument) with Ricardo didn't help. When I asked—okay, confronted—him about how focused he was on his work during class, he declined to tell me what he was doing for his project.

And then he had the gall to assert that he'd be an excellent intern for my dad.

As if.

When I asked him if he wanted the internship, he didn't deny it, which only made me angrier. A teacher does not need government experience. What was his problem?

Huffing, I throw off the covers and sit up in the pitch black. If I can't sleep, I might as well get some work done. Blinking, I allow my eyes to adjust as the lamp on my nightstand flares to life. My eyes move to my top desk drawer, where I used to keep a tin of "mints." They were actually amphetamines I got from Professor Rook, but I haven't taken any since Adrienne caught me with them last semester. It had been sloppy of me not to transfer the pills from that clear baggie to the tin. Nobody thinks twice if they see you eating a breath mint.

I know there are only three pills left in that tin, but I haven't thrown them away yet. I should do it, but something is preventing me. What if I need one of them at some point, just for a tiny boost? This is the most important semester of high school, and I have to excel in all of my classes if I'm going to go to Georgetown. It's a tough school to get into, and failure isn't an option.

Stupid Ricardo. Why did he have to needle me about the internship?

Jumping out of bed, I stalk across the floor to my mini fridge, flinging the door open to see what I've got left inside.

It's empty.

Adrienne, Genevieve, and Ricardo have all been spending a lot more time in my room than ever before, and they've eaten all of my contraband. I'll have to get Mikhail to drive us to the store tomorrow so I can refill, but in the meantime… Pulling on my nubby robe and securing it at my waist with its scraggly tie, I peek out into the hallway. The coast is clear.

Silently, I inch up the hall toward the stairs, stepping carefully in and out of the low light cast by the wall sconces. The dormitory building is a hundred years old, and the floors squeak. I debate my destination as I advance. The vending machine near the administration office has the best snacks, but it's much farther away than the one upstairs in the student lounge.

Biting the inside of my cheek, I head downstairs. It'll be worth the extra walking if I can sink my teeth into an imported chocolate bar.

The foyer is quiet as I pass through, only now noticing that the security guard is nowhere to be seen. He must be making his rounds elsewhere on campus.

A dreaded sense of being watched tingles along my spine, making me spin to look behind me. There's no one in sight. Chiding myself, I continue. Thinking about the threat Gul received is making me paranoid. I feel like I'm constantly being followed. It's ridiculous.

No one has any reason to be following me. I don't have any enemies. I think.

A few weeks ago, I would have counted Ricardo and Gul as my top antagonists, but that has changed. Gul and I aren't exactly friends, but she's not as catty as she used to be before. And Ricardo... I don't even want to think about him right now.

I don't bother to walk quietly as I go down the hall. I'm far enough away from the dorms that no one will hear me. An abrupt sound up ahead makes me pause in the corridor. Light and laughter spill out of the cracked kitchen door as I approach.

Hushing my steps, I edge closer and peek inside.

Adrienne and Mikhail are standing side by side at the counter, kneading dough of some kind. Cal is sitting cross-legged on the counter, drawing on his tablet, and even Ricardo is there, eating nachos on a plate. They look delicious as he lifts one up toward his mouth, the strings of yellow cheese hanging off the tortilla chip.

My stomach grumbles as jealousy stings me. They're all hanging out down here, having a big time, and they didn't even think to invite me. Once again I'm left on the outside.

I expect Daddy to make me feel this way, but never my siblings. Or my bodyguard. Or my fake boyfriend, for that matter.

My lip curls upward in resignation. If they don't want me around, I won't linger. I don't need their pity friendship. Besides, I'd die if they saw me in my old bathrobe. Obviously it was a bad call to wear it outside the confines of my room. A mistake I won't repeat.

Squaring my shoulders, I slink down the hallway and around the corner toward the vending machine. Hopefully Adrienne and the others won't hear the machine spitting out my late night sustenance.

I'm standing in front of the vending machine tapping my

credit card with my long fingernails when a zing slides up the back of my neck. I pivot on the balls of my feet and scan the hall. There's no one here.

Get it together, Charlotte. No one is following you. Gul has made you a paranoid freak. Just get your chocolate bar and go back upstairs.

A door creaks, making me go still.

Utterly ridiculous.

This is an old building. It makes noise. That doesn't mean there's someone lurking in the shadows, waiting to eviscerate me.

Making my choice, I put my card into the vending machine and reach for the screen to tap in my selection.

A low rustle behind me makes my eyes go wide. Before I can react, someone drags a black cloth down over my face. A solid, heavy body brushes against my back. Hands pull the fabric tight over my nose and mouth. Smothering me.

Reaching up, I claw and scratch at their arms, trying to loosen their hold on the cloth. It's no use. Panic unspools in my belly, threatening to rip out every stitch of my self-defense training. Fear is laying siege to my body.

Opening my mouth, I try to call for help, but my throat is dry and sticky. Mikhail and Ricardo are so close by, if they could only hear me. I'm thwarted by rough fingers jamming the cloth down my throat. Choking me.

I can't scream. Can't speak. Hot, humid air presses around my head, making it harder to think. I have to do something before I pass out. Kicking out with my heel, I come into contact with my attacker's leg.

He grunts in pain. It's definitely a he.

Okay, then.

Reaching back with one hand, I make a grab for his twig

and berries. Hit them where it hurts, my self-defense trainer said.

With a muffled curse, my attacker slams me forward into the glass front of the vending machine. Glass rattles under the impact. Candy bars thud to the bottom of the receptacle. Someone had to have heard that.

My eyes water as the tang of metal hits my tongue. My fear spikes higher, clawing its way up my spine until it threatens to consume me. I have to get away before I'm seriously injured. Or worse.

Images of the bruises around Adrienne's neck fill my thoughts, further fueling my panic.

Wrestling my mind away from the cliffs of abject panic, I home in on what I know. The man who attacked my sister is long gone. He can't be the one doing this to me. Then who?

I have to focus. I can do this.

Taking breaths through my nose, I try to get a whiff of my attacker's scent. It's generic bar soap, so no help. I've got to get a look at this guy.

Kicking with all my strength, I hit my attacker's shin again. A louder cry of pain is my reward.

Heavy hands thrust me forward, slamming me into the vending machine again. More brutal than the first time. My nose spurts blood. The fabric of the cloth bag bunches in my mouth, gagging me. Hot blood trickles down my throat. My lungs burn as I struggle to inhale.

When my attacker rasps a threat into my ear, my every muscle goes rigid.

"Stop looking into Rook's death, or I'll kill you."

21

Cool air rushes around me as I'm freed from his cruel grip. Footsteps thud along the hallway, receding. Whoever was trying to hurt me is gone.

My hands tremble as I pull at the cloth over my head, but can't get it off. Wilting, I lean against the wall for support.

Footsteps bang up the hallway toward me. He's coming back to finish me off.

My legs give out and I slump to the floor. I thrash my hands, trying to get the cloth off my head, but I'm shaking too badly. The combination of fear and adrenaline has flatlined my control of my fingers.

The fabric is whisked off my head, and Ricardo's is the first face I see. Behind him, Adrienne and Cal are staring at me with wide eyes. My sister's face is ghastly pale in the low light. Mikhail looms over their shoulders, scanning me with military precision. His eyes narrow.

"What happened here?" he asks, voice demanding.

"Mezanmi, Charlotte. Are you okay?" Gathering me into his arms, Ricardo tries to pull me into his lap.

"Don't touch me," I say hoarsely, pulling away from him and curling into a ball against the wall. Panic has kept its seat on the throne of my mind. "I don't need your help."

My heart is slamming against my ribcage, all too aware of how close I was to suffocating back there. I've always felt safe within the walls of the academy, but after this? I don't know.

Adrienne crouches down beside me, holding out a hesitant hand. "Who did this to you? Misha, go find him," she says to Mikhail over her shoulder.

The bodyguard gives a tight nod before disappearing down the corridor, moving between the shadowed doorways like a ghost. He's broad, but stealthy. Hopefully he catches whoever did this so I can make them pay.

And I will make them pay. Daddy is important enough. I bet he could get the press to call it an assassination attempt. Which is exactly what it felt like. The press would slaughter them in the court of public opinion. They'd be ruined.

"What can we do? Let us help you," Adrienne says, putting a feather-light hand on my shoulder.

I take a deep breath, stuffing down the urge to burst into tears. I will not let them see me cry. "I just want to go to my room. And a candy bar."

"Got it." Ricardo pops to a stand. In a moment, the machine whirs and he holds out a Dairy Milk and a Toblerone. "I didn't know which one you wanted," he says, looking sheepish, "so I got both."

Snatching them away, I mumble a grudging thanks. The boy knows my favorite chocolate bars. Taking my hand, he hoists me off the floor.

I refuse to look at him. I'm still mad at him about the internship, but more importantly, I would never have let him see me all bloodied and weak like this if I had any choice. My resolve hardens. No one will ever see me like this again. Straightening my robe, I lock eyes with my sister. "Walk me back to my room. Please."

Cal holds up a plain black hoodie. "This is what they put over your head. I'm giving it to the police, when they come."

I shake my head vehemently, unable to stop the shudder

that rolls through me. "No police."

My brother and sister have never looked more alike than they do right now, their mouths twin gaping holes of astonishment.

"Why no police?" Adrienne asks. "They can catch whoever tried to hurt you."

Ricardo's eyes flicker toward mine, and I can see in their depths that he knows why I can't allow the police to become involved. At least I don't have to lie to one person in my life, even if he is a thorn in my side.

If I call the police, they might be able to catch whoever did this, but then they'd start asking questions about it. Whoever it was might spill their guts. It might come out that I've been looking into Professor Rook's death. The authorities would be curious as to why a seventeen-year-old girl was interested in a hit-and-run. A simple glance at my credit card statement would unveil that I'd paid to have Cal's car repaired. The dented bumper and hood replacement would be a dead giveaway. They'd think I killed Rook, for sure.

Bata bing, bata boom. Future demolished.

"I'm fine," I insist, reaching up to touch my fingertip to my throbbing nose. "I don't think my nose is broken. No police," I say again, more firmly.

Adrienne crosses her arms. "Fine, but can I ask Dad to assign you a bodyguard, at least?"

Movement to the side makes me whip in that direction.

It's Mikhail approaching, alone, eyes flashing with anger. My attacker escaped.

Swallowing, I look back at my sister. "That's not a terrible idea."

Mikhail found no trace of my attacker when he did a perimeter check last night. No unlocked doors or windows, and no suspicious figure lurking in any of the surveillance footage. Which means that whoever it was, was already inside. My assailant was either a professor, a student, or worst case scenario—one of the security guards.

So basically every guy I see as I navigate my classes is a suspect to be avoided. I've never felt so vulnerable in my life, and it makes me angry. I am a smart, strong, ambitious woman, and one dangerous encounter with an unknown brute has me shrinking away from pretty much everyone with XY chromosomes.

A guy bumps my elbow as he passes, and reaches out a hand to steady me, his apology on his lips. The way my entire body recoils stops him. Frowning, he fades into the crowd.

Immediately, I want to slap myself in the face. *Get a grip, Charlotte.*

Sighing, I keep moving. This totally sucks.

Plus, I'm beginning to realize how much like a fish out of water Adrienne felt last semester. Not only is my new bodyguard, who is nothing like Mikhail, I might add (apparently Daddy didn't want another one of his daughters dating their protection detail), I've also got two black eyes and a swollen nose. No amount of makeup can hide it, which means everyone in the whole school is staring.

My professors wince when they look at me, and I'm pretty sure none of them believe my story that I tripped when my high heel broke and fell on my face. My new bodyguard, Steve, a middle-aged man who is constantly wearing sunglasses indoors, and who insists on clearing every room before I walk into it, only makes it worse.

By lunch the next day, I'm about ready to hide in my room and ditch the rest of my classes. If one more person dares to gawk at me, or ask me how I injured myself, again, I might scream.

Playing the good boyfriend, Ricardo hasn't left my side either. It's terrible. He saw me at my weakest, bloodiest last night, and it makes me want to stage a huge fight and end this masquerade before it gets even more complicated. Usually, I can prevent anyone from seeing me when I'm at my most vulnerable, but last night I had no control. It's shaken me to the very core.

The only thing stopping me using a metaphorical flame thrower on my fake relationship with Ricardo is the way he goes stiff whenever we encounter his mom in the halls. I may not want him around anymore, but for some reason bickering with me keeps his head high whenever she shows up.

Still, restless angst has me so wound up, picking a fight with him might make me feel better. Give me back some of my control. Besides, couples fight. It's inevitable. The eatery is crowded, not my usual choice for a confrontation, but if I don't do something now, I may lose my nerve. Not something I ever thought I'd struggle with, honestly.

Ricardo's arm brushes against my back as he reaches over to take a cherry tomato from my plate. Ordinarily I don't mind sharing food. It's not a huge deal. But right now? It's the opening I need. Steeling my resolve, I swivel toward Ricardo and push his arm off the back of my chair. "Give me some room, will you?" I snap.

Ricardo's eyebrows shoot up.

Across the table, Adrienne's mouth forms a tiny "o" at my outburst, her spoon suspended before her face.

Yeah, I've been kind of rude today, but not outwardly hostile. That changes now.

"What's wrong?" Ricardo whispers, tucking his arm into

his lap as if I've physically injured him. A sharp rap of guilt knocks on my conscience, but I bolt my mind against it.

Ricardo's love language is definitely touch, so that's where I strike first. "You. That's what. You're so touchy feely all the time. Give me a break. You're suffocating me."

Ricardo's eyes widen and his jaw drops, as if he just took a punch to the gut. He takes a slow bite of his salad, his eyes not leaving mine. "That's an interesting choice of words, chérie. Don't do this here," he whispers, eyes skimming over my shoulder.

"Why not?" I rasp. "Maybe it's time we put on a show so everyone has something to talk about other than my face. At least then I'd be at the front of the rumors, instead of the butt of everyone's raccoon jokes."

Mikhail's eyes scan the eatery, watching, evaluating everyone around us. It's comforting, if unhelpful.

"Who's telling raccoon jokes?" Cal asks, his lacrosse stick in his hands. "I'll, I'll…"

Adrienne pulls his stick down under the table, shaking her head.

Ricardo's eyebrows furrow in frustration. "Is that what this is about? You're tired of people talking about your face? It gives me no little pleasure to tell you that you look terrible. Maybe you should have skipped classes today. Taken a chill day. You sound like you need it."

I rear back, scoffing. "How dare you tell me what I need? You know what I actually need? A supportive boyfriend. Maybe you could try that for once." It's a low blow, since he's been nothing but supportive. I know that, but the part of me that needs some distance is in control right now, overpowering the little voice inside me that is begging me not to lay waste to whatever is going on between Ricardo and me.

Ricardo's jaw clenches. "Is that what you think? That I'm not supportive? Okay. Okay." He shoves back from the table. The metal feet of his chair screech over the tile floor as he moves it into position, hoisting himself up onto it so that he looks like a tall, lithe, angry giant. "Hey, everyone," he shouts, throwing his arms wide. "The next person I catch gossiping about Charlotte is going to regret it. So shove it." He slams his body down into his seat, heat emanating off him in waves. He won't look at me.

Everyone in the eatery has gone quiet. We're all staring at him in shock.

There's a flicker in Genevieve's eyes that, if I didn't know any better, I'd call pride.

My heart is thrumming behind my ribs, my resolve to push him away wavering. I had no idea he'd do that. The abrupt, protectiveness of the gesture short-circuits my drive to fight with him anymore. Anger snuffed out like a candle flame, I nibble at my cobb salad.

Gul sidles up to our table and hovers near Cal, her dark hair brushing his shoulder. He takes the hint and gives up his chair. They switch places, Gul sitting across from me and Cal munching on his banana in annoyed silence.

"Trouble in paradise?" She says, eyeing Ricardo and I where we sit next to each other but worlds apart.

I haven't forgotten her pointed questions about our lack of presence on social media. To combat it, I made Ricardo take a few cutesy photos with me so I could post them periodically. They'll keep Gul off my back. Oh, and bother Kenneth.

Gul's eyebrow is cocked in unmistakable skepticism. "So, you fell and gave yourself two black eyes? Your dad hired a bodyguard to protect you from, what, your high heels?" She shoots a pointed glance toward Steve, my new bodyguard.

"Yes. It was a rare moment of clumsiness."

Gul leans over the table, pushing Cal's plate out of the way so it won't soil her uniform. "Is that really the story you're going with? At least make it sound realistic." She swallows, the arrogance in her expression giving way to something softer. "Did someone hurt you?"

The question is so abrupt, it steals my breath. Either I'm imagining it, or there's concern underpinning her words. As if she knows what she's asking about. I'm tempted to tell her about the threat my attacker growled into my ear.

Stop looking into Rook's death, or I'll kill you.

Distrust stays my tongue. I can't tell her that. An admission like that would only give her more ammunition should she decide to annihilate my reputation. No, the fewer people who know about that particular threat, the better. Right now it's just me and my attacker, and I'd like to keep it that way. My siblings are treating me with kid gloves as it is. If they found out my life was threatened, I have no doubt that Adrienne would tell our dad in a fit of do-gooding that would probably end up with us under house arrest, or guarded around the clock by a platoon of secret service agents.

I'm not ready to give up the semblance of freedom I have. I'll take Steve, and leave it at that. Taking a sip of my lemon water, I say, "I'm fine, Gul. But thanks."

Her eyebrows rise. "You're being sincerely polite now? Wow, there really must be something going on with you."

My fingers clench around my glass, but my expression remains placid. "No. Everything's fine. A couple of black eyes aren't going to stop me. Nothing keeps Charlotte Cavendish-Holt down."

Gul sits back in her chair, her mouth flat. She seems… disappointed by my denial. "Right… Good to know." She sighs. "You're not the only one with a new bodyguard." She points to a guy in plainclothes sipping from a thermos in the corner of the room. "I told my parents about the video, and instead of insisting I come home, they send him."

I'm surprised she admitted this, and especially to me. We were never confidantes before this whole mess started. We weren't even friends.

"Sorry."

Gul nods. "Again with the politeness. See you." She gets up and returns to her own table. For the first time, I notice how straight she sits, how still. Like she isn't comfortable there with her friends. It's kind of sad.

Slowly, the ebb and flow of conversation rises around us, everyone assuming that the lunchtime theatrical is over.

It doesn't escape my notice that Ricardo is stiff beside me, careful not to brush my elbow with his, or to let his knee fall open against mine. The distance leaves me cold.

Adrienne's eyes drift past me, and widen. A gasp escapes her lips.

My head whips up at this, and I twist in my chair to see whatever's caught her off guard.

Kenneth has come rushing into the room. He stands in the doorway, his chest heaving as he holds a bag of ice over his shoulder. When he spots me, he comes barreling toward me, frowning, eyes dark. Tossing the bag on the floor at my feet, he kneels in front of me, eyeing my shiners. "Charlotte, I just heard. Are you okay?" One hand covers my knee with a light squeeze.

Out of the corner of my eye, there's no mistaking Ricardo turning away. It's the first time he hasn't risen to Kenneth's presence by pulling my hair or holding my hand. Dare I say, I miss it.

Behind me, Adrienne huffs. She must *really* not like Kenneth, because it's the most unkind sound she's ever made.

"It's nice of you to deign to talk to me," I grumble, pushing his hand off my knee. "What's up with the ice?"

He shrugs. "Broken fridge in the health center. No big deal."

I glance around. No one is paying us any attention, instead chatting with their table mates. Thankfully, Kenneth's and my breakup is old news, so his arrival in the eatery isn't gossip-worthy. Unlike the sparring match I had with Ricardo a few minutes ago.

Only Gul is watching us with interest. Beside her, Grady glances our way before bumping her with his shoulder, distracting her. I'm relieved when she takes her focus off Kenneth and me and takes one of her boyfriend's fries with a smile.

I lick my lips, turning back to Kenneth. "Why have you been avoiding my calls for over a week?"

My ex's eyebrows rise in feigned surprise. "What are you talking about? I haven't been avoiding you."

"Uh huh." I get out my phone and scroll through my call log. "Then what's your excuse for sending my last ten calls to voicemail, and then not calling me back? Did Gordo even tell you I stopped by?"

Kenneth gives a head shake, scooting closer to me. "Look, I've been busy. Between my internship hours and classes, I don't exactly have a lot of free time."

Finally, Ricardo's arm snakes over the back of my chair. Like he's staking a claim to trump Kenneth's. I don't hate it. It's a relief to know that, despite my behavior earlier, he's still with me. It's not something I want to analyze right this second, though.

Crossing my arms, I lean toward Kenneth so only he can hear me. "Are you sure it's that, and not the fact that I saw the footage of you here on campus the night Professor Rook was killed? What were you doing here, anyway?"

Kenneth's expression tightens, and he pushes to a stand. "I was here dropping off the final paperwork for my intern hours. I'd just gotten out of night class, and it had to be turned in before I started here. I knew I wouldn't have time to come by the next day, because it was my last at the morgue. I called you to tip you off about Alan R... er, Professor Rook's autopsy, remember?"

"Sure," I say, watching him walk away. I don't believe him. Kenneth is lying about why he was here that night, and I'm going to find out why.

22

I'm lying primly on my bed with my arms crossed over my chest, taking a break from studying. Staring up at the ceiling, I can't stop thinking about the fight I picked with Ricardo in the eatery two days ago. He was supposed to leave me after that display, decide I was too high maintenance, but he hasn't. He even defended me, in front of everyone. Threatened those who continued to gossip about my woefully black eyes. What I don't understand is why. I'm not exactly the easiest person to get close to, and it's not like there are other benefits to our arrangement, at least for him.

Still, I won't look a gift horse in the mouth. Between him, Genevieve, and Adrienne, I might actually be finding a group of friends who will stick around. Not like my bio dad, or Rhiannon. Or my mom and step-dad, for that matter. At one time or another, each of them has made me feel like I was too much—work, energy, consideration. Just too much.

Rhiannon's leaving wasn't entirely her own fault. I admit I played a role in her departure. But the rest?

My head lolls as I look out the window. The darkness outside is broken by the orange glow of the city lights bouncing off the clouds above. Shivering, I pull my faux fur blanket up to my chest. It's a cold night. Too cold for snow.

"My eyes are going to fall out if I look at this tablet screen anymore," Ricardo says from where he's laying sprawled on his side on the floor, propped up on one elbow. Flopping onto his

back, he stretches out his arms over his head. A groan escapes
him as his muscles relax. His long, lanky body looks completely
at home on my white, fluffy rug, almost like the cover of one of
the romance novels my mom hides in her nightstand. All
Ricardo needs is long, flowing blond hair and one less shirt.

I force myself to look away. Okay, so my fake boyfriend is
not unattractive, but I can't afford to lose sight of the objective.
Make Kenneth jealous. That's the reason I'm keeping up this
farce. Not at all because I've started to care about Ricardo.
That would be ludicrous. No, that's not it at all.

He groans. "Your floor is so hard. Can I come up there
with you?"

I recoil, sitting up. "No, you absolutely cannot. The last
thing I need is your smelly cologne all over my blankets."

Ricardo folds his hands behind his head and smiles as his
eyes glide over me. "What? Is my smelly cologne too irresistible
for the great Charlotte Cavendish-Holt?"

I drape my blanket around me like a cape and hold it
under my chin. "Don't be absurd." Even as I protest, I can feel
my traitorous skin warming.

Ricardo fairly crows with pleasure, his smile growing into a
grin. "Ah, I see it now. You're falling in love with me, and
you're embarrassed. Don't be. I'm hard to resist."

I roll my eyes so hard it hurts. "You have got to be the
most arrogant, cocky boy-child I have ever met."

Pushing off the floor, Ricardo props his elbows on the
edge of my bed and comes within a few inches of my face. "I
am. And you love it."

A tangled ball of thoughts and feelings is pinging around
my insides so fast I can't even tell what's going on in there. But
I know I have to stop this before it goes any further. This
conversation feels more dangerous than any I've had with

Ricardo in the past.

Probably because he's closer to the truth than I'll ever admit.

Scrambling past him, I jump off my bed and scoop up my phone. The cool air cuts through my gauzy thoughts. "Cut it with the flirting. Let's talk about something else. Like who would have the motive to attack me. I'm going to tell you something, but you can't freak out or go all soft on me. Deal?"

Ricardo leans back against my bed, facing me. "As you wish, mon coeur."

I shoot a glare at him, but he just chuckles.

"I'm a nicknamer, Char. Can't help it."

I huff, but leave it there.

"Now, what were you going to tell me that's going to make me go soft on you? Like I said, I already know you're crazy for me."

There's a suspicious flutter in my abdomen at his words. "You wish, but it's not that. The other night, when someone attacked me? I didn't tell you the whole story."

Ricardo's brows bunch, but he stays quiet.

"When he was," my hand rises to my throat, "suffocating me, he threatened me. Told me to stop looking into Professor Rook's death, or he'd kill me."

As I predicted, Ricardo's eyes go liquid. The usual teasing antagonism is missing. Since when has he looked at me like that? He steps closer to me and puts his hands on my upper arms. "Mon Dieu, Charlotte, you should have told your parents. You still should. As your fake boyfriend, I insist you protect yourself, unless your goal is to keep me by your side at all times. Because I'll do it, you know."

The butterflies in my stomach start doing backflips, but I mentally threaten them with pins and glass cases. Gently pulling out of Ricardo's grip, I turn away from his intense gaze. "You're getting all mushy on me, playboy."

He's quiet for a beat before his whisper comes, caressing my shoulder. "Sorry. I'll try to refrain."

Nodding, I pick up my phone, focusing on my objective. "I figure that whoever attacked me was involved with the professor's death, maybe even killed him, and that's why he doesn't want me to look into it. So I need to make a list of all of the people who might have wanted Professor Rook dead. Then we can do some investigating."

Ricardo cocks his head. "Have you ever noticed that when you say "we," you're assuming I'll participate in whatever scheme you're cooking up? Fake dating, fake fights, murder investigations. It's almost as if you think you can count on me to follow your lead, despite all of your blustery attempts to push me away." His mouth twitches as he ticks them off on his fingers.

The shock at being caught out must show on my face, because Ricardo nods. "Yes, I know exactly what you're doing, mon coeur, because I've done it myself. A hundred times." He drops his face toward mine, lowering his voice. "And yes, you can count on me."

I don't believe him, yet, but I want to.

That's when I know this fake relationship can only end one way—with pain. Because Ricardo is right. I do push people away. I always insisted it was easier that way, but for once the truth is too loud in my head to ignore. It was for protection. For my own heart. Because if there's one thing I've learned from the past seventeen years, it's that the people you love? They leave.

Our list of suspects is unsatisfactorily brief, because we really don't know a lot about Professor Rook except for his dealings with the students here. He was a closed book. Therefore, our list is as follows: me, for obvious reasons; Grady; Rhiannon; and his other student clients.

It's an incredibly unhelpful list, considering that I now know I didn't kill him—thanks to Kenneth's revelation that Professor Rook was run over not once, but twice, and my turn was the latter, after the man was already dead. But who would hate the professor enough to run him down in the street, without hesitation or latent regret?

We wrack our brains for several days, but we can't come up with any more enemies of the professor's. There's simply not enough evidence in his abandoned classroom to give us any further leads.

Grady was stuck in Texas when the professor was killed, and Rhiannon had already passed. Even so, we start with Grady. It's the logical place to begin.

I'm gratified to find him exactly where I thought he'd be—in the conservatory on the dormitory roof. When we emerge from the narrow staircase onto the tarred surface, a biting wind swirls around us, making me shove both hands in my jacket pockets, even the one that's laced through Ricardo's. My pocket looks comically large with both of our hands jammed inside.

There's a shadow of someone moving around inside the glass house some of the classes use to study botany. It has to be him.

Nodding, Ricardo urges me forward. We're back to the show of coupledom. It's starting to irk me that Ricardo is so good at pretending like this. It's one area where his skill exceeds mine.

"Grady?" I ask as I step inside the conservatory, letting go of Ricardo's hand to fit through the narrow opening. Warm humidity swirls around me, and I can feel my hair expanding. Straightening my headband, I move further into the space to make room for Ricardo.

"Shut the door behind you," Grady calls from behind a tall plant I can't identify. As he steps out from behind the dark green foliage, a pair of small pruning shears gleams in his hand. Catching sight of us, his mouth opens in a surprised smile. "What brought y'all up here?"

"We wanted to see if you're okay, man," Ricardo says. "I don't want to think about what I'd do if someone I cared about passed away." Stepping up behind me, he wraps an arm around my shoulder and tucks me into his side.

"Especially now that Professor Rook is dead," I add. "We know he and Rhiannon had history."

Grady's expression darkens, and he resumes pruning leaves from the tall, shapely bonzai he was working on when we interrupted him. "You're talking about the drugs he sold her. And whoever told her about them in the first place."

A jab of guilt pierces my composure, making me duck my head. Because that person Grady mentioned? I knew her, once. "I know if it were me, I'd be disappointed Professor Rook was never caught and prosecuted for his crimes."

Grady's eyes flicker over us, as if he's measuring our sincerity. Then he nods. "I was pretty angry when I heard, but after a while I figured that being run over was a kind of justice too. Sure, it wasn't lawful, but it must have been a terrible way to die. I reckon it has to be enough." He hesitates. "Rhiannon's parents are floored, though. You know the police called there to talk to them? See if they hired someone to kill Rook? They were furious. It wasn't a terrible idea on the police's part. Rhiannon's parents are pretty intense."

He sounds so defeated, so numb, my heart goes out to him. Rhiannon's parents though? It's another avenue to investigate. "I'm sorry, all the same."

"I appreciate that, Charlotte." There's a small pile of clipped leaves scattered over the gravel floor at his feet. Turning his back on us, he continues to work.

My mind is humming as Ricardo and I walk across the roof to the door that leads inside. If what Grady said about Rhiannon's parents is true, they're our best lead. And it also means they may be behind the threats to Gul and me. I know why they'd threaten me, if they discovered my part in Rhiannon's downfall, but Gul? That I don't know.

Ricardo doesn't say anything until we're alone on the staircase. "What do you think?" he asks, gliding his hand along the shiny wooden bannister.

I glance up at him, my eyes catching on the reddish stubble along his jaw. "I've heard you're not too shabby at sneaking and picking locks. Are you up for it?"

Catching my gaze with his amber eyes, he smiles.

Doing a little breaking and entering will give us something to do while we're trying to figure out how to investigate Rhiannon's parents. It wouldn't be the first time I've heard of a powerful couple of parents who put out a hit on someone who harmed their child. But if Rhiannon's parents think sending someone to threaten me will keep me quiet, they're sorely mistaken.

23

I've only been fake dating Ricardo for a few weeks, and I've already turned into a girl who waits for her boyfriend after every class. Imagine what it would be like if we were actually dating. Ugh, where is he? My fingers tap on my forearm as I scan the hall for a tall, ruddy brown figure whose strawberry brown curls are getting long enough to hang down over his forehead. I bet those curls would be silky soft wound between my fingers.

Pinching my eyes shut, I chastise myself. Get a hold of yourself, Charlotte. There is no earthly reason I should be thinking about Ricardo's hair, even if it is dreamy. Er, well kept.

"What are you thinking about?" Adrienne asks from her spot leaning against the wall. "You've got a weird look on your face."

"It's her googly eye face. She must be thinking about Ricardo," Genevieve says with a knowing look at my sister.

"Huh, so that's how she looks when she's in love," Adrienne croons, teasing me.

Behind her, Mikhail's mouth tilts up just slightly. Is he laughing at me?

"Shut up," I say, willing my face not to betray my embarrassment. I am NOT in love with Ricardo. How absurd. His hair, maybe. Him? No freaking way.

"Sorry I'm late," Ricardo says as he tucks his chin over my shoulder and slips his arms around my waist from behind.

173

I'm paralyzed as his scent of cardamom and vetiver floats around me, his hands like fire on my waist, his jaw resting against mine. His warmth permeates my form, short circuiting my brain. This is so bad.

Genevieve's eyes flash. *See? I know you.*

Adrienne is giving us obvious hearty eyes as she and Ricardo chat.

Fighting a blush, I look away.

Ricardo banters with her as if it's perfectly normal for him to carry on a conversation with his lithe frame draped over a girl's. Mine. Actually, now that I think about it, it might be. After his first day at the school, I never paid that much attention to him. Until he started buddying up with my stepsister last semester. Okay, that's not true. I noticed his shameless flirting with everything in a skirt the second day of freshman year. Everyone except me. His first day? I need to think about something else.

Adrienne is leaning into Mikhail's hand where it's wrapped around the nape of her neck. He almost smiles when she meets his eyes. They really are cute together. I'll never forget the fear that skated across his face when we found her being choked to death last semester. Fear, and then rage. He pulled that ambassador off my sister and put him down so quickly I'm not even sure how he did it. Then he'd picked Adrienne up and cradled her limp body in his arms, his entire body rigid with tension. I'd known in that moment how much he cared for her. Enough to kill, if need be.

Will anyone ever care that much for me? Or me for someone else?

Genevieve's French-accented tones cut into my spiraling thoughts. "I'm so glad we're going out on Saturday. Couples night at the club is going to be très magnifique. Don't you agree, Char? Plus, we haven't been since last semester, and I'm dying for Ryou to see me in a flapper dress. What do you think, Adrienne? Mikhail?"

"I have received permission from the senator, yes. Mr. Hale will accompany us."

My eyes flick to Bodyguard Steve. I bet he doesn't swing dance, but I guess we're going to find out. Friday night we're busting out of this place and going to our favorite swing club. *Coco. Zelda. Gloria. Louise.* It's been ages, and I miss it.

Now that the older guard is involved, there's no way to leave campus without him knowing. I'm positive he tells Daddy absolutely everything. He can't be bought. I already probed the subject when I asked him to keep my almost nightly excursions to the security office a secret from Daddy. The bodyguard didn't so much as give me a verbal reply.

I admit having to get clearance from Daddy takes some of the thrill out of going to the swing dancing club we frequented last semester, since our excursion won't require clandestine sneaking.

"I'm in," Ricardo says, then lower in my ear. "It'll give you a chance to let your hair down, mon coeur. And trust me. You need it."

I open my mouth to argue, but the faint press of his lips on my jaw stuns me into silence. My eyes blink slowly in incomprehension. He just kissed me right in front of my sister. My best friend. My bodyguard. The whole school! He's brazen. The complete opposite of Kenneth.

Speaking of, I see Kenneth down the hall, slinking back toward the health center.

My brow furrows. Is that why Ricardo kissed me just now? For Kenneth's benefit? If he did, that's great. It was the whole point of this fake dating arrangement, after all. So why the tinge of disappointment rippling through me right now?

"Pardonnez-moi, but I could use some coffee before my next class. Anyone else want to come?" Genevieve's eyes move over each of us.

I shake my head. I'm already hopped up on the giant mocha I had an hour ago.

Adrienne, however, yawns in assent. "I think I will. I didn't get much sleep last night."

Genevieve, Adrienne, and Mikhail move off toward the eatery.

Ricardo withdraws his arms from around my waist, leaving burning strips along my skin.

"Hey," my mouth protests without my permission as Ricardo spins me toward him.

"You went rigid just now. What was that?" he asks, locking eyes with me.

There is no way I'm telling him it's because I wished, only for a nanosecond, that he kissed me because he wanted to and not because Kenneth was around. It would only make his ego bigger than it already is. No, instead I choose to poke the bear. "If you wanted to see me with my hair down, you could have invited me to hang out in the kitchen with you guys that night. Instead I come down for a snack and see all of you palling around without me. What was that?" I'm whispering by the end, realizing how vulnerable I sound. How lonely. I should have kept my mouth shut.

"Oh, mon coeur. I'm sorry." He wraps his arms around me and pulls me into a soft hug. "If I'd known how difficult it is for you to be away from me, I would definitely have invited you."

Groaning even as I laugh, I pull away. "Yes, that's me. Creeping down the hall to be closer to you. Arg, you're the worst. Don't you take anything seriously?"

Laughter rumbles from his throat. "Nope. It's more fun this way."

I'd like to kiss that smug look off his face. That, I bet he'd take seriously. I frown. I can't believe I just thought that. I have to put some distance between us before I do something I regret. "Whatever. See you later." I move into the stream of people navigating the hallway.

"Whoa, whoa, not so fast. Where's the fire?" Ricardo says, snagging my arm as I try to sail past him.

"Nowhere. Just decided Genevieve and Adrienne had the right idea, getting away from you."

"Ouch. Alright, let's get some coffee."

"You weren't invited."

Even though it's been a few weeks, I'm still pleasantly surprised when the crowd parts to let the two of us pass. "I'm your devilishly handsome plus one."

"About that, I think we should break up." No. Yes. No. Yes?

Ricardo stops in his tracks. "No, no, no. That's a terrible idea. This is way too much fun. Plus, you know why I was late? My mom tried to corner me after class, and you were my excuse to leave. All of the girls on campus are nicer to me now that I'm a committed man. And Kenneth isn't jealous enough yet." He looks a little green as he talks. I didn't know he was so hell-bent on avoiding his mom. Or having such a hard time dating only one girl the first month of the semester.

Oh no. It hits me. This Saturday. It's couple's night at the swing club because it also happens to be Valentine's Day. Crap. What am I going to do about that? I can't spend it with Ricardo. That would be way too… real. I should put a stop to this right now, before I dig myself even deeper. I'm already in neck-deep as it is. But the way he's looking at me right now...

"Come on, Char. Give me a couple more weeks? Please?" Ricardo's giving me puppy dog eyes, his hands knotted under his chin, and darn it if it doesn't make me want to concede.

My instincts war within me. Protect myself by pushing Ricardo away. Give in and keep up the act. "Okay," my mouth says before I can make up my mind.

Ricardo grins. "Great. You won't regret it. Wait until you see my moves when we go dancing. I've been practicing." He waggles his eyebrows at me, and I can't help but laugh. Even though I'm pretty sure he's wrong about regretting this whole mess after it's over. Ricardo's shoulders relax as he throws his arm around me and we resume our walk toward the eatery.

"Oh, hey, before I forget. You talking about creeping in the halls reminded me of something weird. I saw someone lurking toward the classrooms one night over break, but didn't think much of it at the time. I'm pretty sure it was a girl. We should go back through that footage and see if we can identify her. It's a far away shot from the camera at the front door, but it's worth a try. At the least, it could give us another suspect in the great mystery of who killed Professor Rook."

My lips purse. A girl? I'm not sure how that would connect to Professor Rook's death. The person who attacked me was definitely a guy. Still, anticipation courses through me at the possibility of finding another piece to the puzzle. "Can we go tonight? I want to see who it was."

Ricardo's head shakes. "Sorry, mon coeur. I'm not on duty again until Saturday. If you come visit me then, I'll show you. Then we can go dancing with everyone. It'll be great."

"I have to wait until Saturday? But what if it's important?"

"It'll still be there."

Thinking back to how easy it was for Ricardo to delete me

from the footage of the night Professor Rook was killed, I have my doubts. Still, if some girl was skulking around the classrooms, I want to know about it. They might have been doing the exact thing I've been dying to do, even though I haven't yet found an opportunity.

Break into Professor Rook's desk and look through his student files.

Okay, I'll say it. Watching Ricardo pick the lock on Professor Rook's desk is doing it for me. He's hunched over in the shadows behind the desk, the curls of his hair draping his neck as he works. I clasp my hands between my knees to keep from reaching out to caress Ricardo's hair.

The academy building is silent around us, as if the ancient building itself knows the importance of our task and has taken a vow of silence. As with the other times I've snuck around where I'm not supposed to, my heart is dancing in my chest. Adrenaline sings through my veins, making me antsy with anticipation.

The infinitesimal click of the drawer's lock giving sounds audibly, making me lean forward in anticipation.

Ricardo grins at me over his shoulder, and in this moment I'm so very glad we made the no kissing rule. Because if we hadn't? I'd probably jump him right now. An image of me shoving him against the desk and pressing my lips to his makes my skin tingle. I'm in way deeper than I realized. I freeze, not sure how I feel about this turn of events.

"Mon coeur?" Ricardo whispers, his eyes sparking pools of liquid heat. "If you don't stop looking at me like that, this evening is going to take a very unexpected turn."

His earnest tone is what snaps me out of my decidedly less-than-innocent reverie.

"Let's just do what we came here for," I whisper, kneeling beside him and pulling the drawer open with a slow, silent hand. Once it's open, I pause, listening. All is quiet. When we came down here, the security guard was on rounds, so we may not have much time. He could come up the hall at any moment, and I have no doubt he'd go straight to the headmistress if he found the two of us in here, poring over files from a drawer that was supposed to be locked. He'd accuse us of cheating, probably, which would mean immediate expulsion from the academy.

Adrienne told me that Professor Rook kept indicators in his files of who his clients were, and I need that list if I'm ever going to figure out who would want me to stay away from the investigation of Professor Rook's death.

Skimming over the files, I begin to notice a pattern. Beside a good number of the names, there's a small dot. Looking over the names, I tally them up in my head. Looks like my sister was right. The students whose files are marked with a dot are those who had purchased drugs from Rook. Rhiannon's name is accompanied by a dot. So is mine.

"So many," Ricardo says, frowning.

"Let's just take the photos and get out of here." Whipping my phone out of my pocket, I take a photo. The shutter sound is amplified by the quiet, reverberating through the room. I go still, praying no one heard it.

Crap. Footsteps sound at the end of the hall.

Ricardo makes a "hurry up" motion with one hand, and I flip through the rest of the files as quickly and quietly as I can, capturing the rest of the photos I need with a silent phone. I take Ricardo's extended hand, and he helps me stand.

"Let's go," he mouths, gliding toward the door. But when he peeks out, he quickly withdraws his head back into the classroom. Oddly, he's smiling.

"What's so funny?" I whisper.

"This is the second time I've hidden in this very room after breaking into that desk."

"It's not funny," I mouth, worry edging my words. "If we get caught in here…"

In the hallway, the security guard draws closer, and pauses.

My breath hitches as I press against Ricardo's side, hoping the guard doesn't take more than a cursory glance into the room. I scan the room, looking for signs that we've been here. The throbbing in my chest is so loud, I'm positive it's audible. The desk drawer, I left it open.

"If the two of you wanted to be alone, there are better places for it."

I jump nearly out of my skin before I recognize the voice. It's Mikhail standing in the doorway, the hint of a smile warming his expression.

Ricardo busts up laughing. "Your face." He tries to imitate me, and doubles over, clutching his stomach.

"You saw who it was!" My body heats with embarrassment as I shove Ricardo away from me.

"It was worth it," Ricardo gasps between guffaws.

Ignoring him, I face Mikhail. "What are you doing down here? Aren't you off duty?"

Mikhail shrugs. "Adrienne has banished me from the kitchen. I believe she is planning something for Valentine's Day tomorrow. She does not know I have something for her as well." He pats the pocket of his suit jacket.

Intrigued, I move closer. "Show me!"

Finally done laughing, Ricardo sidles up next to me and slings an arm around my waist. I peel him off, but I can't hold a mad face. He did get me pretty good. When he snakes his arm around me again, I let it be.

Mikhail pulls a small, black velvet box out and hands it to me. Inside are two shiny moss green stud earrings. Agate, I'm guessing. It's not a super expensive stone, but the color is perfect for Adrienne. "She's going to love these," I whisper, closing the box gently and handing it back to Mikhail.

"I am glad you approve." So saying, he tucks the box away for safe keeping.

Ricardo leans his head against mine, a surprisingly tender gesture. "Don't get any ideas, mon coeur. We're not to the jewelry stage. Yet."

Now it's Saturday afternoon and Adrienne, Genevieve, and I are in one of the community bathrooms getting ready to go swing dancing. The dormitory is decorated with glittery pink and red streamers, and Ms. Poppin left a small treat at each of our doors. Mine was my favorite candy bar, and I ate it immediately.

There's been a flurry of activity in our dorm all afternoon as girls got ready for their hot dates in honor of Saint Valentine. Gul came by our room just to show us the outfit she chose for her surprise date with Grady. She grinned as she told us that he hadn't given her any hints as to where they were going. Then she was gone, eyes sparkling as she strutted down the stairs to meet him.

Looking at my friend in the mirror, I concede that she was right; we all need this break from the academy. There's way too much pressure within these walls, what with Professor Rook's death still unsolved, my attacker being on the loose, and the possibility of running into Kenneth or Mrs. LaGuerre around every corner.

I'm standing in front of the gilded mirror in our

community bathroom, which I commandeered from a pack of giggling freshmen. With a deft swipe of my wrist, I put the finishing touches on my makeup. My mouth is stained cherry red, and my eyes look wide and upturned thanks to the perfect cat-eye I'm rocking. The emerald green, beaded Emily Allison frock I scored last weekend hugs my willowy frame perfectly, making me look curvier than I am. I'm going to knock Ricardo dead. Just because. It has nothing to do with Valentine's Day. I even eschewed traditional V-day colors, specifically.

Beside me, Genevieve is curling her cinnamon brown hair. Catching my eye in the mirror, she smiles. "So, you've been pretty tight-lipped about you and Ricardo. We want to know what's going on. Please tell us."

"Yes, please," Adrienne trills from where she's sitting on a tufted velvet stool between us. Her fuchsia, sweetheart neckline fits her like a glove, and she looks fantastic. Every line of her body is buzzing with excitement. She's ecstatic about the prospect of dancing with Mikhail tonight. I don't blame her. He's an excellent dancer. She puts a hand on my skirt. "Every time I try to ask you about him, you clam up. I want the details."

I spin slowly in the mirror, pretending to examine my reflection while looking around the cream and champagne bathroom for something to distract them, but there's nothing diverting enough to deter them from wanting to know about Ricardo and me. I sigh. My sister is right. I've been avoiding this conversation since I announced I was dating Ricardo, which must appear weird to them. If I was in love with my boyfriend, wouldn't I want to gush about him to my friends? I mean, I used to brag about Kenneth. Why not Ricardo?

My stomach tightens, and I run my hand over it as if they can see the knots there. I'm not gushing because I'm faking it with Ricardo, that's why. Or he's faking with me. Honestly, it's hard to tell fact from fiction in our relationship anymore. My mind says it's all fake, but my body… It's whispering another story. As much as I deny it, being around him lately has given me unidentifiable flutters in the general region of my stomach. But Ricardo? I have no way of knowing if he still thinks of me as an excuse to duck his mom, or something more. I can't bear to tell my sister and closest friend that I'm beginning to have feelings for a boy I profess to hate, only to be shot down. I'd never be able to save face after all that.

"Are you sure you don't want to talk about something else? Like the peace talks in the middle east? Or the new gun laws in California?"

"Charlotte," Adrienne scolds, standing and putting her hands on her hips. "I do not want to talk about gun laws right now."

"Or ever," Genevieve says, shivering. She's not a fan of firearms.

I relent, my expression softening. "Okay, what do you want to know?" I say, pulling Adrienne toward me so I can do her eyeshadow.

"How did this happen? I thought you hated Ricardo," Adrienne says, blinking.

"Look down at your fabulous new shoes," I order, and she complies.

"I did too," Genevieve says, dropping a perfect curl and wrapping another strand around her curling wand. "I'm surprised you'd talk to him at all, after how he treated both of us."

My lips purse in concentration as I blend the colors I'm putting on my sister's eyelids. "I know, and I'm sorry. It just sort of happened. And he's not so bad. Really. He went to bat for me last week when everyone was talking about my black eyes, you know? No one's ever done that for me before. Plus, when I'm with Ricardo, I feel like he sees me. Does that make sense?"

Genevieve and Adrienne nod. My stepsister is grinning. "Don't move."

"Sorry." But she's still smiling.

Their warm reception of my pretend gushing is all the encouragement I need to keep going. And let's face it; everything I've said about Ricardo just now is true. I do feel seen by Ricardo, more than by anyone else in my life. We may push each other's buttons just because we can, but it doesn't feel spiteful anymore. The crackle of energy between us is… intriguing.

"His hair kills me. It makes me want to shove my fingers into it and never let go." My eyes go wide. I cannot believe I said that out loud.

"Charlotte and Ricardo sitting in a tree, K. I. S .S. I. N. G." Adrienne squeals, meeting my eyes.

My face flushes hot at the images of kissing Ricardo that flit through my mind. Our lip lock during that game of truth or dare. A secluded corner of the academy, three years ago...

Genevieve's answering smile shows her white teeth. "He is a good kisser. I'll give him that."

Concern ripples through me, and I look past my sister to where Genevieve is standing at the counter. "You're really okay with this? If it hurts you at all, I'll put an end to it right now. It's not worth hurting my bestie."

She meets my gaze in the mirror. "It's fine. We were never a great fit, anyway. It always felt like work, you know?"

I nod. I think I do, because that's how it was when I was with Kenneth. I always felt like I had to be on my best behavior, appear mature and put together for him. I didn't even realize how draining it was until it was over. Not that it's a cake walk with Ricardo, but being with him doesn't leave me emotionally and mentally drained. Instead, sparring with him revs me up and gives me energy to conquer the world. So why am I trying to make Kenneth jealous, again?

"Seriously, though," Adrienne says, biting her lip. "I know what you mean about him seeing you. Last semester when everyone was convinced I'd killed Na, he was one of the only people who treated me like a person. Aside from you, Char, everyone treated me like an alien from a strange planet. Ricardo kept me grounded. He's good at that."

"What do you think?" I step back from Adrienne, finished with her eyeshadow look. It's a smoky cherry color that compliments her dress perfectly.

Adrienne's eyes widen when she catches sight of herself in the mirror. "I look so grown up," she says.

"You look amazing," I say.

Genevieve agrees.

Golden afternoon sunshine flows in through the frosted window, wreathing my sister in an aura of yellow light. She smiles, her cheeks a rosy pink.

Glancing at my phone, I say, "It's almost time. I'm going to meet Ricardo in the surveillance room. We'll catch up with you in the foyer."

Genevieve blots her lipstick and Adrienne grins. "Have fun."

"Will do." I pull my faux fur coat on over my gorgeous dress, and descend the stairs, ignoring Bodyguard Steve's quiet tread behind me. Instead, I revel in the sensation of my heels sinking into the plush carpet. Man, I love how beautiful heels make me feel. And liberated. Like, yes, I am wearing six inch heels, and yes, I am a powerful, intelligent, magnificent woman. Thank you very much. Tonight is going to be amazing. An evening of dancing and delicious mocktails sounds absolutely perfect.

Since it's Saturday, all of the professors and students have abandoned the classroom hallways, either in favor of their own rooms or whatever weekend plans they have off-campus. It's quiet as I pass through the empty corridor toward where the security office is located at the end. My instincts hum. It's almost… eerie down here.

The late afternoon sunlight streaming through the windows into the classrooms is weakening as I tap on the closed door of the security office. No answer. Ricardo must have earbuds in or something.

My security detail settles against the wall, his eyes hidden behind those ridiculous sunglasses.

After listening for sound from within and hearing nothing, I knock again, louder this time.

A hint of frustration flares through me as I pull out my phone and call Ricardo. What's he doing in there? Behind the security office door, his ringtone sounds loudly, playing all the way through without interruption.

That's weird. Ricardo doesn't use his phone a ton, but I'm surprised he'd leave it here if he stepped out. A twinge of worry shoots through me, filling the air with nervous energy. "Ricardo?" I call.

No answer.

Glancing down the hall, I notice how dark it's gotten while I've been standing here, waiting. Instead of sunlight bathing the wooden floors, they're swathed in shadow. The brass sconces dotting the walls have lit up, illuminating us.

Now that I think about it, it is kind of odd that there's not another soul around right now. Even though it's Saturday, there's usually a professor working in their office, or a student using a quiet room to catch up on some studying far from the noise and distraction of the dormitory. Where is everyone?

"Ricardo?" I call, louder this time. His ringtone drums and bops as I call him a second time without a response. Gripping the cold metal knob in one hand, I twist. It doesn't budge. The door is locked. That's strange.

The coil of anxiety in my chest twists tighter. Morphs into something akin to fear.

Turning to my bodyguard, I look at his sunglasses, guessing at where his eyes rest behind the dark frames. "Steve?"

"Yes, Miss Cavendish-Holt?"

I lick my lips. "Can you pick this lock for me?"

He shifts uncomfortably. "I'm not authorized to be in the surveillance room, Miss."

Taking a step closer, I put a hand on his forearm. "You don't understand. I'm supposed to meet my boyfriend here, and he's not answering. I'm starting to worry that something happened to him." It's the bare truth. I *am* starting to worry. My instincts are screaming at me that something is wrong.

The man shrugs. "Maybe he's running late."

I know immediately that's not it. Even though Ricardo puts off a laissez-faire vibe, he's a great student, and he's almost never late. Whether it's his nature to be on time or he merely realizes how irritated I would be if he were to keep me waiting, he's always been prompt since we started spending time together.

My stomach twists as alarm bells go off in my brain. I need to get through this door.

"Fine, if you won't do it, I will." I hope. Kneeling, I take my emergency stash of hair pins out of my buttery soft new clutch purse and take a deep breath. I watched Ricardo do this. I can do it. I hope.

"Wait, Miss. If you're that desperate to get through that door, I can help." Bodyguard Steve takes the hairpins from me, working them with expert hands. In seconds, there's a tiny click and the door swings open.

Frigid air brushes over me, making goosebumps pebble my skin. It's freezing in the surveillance office. My eyes sweep over the interior of the room, and a cry screeches from my throat. Ricardo's phone has been abandoned on the desk. Its screen flashes with notifications. The desk chair has toppled over and lies on the ground, its back snapped where it hit the hard floor.

The worst part?

Ricardo is sprawled on the tile floor where he fell out of his chair. Eyes clamped shut. Unconscious. And his lips are blue.

24

I fly toward Ricardo's prone body, but Steve wraps his arm around me and drags me back. "I cannot allow you to touch him, Miss. Let me assess the situation first."

I shake my head and lunge toward Ricardo again. He's unconscious on the floor. In need of help. My face pales. He could be dying as I stand here.

Bodyguard Steve's arm tightens around my waist and he meets my eyes. "Let me do my job, Miss Cavendish-Holt."

I sag, still fighting the compulsion to erase the distance between me and my fake boyfriend. "Fine. Do something. I'll call 911." With shaking fingers, I dig my phone out of my clutch and make the call. My voice trembles as I answer the operator's questions. No, he doesn't have any allergies or underlying conditions that could lead to spontaneous loss of consciousness. He's perfectly healthy, isn't he?

My bodyguard takes Ricardo's pulse and checks his breathing. Nods in my direction. Ricardo's still alive.

I squeeze my eyes shut, but pop them open again. If Ricardo is dying in front of me, I don't want to miss it. I want this image seared onto my brain.

Once I'm finished with the emergency operator, I hang up. Wrapping my arms around myself, I huddle in the doorway as the bodyguard lifts Ricardo's arms gingerly and pulls him out of the security room. Standing up, he moves toward the surveillance office.

I don't wait for permission. Kneeling beside Ricardo, I reach for his face with gentle fingers.

"Don't touch him," my bodyguard orders. "He may have come into contact with something that did this to him."

I frown even as I retract my hands, twisting them in my lap. "I'm not allergic to anything."

Bodyguard Steve's face is expressionless, his tone somber. "That's not what I mean. It could have been a toxin or contaminant that did this to him, and it's my job to keep you from harm. Don't touch him."

My blood runs cold as I stare down at Ricardo. Someone could have done this to him? It didn't even occur to me until my bodyguard said it, but as soon as he does I know it's true.

This can't be an accident. Not after Professor Rook's death. That video threat someone sent to Gul. My attack.

Someone just tried to kill Ricardo. And from the look of it, they almost succeeded.

Resolve chills my veins to ice. My fists bunch my skirt. I'm going to figure out who is behind all of this shit, and I'm going to make them pay. I lock eyes on Ricardo's face. Memorize every curve and line. I want to commit it to memory so I can feed on this image later, when I'm foisting justice on the bastard who did this to Ricardo.

The older man examines the surveillance room inch by inch without touching anything. There's nothing there. No loose powders or weapons or traces that indicate that someone else has been in this room in the past few hours. "Are you sure he doesn't have any underlying conditions?" The man asks, glancing at me from where he's standing in the middle of the small room, scanning the walls with a practiced eye.

I shake my head, my fingers itching to touch Ricardo. Sitting here doing nothing makes me feel helpless. My eyes flash as an idea hits. Digging my black leather gloves out of my clutch, I slip them on. Ignoring my guard's shaking head, I pull Ricardo's head into my lap and stroke his soft curls. My eyes sting as they rove over his face. He'd look serenely asleep if his mouth didn't look like he recently made out with a blue popsicle. Doesn't that mean he's lacking oxygen? But how could that be?

One of the on-duty security guards comes jogging down the hall toward us. "What's going on here?"

Bodyguard Steve fills him in.

I tune them out, focusing on the boy lying perfectly still on the floor. Hoping it doesn't end like this. Whatever *it* is.

My gloved fingers work through Ricardo's hair. I wish I could slip off my gloves and caress his tresses with my bare hands. A quick scan of his face makes hope alight in my chest. I'm pretty sure his lips aren't as blue as they were.

"Hey, Ricardo," I whisper, hoping the men can't hear me. "Wake up. I'm not done arguing with your stupid face yet. Plus, you have to be around so I can beat you to that internship in Daddy's office. It won't be as fun winning if you're not the one I'm beating. And… and Kenneth isn't jealous enough yet." Not the real reasons I want him to wake up, but I can't bring myself to say them aloud, even if he can't hear me. "Also, Adrienne will never forgive you if you leave." Still not the real reason. "I won't forgive you either." I swallow. There it is. The truth. I will never forgive Ricardo if he leaves me like this. It's just not right. I refuse to examine why there's a deep desperation churning through me at the possibility of losing him right now.

A warm hand reaches up and gently takes my wrist. "So, you kind of like me, huh?" His voice is hoarse from disuse.

My eyes fly to Ricardo's dark, luscious eyes, which are open and sparkling up at me.

"Ugh, you're the actual worst." I swat at his chest, but he catches my other hand. Doesn't let go.

"I absolutely do not like you. At all," I lie.

"You do," he murmurs, not taking his eyes off mine. A sly smile apparent in his features.

"No comment."

He coughs out a chuckle and tries to sit up.

I shove him back down into my lap. "Stay down until the paramedics get here."

"Yes, ma'am." Taking my hands again, he pulls them down around his neck and covers them with his own.

My brain is jumping through hoops trying to figure out why having my arms around Ricardo like this feels so comfortable, so right. There can only be one conclusion.

I am in deep trouble.

Mercifully, Bodyguard Steve interrupts my introspection. "How often does someone clean the air vents?"

The security guard shakes his head, but my security officer doesn't take his eyes off the AC vent high on the wall above the desk. Mumbling something under his breath, the bodyguard climbs onto the desk and, taking a multi-purpose tool out of his pocket, tests the screws in the vent cover. "Strange. These are already loose."

He's got my full attention now, despite Ricardo's thumbs swirling across my palms. I can't look away as he works to pull out the screws, pocketing them.

The scrape of the vent cover being pried off the wall makes me wince. The bodyguard hands the cover to the man below him and carefully slips a gloved hand into the vent, feeling around for something. Plastic crinkles under his fingers. "Bingo," he mutters, pulling out two partially melted bags of dry ice. Despite Bodyguard Steve's gentle movements, liquid droplets spatter over the desk.

Dry ice. "The stuff that emits carbon monoxide as it melts?"

"Correct. It can cause headaches, nausea, dizziness. Eventually victims lose consciousness, and if they aren't removed from the source of the gas, death. Judging by the size of this bag and assuming it was full when placed in the vent, anyone in the nearby rooms would have experienced symptoms."

Suddenly the absence of anyone in the wing of classrooms makes sense. Anyone who began to feel sick would probably retreat to the dormitory. But Ricardo may not have had time to react, being so close to the source of the poisonous gas.

My hands tighten around Ricardo's. I was right. This wasn't an accident. Someone put that dry ice in the vent in order to hurt another person. And pretty much everyone at school knows Ricardo has been in the surveillance office on Friday afternoons since the semester started.

My eyes lower to Ricardo's face. "Someone tried to kill you."

25

I read the same calculus question for the umpteenth time, but it still doesn't penetrate the nervous buzz in my skull. My brain simply won't focus on my homework until I tell Adrienne and Genevieve what's going on. And frankly, it's about time I came clean with them. They deserve my honesty, and I've been feeding them lies. "I have something to tell you both. It's important."

Adrienne looks up from her e-reader, her auburn brows scrunched together.

Genevieve, too, looks up from her laptop. "What is it? You can tell us."

I lick my lips. After Ricardo's near-death experience, it was obvious to me that somehow, faking a relationship with him had lead to real feelings. Even though I denied it, I knew the truth. I was falling for Ricardo. And knowing that, I can't stand to lie to my sister and my best friend anymore. Even though I'm afraid of how they'll react.

"You know how my relationship with Ricardo came out of nowhere?"

Genevieve and Adrienne nod in tandem.

Taking a deep breath, I spill it all before I lose my nerve. "That's because it did. The first day of school, when we ran into Kenneth in the hallway. I was still upset over our breakup, and I knew Ricardo wanted an excuse to avoid his mom, so... I made it up. I told everyone we were dating, but we weren't.

We've been faking it."

Adrienne's mouth drops open, even as Genevieve sits up straighter, her eyes fixed to my face.

"You mean, you and Ricardo aren't madly in love?" Adrienne says, looking as if someone just smashed her favorite rolling pin to bits.

"You made it up," Genevieve says, deadpan.

Flinging myself down on the rug beside them, I hold up my laced hands in supplication. "Forgive me. Please. I never would have done it if I thought it would come between us."

Genevieve's jaw works as she stares at me, considering my words. A flicker of sadness moves over her face. She's not going to forgive me. This is the end of our friendship, right here. And I can't blame her for it. Lying is unforgivable.

Putting her pen down gently on top of her notebook, she shifts onto her knees. She's going to walk out without even letting me explain. "You've been fake dating Ricardo for the past month and a half, as a way to make Ken Doll jealous."

I nod, daring to look past her toward where Adrienne is sitting, frowning. She runs a hand through the lush pile of my faux fur rug. "I can't believe you both were faking it this whole time, and you both kept it from me. I have to say, I'm hurt, Charlotte."

"I'm so sorry, to both of you." There aren't any excuses I can make that will make the situation better, so I stop there.

Genevieve's lips purse. "I forgive you." It's simple, straightforward, and given willingly. I don't deserve a best friend like Genevieve.

"Me too," Adrienne says.

Relief courses through me as I throw my arms around them, pulling the three of us into an awkward group huddle. "Thank you. Thank you. Thank you. You have no idea how glad I am to hear that. I had no idea how complicated fake dating would get, or that it would last this long. And I never thought I'd fall for him, but I…" I cut myself off with a hand clamped over my mouth. I didn't mean to tell them that. I haven't allowed myself to acknowledge my feelings toward Ricardo, but in this moment I know my words are true.

Genevieve leans back to look at me, her eyebrows in her hair. "You what?"

Adrienne is grinning. "Say that again."

I shake my head vehemently, embarrassed.

"You said you fell for Ricardo. You like him? For real?" Adrienne looks like she's just won a million bucks.

Casting a furtive glance at Genevieve, I nod. She blows out a long breath. "Thank goodness."

"What?"

"It's been obvious to me for weeks that he's crazy about you, Char. He looks at you as if you're the best thing in the world to him, and despite my feelings about him, I couldn't stay mad when it seemed like the two of you were so happy. And then you tell me you're faking the whole thing, and I don't know what to think."

I feel hollowed out and filled up again with something warm and soft. Can it be true that Ricardo has real feelings for me? "He hasn't said… He acted so… Are you sure?"

"Just don't go overboard with the PDA, all right? Spare us that." Genevieve smiles.

I grin. "Deal. If he'll have me."

"Oh, he will," Adrienne says, climbing to her feet. "I can tell Mikhail, right? I'm going to tell him. I'll be right back."

I open my mouth to protest, but stop. It won't hurt for her to tell Mikhail about Ricardo and me. Besides, he's so observant, he probably guessed the whole situation anyway.

Really, I should be thanking him for keeping his mouth zipped about it this whole time.

With another smile at Genevieve, I turn my attention back to my calculus homework. It's going to be a breeze.

As soon as I hear that Ricardo is back from the hospital, I hurry up to his room, telling myself the whole way that I'm anxious to see him because he's been helping me investigate Professor Rook's death. No other reason. Ignoring the curious looks I get from everyone in the student lounge as I pass, I walk as casually but as quickly as possible to Ricardo's room.

You kind of like me, huh?

My cheeks warm at the memory of his long, warm hands wrapped around mine. Yep, deep trouble. Assuming that Genevieve is right, and he has feelings for me too...

I knock on his door, and Ricardo beckons me inside. He's stretched out in his hammock, tucked into a blanket like a rolled taco when I enter. My stomach flips at the sight of him relaxing in a clean white tee. His black socked feet peek out at the bottom of the blanket.

Mrs. LaGuerre is sitting in the desk chair, ankles crossed, with a book open in her lap. Sun from the window is the only light in the room, fanning over the spread pages of the tome. Keeping vigil.

Ricardo looks from me to her. "Can you go now, Mom? Since I have company?"

A pitter-patter of anticipation slides down my spine at his words. Will she actually leave us alone in here? If I ever brought a guy home, my mom wouldn't even let us go upstairs to my bedroom, much less leave us unchaperoned in there.

Mrs. LaGuerre's shoulders slump, but she nods. "If that's what you want, my son."

"It is." Ricardo's tone is stubborn as his mom scoops up her purse and stands.

"I'll talk to you soon?" she asks in resignation.

Ricardo merely shrugs, not taking his eyes off me.

It occurs to me that I should encourage him to spend some time with his mom. Talk to her. Reconcile, because that is clearly what she wants. But I can't make myself do it at the moment. The urge to be alone with him is stronger than my inclination to fix the broken relationship between mother and son.

Mrs. LaGuerre leaves the door open a crack, and then it's just the two of us.

"Couldn't wait to see me, could you?" Ricardo hits me right in the chest with an intoxicating grin.

"You want me to leave? Because I will." Spinning on my heel, I make for the door, shooting an eye roll over my shoulder. This was a mistake. Clearly, Genevieve is mistaken, and Ricardo simply enjoys yanking my chain to get a reaction.

Struggling to pull his hands out of his tightly wrapped blanket, Ricardo holds them out toward me. "No. No, wait. I'll try not to flirt."

With hands on my hips, I turn toward him. I'll believe that when I see it. "That would be like you not breathing. Don't do that again. Once is enough."

The corner of Ricardo's mouth tips up as he relaxes into the hammock. "As you wish, mon coeur."

"You know I don't like that nickname," I argue, halfheartedly, even as I'm crossing the room toward him. I've already realized that arguing with Ricardo about that mushy nickname is futile. Almost without thinking, I reach out and touch the stubble along his jawline. It's a liberty I've never taken with him, and I'm not sure how he'll react.

Ricardo's eyes are heavy-lidded as he looks up at me. "Is that why you've gone all pink and glowy?"

I snap my fingers away from his face, touching my own warming cheeks. "Shut up."

Ricardo rolls his head in amusement. "Do you know why all of my relationships up to now have ended after only a couple of weeks?"

"Because you're a commitment-phobe who doesn't take anything seriously?"

He huffs, but when his eyes find mine, there's something new in their depths. Vulnerability. "My mother left us when I was eight. For a long time, I assumed it was because she didn't want me. I thought I wasn't enough for her. That it was my job to keep our family together, and I failed. I was so absorbed in my own pain, that I didn't see how much her absence affected my dad. But after a while, I saw how much he had changed. Before my mom left, he would get home from the office in time for us to sit down to a family dinner. He was always happy, eager to be with us. Smiling. You know? But after she left… He wasn't the same. He started working longer hours, stopped smiling. Family dinners became me eating alone in the kitchen while the cook did the dishes. It made me realize. My mom… she left him just as much as she left me, and it destroyed him. I learned that love is dangerous, especially when it's not returned in equal measure. I figured, if I didn't let anyone in, they wouldn't see that I'm not enough. They wouldn't see that I'm lacking."

I can't speak. I have never understood Ricardo as much as I do right now. In this moment. Because what he's saying, I understand it. I've been the little girl left behind with an anguished parent. The child wondering if I'd only been more, maybe my father would have stayed. Only in my case, my mom remarried. Found happiness again. From what I know, Mr. LaGuerre has never remarried. Ricardo has spent his entire life under the weighty cloud of his mom's absence. No wonder he's jumped from relationship to relationship without a backward glance. He's never stopped running.

"But recently, I've realized something. It wasn't me who wasn't enough. It was her. Something about her kept her from being satisfied with our life as a family. It wasn't my fault. You want to know what my dad said when I told him?"

I bob my head, unwilling to speak, to break the spell being woven between us.

"She planned to come back for me, once she was settled. She wanted me with her, at the time. She didn't leave because I wasn't enough. She left because our family had too much. She felt guilty staying when so many in our country had nothing. I don't agree with what she did, but it helped to hear it. You know?"

This is all too much, the similarity between Ricardo and me. For all of my life, I've wondered what I lacked. What indefinable quality was missing from me that led my biological father to walk away from us, his family. And now to discover that Ricardo felt the same way...

Ricardo's amber eyes home in on mine, and he cups my cheek with one hand. "Charlotte, I like you, and I think you like me too. Can we drop the pretense?"

I snag the inside of my lip between my teeth. Debating. I do not like relinquishing control like this. To anyone. If I admit to Ricardo that he's right, I'll be giving up some of my power. But I do like him. And after hearing his explanation tonight, I think I can trust him too. Gathering my courage to me like a soldier beckoning his comrades in arms, I meet his gaze. "Okay."

A wide grin spreads over his features. "Then come here." Pulling the blanket back, he pats the woven fabric of the hammock beside him.

Finally allowing myself to embrace the squishy feelings in my chest, I relent. Climbing into the hammock beside Ricardo is awkward, but once I'm safely tucked against his side he pulls the blanket up around both of us. I rest my head on his shoulder, and his cheek touches the top of my head. It's so warm, like we're wrapped in a cocoon of our newly admitted feelings. Cushioned on a cloud.

"So..." He begins.

"So..."

Laughing, he nudges my chin up and meets my eyes. "We're doing this? Dating? For real?" There's a trace of something in his voice. Could it be insecurity?

My throat goes dry, so all I can manage is a nod.

"Excellent. Can I kiss you now? Because I've been dying to since that stupid game of truth or dare. Your sister is more devious than we give her credit for."

My mouth curves up. "You better."

Sliding his hand from my chin to the side of my neck, Ricardo puts his lips on mine. Fireworks shoot through my body, making me feel like I'm flying. I'm reminded of how it felt to kiss Ricardo during that truth or dare game. Warm. Consuming. Exhilarating. Kissing has never felt like this before.

Except for my very first day at the academy, two and a half years ago. A tall, cocky boy with ruddy brown skin and strawberry brown hair had come over to me unannounced, and grinned when I didn't back away. "I'm Ricardo," he'd said, "and I can tell you and me are a perfect match."

I'd laughed, pleased at the attention. I'd been looking for a way to stand out that day, shimmer out of the sea of privileged geniuses I found myself thrust among. So I'd gone for it. Lifted up on tiptoe and kissed him, stealing his breath. He'd been stunned for a second before falling into it with me. It had been my first kiss, and it had been exhilarating. Until it wasn't.

I don't want to think about that right now.

Ricardo's fingers slide into my hair, giving the gentlest tug. Tingles tiptoe across my scalp.

Sinking further into the kiss, I shift my weight, turning into his body. The hammock rocks violently underneath us. My stomach dips, pulling me out of my kiss-induced trance. Laughing, I try to sit up. "Maybe we should stop."

"Just one more," Ricardo says, using his hand in my hair to drag me toward him.

I relent, giving him one more chaste kiss before slipping out from under his blanket and managing to dismount the hammock with a modicum of grace. Feeling the need to put distance between us, I drag his desk chair to the other corner of the room and sit in it.

My breathing is ragged as I watch Ricardo swing his legs off the side of the hammock and sit up. His eyes don't leave my face, his gaze intense. There's a fire in his eyes that makes me all tingly. Alive.

He moves to stand. "Can I just—"

"Stay right where you are."

Ricardo sinks back into the hammock with a smile. "You don't trust me, mon coeur?"

"Not in the slightest." I'm gripping the chair in an effort to keep my seat. I don't trust myself either. The bubbling sensation moving through me is heading toward my brain, making me liable to give in and kiss Ricardo until we're both senseless. I mean, it would be fun…

Nope.

The last time I did that, I ran over a dead body.

"You want to know something funny? Now that we're dating, everyone is treating me better. Taking me more seriously. It's because of you."

I shrug. "They're probably scared of me."

"No, I don't think that's it. My teachers don't act surprised when I do well on an assignment anymore, even though I've always been a good student. And all the girls around here are actually nice to me, instead of treating me like an arrogant jerk. I think it's because they respect you, and since you're with me... They think I'm better too. It's nice."

I don't know what to say to that. I already knew everyone treated me carefully, but I genuinely thought it was because people are afraid of me. Could Ricardo's theory be true? That people treat me with kid gloves because they respect me? It's something to chew on.

If it is true, it makes me even more determined than ever to figure out what's going on here at school. Who killed Professor Rook? Threatened Gul? Attacked me? Tried to kill Ricardo? Sticking my head out into the hallway, I verify that we're alone. Satisfied, I face Ricardo. "I don't think you should help me investigate anymore."

Ricardo looks taken aback. "Why? We make such a sexy team."

My eyes roll of their own accord, even as a tendril of guilt weaves itself around my heart. "Because it's dangerous. You almost died yesterday. I don't want any more blood on my hands."

Ricardo's eyebrows bunch. "More blood? I'm not following. I thought you said you didn't kill Professor Rook."

I study the industrial carpet. If I confess now, will it make him think of me differently? Rethink the decision we just made to date for real? Steeling myself, I look up at him. It doesn't matter what happens. Even if it results in my heart being pummeled, I have to be honest with him. He deserves to know what I've done.

My hands clench in my lap. "It might be my fault you got hurt. If I hadn't dragged you into this, you'd never have been targeted."

Ricardo springs out of the hammock as if he can't hold himself back any longer. Striding over to me, he kneels and pulls me into his arms. "Don't talk like that. None of this is your fault. You haven't hurt anyone. You're innocent in this."

The guilt is squeezing harder now, a pinch in my chest.

Closing my eyes to block him out, I whisper, "That's not entirely true."

Gentle fingers lift my chin. "Charlotte, open your eyes. Tell me what you're talking about."

Dragging in a long breath, I meet his eyes. "Rhiannon's death. It's my fault."

His head shakes slightly as he gazes at me. "No, that's not possible. She died in rehab. She overdosed. That's not on you."

I swallow, afraid to say out loud something I've never told a soul. "It is. We were friends last year, and I knew she was struggling with some of her classes. I was the one who told her she could get something from Professor Rook to help her focus. If it weren't for me, she might not have ever tried drugs. But I, I led her into it. And now I'm leading you into this investigation, and someone tried to kill you for it. I can't have another death hanging over my head, Ricardo."

Ricardo hugs me tighter to him. "Rhiannon's death was not your fault. You gave her some information. She's the one who chose to use it, chose to take drugs. Look at me. That is not your fault. And neither is the fact that I got hurt yesterday."

He sounds so sincere, his arms curled warmly around my back.

But what if he's wrong? What if everyone I touch ends up hurt, or worse? First Na, then Adrienne. Rhiannon. Professor Rook. Gul. Now Ricardo?

What if, without realizing it, I'm the root cause behind all of the violence at the academy?

26

Despite my misgivings, Ricardo convinces me to let him keep helping me as I investigate everything that's happened at Brat Academy. There are a lot of threads I'm trying to keep track of, and I haven't gotten to the end of any of them yet.

The police are remaining tight-lipped about Professor Rook's death, and I haven't been able to talk to Kenneth to ask if his friend at the morgue has any more information. So that's up in the air.

Genevieve's room is my next stop. When I breeze through her cracked door, she's at her desk, sound-cancelling headphones on, her fingers a blur over her keyboard. It's keys are inset with lights that move slowly through the rainbow, from yellow to orange to red and on through to purple before transitioning once more to yellow.

I stand rooted in place, watching the colors melt into each other. It's oddly satisfying.

When Genevieve looks over her shoulder and sees me, she startles, her fingers flying off her keyboard and her knees hitting the underside of her desk. Pulling her headphones off one ear, she exclaims, "Mais enfin, Charlotte! You scared me."

I press my mouth closed to keep prisoner the laugh that rises in my throat. "Sorry. I'm sorry. I figured you'd hear me." As I move closer, the music emanating from her headphones becomes audible. It's so loud, I'm no longer surprised she didn't hear me come in. "Have you had any luck?"

She tuts. "No. Whoever sent that video to Gul made an anonymous account to do it, and as far as I can tell they haven't used it for anything else. I'd need the government's permission to get the IP information, and they've got much larger problems. Sorry." She frowns.

Disappointment slithers in, wrapping itself around my chest. I was positive that Genevieve would be able to figure out who sent the video of Professor Rook's death to Gul. She's kind of a badass with a computer. One of her hidden talents. But from the sad look Genevieve is giving me, it's another dead end. Gul is not going to be pleased.

"Thanks anyway for trying."

I was right. Gul was pissed that I couldn't figure out who had threatened her. And I felt bad enough that I invited her to my upcoming birthday party, even though I don't really want her there. She'll bring Grady, of course, who isn't so bad. Maybe he'll act like a sort of buffer between Gul and the rest of my guests.

Putting down my cell phone, I check another item off my list. Good thing the caterers were flexible about me adding to the headcount for my party. Now to figure out who Ricardo saw sneaking down the classroom hallway over Christmas break, the week before the professor was killed.

My fingers rap along the surface of my desk, following a classical tune I've known since I was a little girl who watched cartoon reruns on Saturday mornings. Getting back into the surveillance office is going to be tricky, since Ricardo has been banned from being alone in there as a result of the attack. When the police interviewed us about it the next day, I tried to weedle information out of them, but I got nothing. They wouldn't even tell me if they found any suspicious fingerprints on the bags of dry ice or AC vents. They were unhelpfully taciturn.

The surveillance room is never locked, but it's also pretty much always occupied. So whoever planted the dry ice had to lie in wait for whoever was on duty to go to the bathroom before they took action. Or be a guard. Plus, whoever it was knew where the cameras were and was able to avoid them. After talking to all of the security personnel on campus, Bodyguard Steve doesn't think any of them were responsible, but I can't totally rule out the possibility.

Ricardo and I haven't been able to watch the surveillance video of the foyer in the hours leading up to the time I found him unconscious, but it was a Saturday so I'm assuming people were in and out for most of the day. Besides, anyone could have brought the ice in the back door and put it in the vent without being caught on camera. It's another dead end.

I considered trying to track the bad guy by tracing where he or she sourced the dry ice, but it's available at upwards of ten stores within a five mile radius of the school. Despite my charming telephone voice, none of the store managers I talked to would agree to give me access to their receipts or security footage for last week. Teen detectives on TV make it look much easier than it is in reality.

Seven days after the attack on Ricardo, I'm so frustrated that I'm skirting the edge between rudeness and downright spiteful behavior. Ricardo keeps reeling me back in. Turns out flirty sparring with Ricardo takes my edge off and makes me a lot easier to be around.

Still, the lack of progress is driving me up the wall. Which is why Ricardo and I concocted a plan to visit the surveillance office tonight and try to access the footage he told me about.

"I hope this works," Ricardo says as we walk casually

down the stairs hand in hand.

"It has to work. If it doesn't, I fear for your safety."

His eyebrows rise playfully. "My safety?"

"You'll make an excellent punching bag," I say with a smirk.

"Hit me with your best shot," he retorts. "I'll be ready for you." He gives my hand a squeeze, and I squeeze back.

"We'll see."

My guard keeps pace a step behind us, his body on full alert. When we arrive outside the security office, he stands against the wall with his hands folded over his front.

The security guard on duty gives Ricardo an annoyed look when we walk into the small room and look at the monitors. "What are you doing here? You aren't supposed to be down here anymore, remember?"

Ricardo gives him a sincere smile. "I'm sorry, Freddie. I really am. How'd your wife take being left home alone on another Saturday night?"

The man rakes a hand through his hair. "She sure wasn't happy about it, I'll tell you that. She was getting used to me being home early those nights."

"Sorry man. I'd relieve you if I could without getting suspended."

"You're not kidding. The headmistress is strung pretty tight with all the happenings this semester. Word is, some of the parents have requested she beef up security even further. Motion detector lasers. Interior security cameras. The works."

Ricardo nods. "Look, I feel bad. Why don't you take a quick break and call your wife? I'll watch the feeds for you."

Freddie looks from Ricardo to me and back, wheels turning in his head. A smile spreading across his features. "Looking for some alone time, eh? Wish I could, but I'd lose my job for sure if anyone found out I left you alone in here after last week. No, thank you."

Ricardo winks at him. "Had to try. You know how it is."

The man guffaws. "Yeah, I sure do."

The level of machismo in this room right now is making me want to gag, but I suppress the urge. A flicker of movement on one of the surveillance feeds snags in the corner of my eye. Ignoring the laughter among my boyfriend and the guard, I focus on the feeds. My body goes rigid. There it is again.

Outside in the dusk, someone is prowling around the academy parking lot. Eyes widening, I point. "Do you see that? There's someone in the parking lot. What if they're here to hurt someone else?" My voice rises to an ear-splitting pitch.

"What?" Freddie swivels to stare at the screen just as someone skulks between two cars. The figure is dressed all in black, and is careful to keep their face away from the cameras. Whoever it is, they're a pro.

The guard radios his partners and shoves out of his seat. "You two stay right here," he says, waving his phone at us. "Don't move until I get back. Understand?"

"Yes, sir," Ricardo says, putting an arm around me and pulling me into his chest. "We'll stay right here."

The man runs down the hall, yelling into his phone as he goes.

"Everything okay in here?" Bodyguard Steve says, standing in the doorway.

"We're fine, thanks," I say, schooling my voice and smoothing my features despite the pounding of blood in my ears and the skittering of nerves up my spine. I shove the fear away. I can't think about what's happening in the parking lot right now. I have to focus on what's right in front of me.

The man recedes into the hallway.

"Quick," I whisper once Ricardo and I are alone again. "You've only got a minute or two."

Plunking himself down into the chair, Ricardo rolls up to the desk and starts typing quickly on the abandoned keyboard. Pulling up several video files, he emails them to himself before wiping down the keyboard and repositioning the mouse where Freddie left it in his haste to get to the parking lot.

The files upload slowly, and beads of cold sweat roll down my spine. I don't even want to think about what will happen if anyone catches us in here stealing security footage. But we have to get it. The person Ricardo saw lurking around over break is our only lead, and even that's a thin one.

Footsteps approach along the hall.

"Hurry," I whisper louder, putting pressure on Ricardo's shoulder. "Someone's coming."

"Almost uploaded," he says.

We stare at the progress bar, willing it to tick by more quickly.

The approaching footsteps are almost upon us.

The bar reaches 100% and the email sends just as the security guard jogs into the office.

Ricardo jumps out of the chair. "Just checking my email," he says, inching toward me.

Freddie wipes the sweat off his forehead with his arm as he retakes his seat. "Clear out, both of you. I have to look back at that footage to see if we can get an ID on the prowler."

"He got away?" My words are laced with panic. "Is it safe here tonight?"

The guard glances up at me, worry written all over his face. "Yes, of course it's safe. But the faster we work, the better chance we have…" He trails off, already lost in the replay of the footage of the figure slinking through the parking lot.

"We'll leave you to it, Freddie." Ricardo puts an arm around me and leads me out of the office.

My heart is pounding as we walk back upstairs to the dormitory, Bodyguard Steve on our heels. I can't help but peer out each window as we pass, looking for signs of campus security or a shadowy figure. Several guards are bunched outside the booth at the gate, conferring and gesturing toward the school buildings. They haven't caught them yet.

We stop outside Adrienne's room and thank my bodyguard for escorting us back. Then we duck inside my sister's room. I almost screech at the sight of a figure clad all in black standing in the middle of the room, a black knit cap pulled low over his head. His back is to us, and he's bent forward over someone, the only glimpse I can get of small, white hands.

A familiar giggle is what stops me.

Busting up laughing, I lurch for them. "Oh my God. You scared me. How did you get back in here so fast?"

Mikhail swivels around, smothering a grin, pulling Adrienne with him.

She's flushed and smiling shyly.

I'm pretty sure I just caught them making out.

"It was not difficult to sneak back inside the school," Mikhail says with a wink. "Did they see my face on camera?"

Ricardo shakes his head. "No. I told you where all the cameras were located, didn't I?"

"You did."

"Mikhail, you're the best. Thank you so much for doing this," I gush, thrilled that our plan paid off.

"Did you acquire the footage you sought?"

My smile widens. "I did. Now maybe we can get to the bottom of this." That's my hope. If we can identify whoever was sneaking around campus during Christmas break, maybe it will be the lead we need to unravel the puzzle and identify Professor Rook's killer. My gut is telling me that once we do that, our mystery will be all but solved.

Sitting at Adrienne's desk, Ricardo downloads the videos and opens them. He scans through them quickly until he finds the footage he was talking about. The lights are dim, indicating that it's late at night as a figure descends to the foot of the dormitory stairs and inches toward the classroom wing.

She keeps her face averted from the camera, but I recognize the confident, leisurely gait. The long curtain of black hair. The silvery bracelet on her wrist. "Gul?"

27

The wait staff at school have outdone themselves. The Eagle banquet room looks perfect with white roses and gold tablecloths. A girl couldn't ask for a prettier backdrop for her eighteenth birthday. Well, actually I could—the swing club— but they were already booked for another private event.

Ricardo squeezes my hand. "Welcome to adulthood, mon coeur," he says. "You look gorgeous."

I flush under his compliment. I'd hoped he'd like my asymmetrical black cocktail dress, because I look fantastic in it. "Like you're so practiced, with your two whole months of being eighteen behind you."

"You know I make eighteen look fine," he says, smoothing the lapel of his coat jacket and waggling his eyebrows at me.

Laughter spills out of me as I go up on tiptoes to give him a quick kiss. "You're ridiculous."

"And you love it." He leans in to kiss me again, wrapping an arm snuggly around my waist.

"Um, are we interrupting?"

I break the kiss to find Adrienne and Mikhail standing in the doorway, her smiling and him eyeing the banquet room appraisingly. My sister looks enchanting in a frothy pale mint green frock.

Running my hands down the front of Ricardo's jacket, I pull away from him and smooth my skirt. "Nope, not interrupting at all, but the party doesn't start for half an hour."

Adrienne steps closer. "We just wanted to see if we could help set up? Do you need anything?"

I scan the room, watching the staff working at the buffet table on one wall. The tables are arranged to perfection with low floral bouquets and gilded china. My favorite 1920s crooner's voice filters out of the hidden speakers, weaving an enchanting spell over the room. "I don't think so. We're all set."

"Where can we put the presents?" Adrienne whips a gift bag out from behind her back.

"You didn't have to do that," I say, taking the bag and setting it down on a side table. "I said no gifts."

"Only because you return everything you get and exchange it for something else," Cal says, sauntering into the room.

Adrienne's eyes go wide. "Is that true?"

"Of course not," I say, crossing my arms. It's totally true. I try to steer my family members toward things I want or need, but they never cooperate. Something about it ruining the surprise. But the shy disappointment on my sister's face right now makes guilt blink to life in my ribcage.

Ricardo chuckles. "What did you get her for Christmas?"

My sister looks between us. "I bought her a really nice scented candle. It smelled like citrus, like her perfume?"

"Have you seen it since?" Cal asks.

Snagging her lip between her teeth, Adrienne shakes her head.

"Sorry," I say, blowing out a breath. "I'm not much of a candle person."

"Well, I'm glad I didn't get you the fabulous Christmas gift I had planned," Ricardo says, eyes sparkling.

"Shut up. You didn't have something planned." Did he?

We had just started talking then, after Kenneth dumped me, so it's unlikely that Ricardo actually had a gift in mind for me. But pleasure moves through me anyway at the suggestion he was thinking about me, even then.

"Okay, I didn't, but I do today."

Huffing, I shake my head. "Doesn't anyone understand the phrase, 'No gifts necessary?'" My eyes turn to the doorway, waiting for Gul. Mom was pleased I had invited her, for diplomatic reasons, but I'm actually hoping she'll show up. It'll give me an opportunity to corner her and ask her why she was lurking around the classrooms late at night during Christmas break.

Even more interesting?

Ricardo and I spotted Professor Rook leaving the classroom wing minutes later.

The question is, were Gul and Professor Rook meeting? If so, why?

As far as I know, she's never bought drugs from him before. She didn't have a telltale dot next to her name in his files. Which leads me to wonder if there was something else going on between them. Maybe she was outside that fateful night to meet him, away from the prying eyes of everyone on campus? Maybe she was cheating on Grady with the professor? I bite my lip, chewing on the thought. If so, sucks to be Grady.

Honestly, Gul doesn't strike me as the cheating type. She's a gossip hound, but she's conversely intensely private about her home life, personal relationships, and those sorts of things. Cheating on a boyfriend with a professor would be both underhanded and bold. Not qualities I attribute to Gul's personal relationships. But what do I know? We aren't exactly besties.

As if I've conjured her with my musings, Gul walks into

the room wearing a gold lamé dress that skims her knees. Beside her, Grady adjusts his tie.

I grin. I've always wanted to have a dressy birthday party, and eighteen seemed the perfect time to do it. Having everyone wear cocktail attire was a stroke of genius. We all look amazing under the soft light of the antique chandeliers. Plus, we're going to have a blast putting the dance floor I rented to use.

The sight of Kenneth entering the room puts a damper on my enthusiasm. He looks uncomfortable, with his hands in his pockets and his eyes on his shoes. I'm regretting asking him, but when he wished me a happy birthday this morning, I felt bad and told him about the party. It was a total pity invite, which he should have had the sense to decline.

Ricardo sets his eyes on my ex and tenses. An air of awkwardness permeates the room.

Ms. Poppin interrupts as she enters from the staging area to tell us that dinner is ready if we'll be seated.

Perfect timing.

The food looks amazing, despite the fact that the chef had to figure out how to make Thai food without peanuts. A certain Pakistani girl is allergic, and I can't have anyone croaking at my birthday party.

Despite the motley assortment of people gathered around the long table, conversation is going well. Kenneth is seated all the way at the other end of the table, and I put Grady and Gul down there with him. They seem to be engrossed in conversation about something, but I can't hear any of it. I'm too busy listening to Adrienne and Genevieve chatting about an online vintage clothing auction site they found.

I lean toward Ricardo to ask him to pass me the noodles. He surprises me by burying his nose in my hair and taking a whiff. "Kèt, you smell good."

Laughing, I meet his eyes. "You're too much."

"I don't think so." He hesitates. "Are you happy?"

My brows knit together in confusion. "Am I happy? Why wouldn't I be?" I gesture toward the food and the company to make my point.

"But you're happy, with me?"

My lips part in surprise. Reaching up to run a hand along the side of his face, I smile. "Of course I'm happy."

Ricardo grins at this, and we go back to eating.

I chew my food, unsettled by his question. Why did he ask me that? Putting it out of my thoughts, I try to enjoy my party. I sneak a glance down the table at Gul. I still have to find an opportunity to talk to her.

Finally there's a lull in the conversation around the table. It's my chance. I glide around the table and slide into Grady's vacated seat. He's going for round two at the buffet. "I'm so glad you and Grady could make it," I whisper to Gul. "How's dinner?"

"Delicious, but we both know you didn't come over here for small talk." She shoots an annoyed look at me.

I smile. "I've always liked how straightforward you are, which is why it's so strange that you won't tell me why you were outside the night Professor Rook was killed. Here's the thing. Ricardo showed me a video of you sneaking into the classroom wing one night over break, and soon after the professor leaves the area. So I'm wondering: what were you doing there? Were you meeting Professor Rook? Care to tell me why?"

Gul pales, her eyes falling to her plate. "I wasn't meeting him, okay? But I can't tell you what I was doing there."

"Are you sure? Because I'd hate for a rumor to start about you and the professor. Especially now that you're with Grady, and he doesn't deserve to have his heart broken. Again." I lick my lips. I would never start a rumor about Gul. It's beneath me, but she doesn't need to do that. Bluffing is a significant part of politics, which means I've spent enough time to master it. It comes in handy often.

Gul's expression hardens. "I'm not telling you anything. I wasn't meeting Rook." She takes a careful bite of her panang curry.

"Are you sure? Because it's pretty coincidental that you were seen in the classroom wing when he was there, alone, and then you just happened to be outside when he was run over. Are you sure you weren't meeting him? Maybe you knew he was going to be run over. Maybe that's why you were outside. You were in on it." My eyes widen as the thought hits me.

Gul's face has gone from pale to blotchy red. "You don't know what you're talking about," she splutters, throwing her fork down. Her fingers curl around her throat as the redness spreads over her face and throat. She wheezes. "What have you done?" Coughing, she pushes back from the table.

Grady hustles over from the buffet table, concern washing over his face. "Gul? Are you okay?"

Gul struggles to speak, clutching her throat. "Allergic reaction," she rasps. "Get my EpiPen." Her gasps for breath fill the room, alerting the rest of my guests.

Everyone goes silent as they watch Grady rifle through his girlfriend's purse. "Did you make sure there weren't any peanuts in the food?" He shoots a harsh look at me. "She's deathly allergic."

I fly out of my seat. "I know that. I made sure of it. I triple checked with the chef. It's not the food." But I'm not so sure. Accidents happen. Running toward the buffet table, I whip the lids off the chafing dishes. Sniff each dish for the scent of peanuts, but there's nothing.

Ms. Poppin comes out of the kitchen as the chafing dishes clang, and spots Gul. She hurries over and hovers near Grady. "What can I do?" she asks.

Gul's gasps grow louder, piercing the air, a jarring juxtaposition with the swing music still playing through the artfully hidden speakers.

"Someone call 911," Grady cries as he dumps out Gul's purse in search of her EpiPen.

Adrienne is already on the phone, talking to someone whom I suppose is an emergency operator. Mikhail stands like a pillar beside her, taking in the scene.

"Found it!" Grady shouts. "What do I do with it?" His skin is clammy as his eyes skitter over the rest of us, holding out the small implement in one hand.

"Give it here," Kenneth says, snatching the EpiPen from Grady's outstretched hand and approaching Gul. "I'm going to administer this, okay?" he asks, and injects it into Gul's thigh almost before she can nod in assent. Once done, he guides her to a chair and makes her sit, kneeling in front of her and watching for signs the medicine is taking effect.

Grady paces behind Gul's chair, not taking his eyes off his girlfriend.

In mere minutes, the EMTs arrive. They work quickly, strapping Gul to a gurney and rushing her out with Grady chasing after them.

Headmistress Morgan arrives with several of the security guards in tow. "We're here to assess the scene," she says, scowling at us. "With all of the accidents happening on this campus this year, there will be a thorough investigation."

Ms. Poppin steps toward the older woman. "We made sure there were no peanuts in the area when we prepared the food," she says, but she too is prodding and stirring each dish with a fork. "Our staff are experts at avoiding food contamination. I don't know what happened."

The headmistress's expression is like steel. "Everyone, put your personal belongings on this table and step back. We're going to search through them." She taps the gift table firmly, making the wrapped boxes and bags crinkle in protest.

"You can't be serious," I say. "None of us did this to Gul."

Headmistress Morgan doesn't deign to respond. Instead, she taps the table again once with a pointed finger.

"It's fine," Adrienne whispers to me. "They'll go through our things and they won't find anything. Then they'll let us go."

Ricardo moves to my side. "You're right. We've got nothing to fear, unless you took the opportunity to poison a girl we know you're not fond of?" Ricardo is teasing as he speaks, but I don't find it funny. My answering glare wipes the smirk off his face.

My bag feels heavier than it should as I lift it off the back of my chair. Opening it, I peer inside. Wallet. Lipstick. Emergency first aid kit. Breath mints. I stop dead in my tracks as my heart starts to pound.

There's a tiny glass bottle in the bottom of my bag with the residue of a tan, powdery substance inside. Turning away from the headmistress, I lift the bag to my face. A distinct, nutty scent fills my nostrils.

No.

I look around at everyone as they shuffle toward where Headmistress Morgan is collecting wallets, purses, jackets, and coats.

Someone in this room planted a tiny vial of ground peanuts in my bag.

They're trying to frame me for the attack on Gul.

But who?

28

The vial is still warm as I wrap my fingers around it. Blood roars in my ears, blocking out the chaos in the room all around me.

"Miss Cavendish-Holt, I'm waiting." The headmistress's voice brooks no argument. Impatient. Cold. That witch always hated me. If she catches me with this vial of peanuts, Gul won't be the only one whose fate is hanging in the balance tonight.

Think, Charlotte. Think.

Eyes wide, I tuck the vial into my bra, pretending to adjust the cups as I withdraw my hand. Ordinarily, I would never be seen adjusting my underwear in public—it's a huge faux pas—but drastic times call for drastic measures.

"I'm coming, Headmistress." Spinning in my high heels, I stride to where the older woman is standing and plunk my purse down on the table. "Here it is. I expect it back promptly."

With a cocked eyebrow, Headmistress Morgan gestures for one of the security guards to step forward. "Now that we've got everyone's things…" Her cold eyes brush over me from head to toe before she turns to the guard. "Start with this one," she says, pushing my clutch toward his waiting hands.

My cheeks flush as I watch Officer Morris paw through my things, examining each item as he pulls it out of the bag.

"I wouldn't open that if I were you," I warn when he withdraws the small, pearlescent zipper pouch I always keep on

224

me.

"Sorry, Miss. Orders are orders."

I shrug. "Suit yourself."

Unzipping the pouch, he pokes a finger inside before yelping and dropping the bag to the table like he's been bitten by a snake. A tampon rolls out over the tabletop.

With a quick roll of my eyes, I snap. "Sanitary products are not deadly, Officer Morris. You won't contract the plague by touching a tampon. Contrary to public opinion."

I don't miss the snicker Adrienne tries to hide behind her hand as I shove my tampon back into the zippered pouch. "Are you done with my things?"

When the guard nods in embarrassment, I whisk my bag off the table and lock eyes with my sister. "Adrienne, I'll meet you in my room, okay? I have to go. Cal, your keys?"

Cal nods and hands me the keys from his pocket. "Let us know how she's doing, okay?"

A quick nod in response. "Will do. Ricardo?"

"Ready, mon coeur." He matches stride with me as I scurry out of the banquet room toward the front door, shrugging into my faux fur coat. Officer Morris moves on to the next bag on the table as we exit the banquet room.

Ricardo pulls on his pea coat before holding the front door open for me.

A frigid wind cuts into us as we step out into the parking lot. The night is dark and ominous as we hurry to Cal's car, slamming the doors behind us to shut out the chill.

Starting the engine, I wait just long enough for Ricardo to buckle his belt before I floor it out of the parking lot and around the corner where the perimeter cameras won't be able to see us.

My heart is still pounding as I cut the engine and turn to

Ricardo. "Quick, turn off your phone." Digging my own out of my bag, I turn it off with a violent stab at the button. Wait for Ricardo to do the same.

His brows are furrowed when he meets my eyes. "What's going on? How the hell did peanuts get into Gul's food?"

Swallowing, I pull the vial out of the front of my dress.

Ricardo's brows shoot into his hairline as he looks from my face to the glass bottle in my hand. "What's that? And why was it in your bra?" He keeps his eyes studiously away from my chest.

"Smell it." Twisting off the top, I hold it under his nose.

He takes a sniff, and his eyes nearly pop out of his head. "Why do you have that? Poisoning someone isn't your style, Char."

"You're right. I'm more the stab you in the heart with a stiletto type, but this isn't the time for that. Someone snuck this into my clutch at the party."

Ricardo's head snaps back toward the academy as if the answer is visible through the car's rearview mirror. "Someone at the party put that in your bag?"

I nod.

"You have to give it to the police, ma chérie. They can fingerprint it and find out who was behind the attack tonight."

"And have them wonder how I got it? No, thanks. I'm sure they've heard the 'It wasn't mine' excuse one too many times before. There's no way they'd believe me. I can't give this to them."

Ricardo starts to argue, but I press a finger to his lips. "Don't. There's more. I asked Gul about that video of her. She denied meeting Professor Rook, but I could tell she was lying about it. There's something going on with her. I thought maybe she was involved in the hit-and-run, but now, I don't know. If she was responsible, that doesn't explain what happened tonight. I don't think she's hard core enough to poison herself to throw off suspicion. Do you?"

He shakes his head. "I don't know."

Sucking my lip between my teeth, I chew on it absently as I think through the events of this semester so far.

Professor Rook.

The threat on Gul.

My attack.

Ricardo's brush with death.

Tonight's peanut incident.

Someone is trying their hardest to get at Gul, Ricardo, and me, all because we're somehow linked with the investigation into Professor Rook's death. I get why they attacked me, and Ricardo, but Gul?

Ricardo licks his lips. "What if the killer tried to poison her tonight because they think she knows who they are. Like she saw them driving the car?"

His words reverberate through the car, and as soon as they hit my brain I know he's right. Whoever the culprit is, they're afraid Gul saw them when she was outside that night. That's why they attacked her tonight. I still don't know why she was outside in the first place, but that doesn't matter now.

The chemical smell of industrial cleaning supplies nearly makes my eyes water as I argue with the nurse at the station closest to the ER. She crosses her arms and turns away from me, unwilling to tell me anything about Gul, wouldn't even admit she was being cared for in the ER, even though I literally followed the ambulance here and know she's somewhere behind the heavy metal door. No matter how much I turn on the charm, use my politician's smile, the woman isn't budging.

Pursing my lips, I pace over the shiny linoleum floor to where Ricardo is sitting in a chair in the waiting area, chin in his palms. Running one hand over the nape of his neck, I coil my fingers in his curls.

The sounds of nurses making announcements over the intercom blurs as I tune it out, along with the beeping of hospital machines, and the ding of the nearby elevator.

Reaching up, he grabs my free hand and brings it to his lips. "You okay, mon coeur? We're going to figure this out and catch whoever is responsible."

I sit down beside him, and he slings his arm around me, drawing me closer so he can rest his head against mine.

A sigh takes shape between us. "You're a lot sweeter than you pretend to be. Why the front, playboy?"

I can feel him smiling against my temple. "Because if anyone knew I was a big softie, I wouldn't get nearly as many girls."

I snort. "Please. Girls love big softies. Even me. My parents too."

He looks down at me, one eyebrow quirked. "You asking me to meet your parents? I accept. I'll charm them so well they'll vote to keep me instead of you."

"You're not so far off," I whisper, shoulders slumping.

"Hey, hey," Ricardo breathes, lifting my chin until I meet his eyes. "I wasn't serious. Your parents love you dearly. Even if they're terrible at showing it."

Swiping at my eyes to combat the prickling sensation behind my lids, I nod. "You're right." But I'm not so sure. Ricardo is handsome, charming, intelligent. I'm pretty sure my parents would love him. Which is why I have to win that internship and prove myself. I'll be the best political intern ever, and then Daddy will have to take me seriously.

"There's something else I've been meaning to talk to you about," Ricardo whispers, his breath hot on my face. "I talked to my mom the other day."

I rear back, surprised. "You what? I thought you were stonewalling her. What happened?"

He shrugs. "She's been so persistent. I got tired of ignoring her. It's exhausting, so I let her talk, and heard her out."

My eyebrows rise in a prompt to bid him to continue.

It's Ricardo's time to duck his gaze away from mine. "She wants me to go back to Haiti with her. Finish my schooling there. Work with her at the community center she started. They need teachers, apparently."

My mouth drops open. "You're not going, are you? That would be insane."

He gives a forced laugh. "And leave my best girl? Of course not. She hasn't been in my life for ten years, and I'm fine. I don't need her now."

But I can tell by his furtive glance that he doesn't mean it. Despite the fact that she abandoned him over a decade ago, he wants his mother back in his life.

I can't blame him. But a larger part of me—the selfish part—doesn't want him to go. "First of all, I'm your only girl. Second of all, you cannot drop everything to go back to Haiti. You'll have all summer to see her, right?"

He gives an assenting jerk of his chin. It's not very reassuring.

A commotion down the hall pulls my attention away from Ricardo.

A nurse is walking backward, trying to console a woman in a bejeweled salwar kameez and head scarf. Her pristine English is sharp with pain. Next to her is a portly man in an impeccably tailored suit.

Gul's parents are here.

I'm out of my chair even before I can formulate what I'm going to say. "Minister Abidi. Mrs. Abidi, on behalf of myself and everyone at Embassy Academy, we are so sorry for what happened to Gul."

Gul's father barely glances at me before dismissing me. He's always been that way, preferring to speak to my father and Cal. It's a common ailment among men in politics, which is one of the reasons I'm determined to succeed. Make the arrogant men take note of a pretty, intelligent, powerful woman.

Mrs. Abidi, on the other hand, sobs and pulls me in for a hug. She murmurs as she holds me tight against her chest. "Thank you, thank you. They tell us she's going to be fine. We're going in to see her now. Would you like to come?"

Success! I bite back the smile that bids for placement on my face, knowing now isn't the time. "No, please. I wouldn't intrude on your time with your daughter, but later, once everything has settled down, I'd like to see her. Would that be all right?"

Mrs. Abidi nods, grateful, and then the two of them follow the nurse behind the double doors into the ER.

I retreat to where Ricardo is sitting and plop down in the chair beside him. Now all we can do is wait.

<h1 style="text-align:center">29</h1>

Angry, red patches mar Gul's face and neck, congregating around her swollen, red lips, which cut like a malicious slash across her puffy face. Her hair streams over the pillow in snarls and knots, like a den of snakes startled by a rock thrown into their midst. She purses her cracked and dry lips together as I step behind the curtain into her little cubicle, her eyes never leaving me.

"I don't have long. Your mom said I could come back to say hi."

Gul crosses her arms, careful not to knock the IV embedded in the back of her hand. "What do you want?" The words grate over my ears as they claw their way out of her throat. Her eyes skim past me to where Ricardo is standing just inside the curtain that separates this cubicle from the main floor of the ER.

Somewhere nearby, a machine begins beeping loudly, followed by a hospital worker calling out a code over the intercom system.

I tune out the noise and sit boldly down on the edge of Gul's bed. "I'm sorry about tonight. I can assure you that I took every precaution to make sure this wouldn't happen."

Gul's dark eyes are wide and luminous when I meet them. The accusation there is unmistakable.

I glance over my shoulder at Ricardo, who nods. "I found something I need to show you."

Gul shifts under the scratchy blue hospital blanket. She takes a slow sip from the large tan plastic tumbler on the rolling stand beside her bed, as if the water burns as it slides down her throat. "Okay."

I tell her everything. My suspicions about her involvement in Professor Rook's death. The vial of peanuts in my bag. The gut instinct that's screaming at me that someone at my party tried to kill Gul to get her out of the picture.

By the time I'm done, Gul's dark eyes are shining. She brushes her mussed hair behind her ears with trembling hands. "I swear I didn't kill Professor Rook, or hire anyone to kill him. There wasn't anything going on between us, and I definitely didn't *buy* anything from him. If my father found out…" She shivers, whether from the cool air in the room or apprehension, I can't tell.

Pulling the extra blanket up from the foot of the bed, I tuck it around her waist. "Look. I don't want to push, but you've got to tell me why you were outside that night. What were you doing out there if you weren't waiting for the professor?"

The girl in the bed looks so small as she chews on her lip, eyelashes fluttering as she cuts a gaze toward me. She focuses on her fingers as they wring the blanket in her lap. "I was on the phone with my mom, okay?" It's a whispered admission.

My head cocks to one side. I don't understand why it's such a big deal, but by the heaving of her chest, I can tell it cost Gul to admit it to me. "Help me understand."

She sighs. "I don't like calling my mom from the dorm, okay? Because if I do, she'll see how it is at school for me."

"I'm still not following."

"I don't have any friends!" Gul's voice breaks on her last word, and her eyes well.

I stare at her in shock. Speechless.

"There. Are you happy now? You can gloat over poor little me with no friends, while you have many."

Finding my voice, I speak. "You sit at a table full of people every day. You've got a posse that follows you wherever you go. You have friends."

Gul shakes her head, dropping the blanket from between hooked fingers. "I have minions. It's not the same thing. You can bet that any one of them would spread a rumor about me without even blinking, if I ever so much as do something even remotely worth gossiping about. So I don't." She hesitates, and I get the sense that she wants to keep talking, so I remain quiet. Still.

After a few beats of silence, it's apparent to me that whether she wants to or not, she's not going to confide anything else to me. Instead, she plucks her phone off the tiny stand beside her bed and looks at it.

Disappointment curves around my throat at her silence, a not unwelcome surprise.

"Okay… What about the night Professor Rook was killed. You made the call to 911, but I can't help but wonder if you saw more than you told the operator. Did you?"

Gul gasps. "Look." Holding her phone out to me, she shows me a message.

Keep your mouth shut, or next time it'll be fatal.

"What?" I screech. "Who is this from?"

I try to stop the shaking of my hands as I take the phone from her and examine the message. It's anonymous, just like the last one. I have no way to trace it, but maybe the police will.

Feeling like a hypocrite, I urge her to go to the authorities. She refuses. "If I say anything, they'll kill me."

"That's exactly what they want you to think. They almost

killed you anyway. You have to tell the police what you saw that night."

Shaking her head, Gul shoves her phone behind her pillow, hiding it from sight. "Don't you get it? I didn't see anything. I don't know who ran over Professor Rook. And now they're hunting me for it." Girding her expression, she locks her eyes on me. "You need to leave. I can't be seen talking to you anymore. Not until this is over."

I don't argue. If she wants me to stay away until the investigation is over, I will. But I'm not going to stop looking into this.

"Glad you're doing okay," Ricardo says, patting the railing at the foot of Gul's bed. "See you." He follows me through the curtain and back to the waiting area, where Minister and Mrs. Abidi are huddled together on a couple of the green vinyl hospital chairs, whispering softly. Mrs. Abidi smiles when she sees us coming. "Thank you for coming to see Gul. I know it means a lot to her, to have good friends close by."

I'm stunned and only manage a polite nod as Ricardo bids goodbye to the adults before ushering me outside. His hand swings mine confidently between us as we cross the parking lot to the car. He says something to me, but I miss it, unable to focus on anything outside the musings in my head.

Someone tried to frame me for attempted murder tonight, and I won't stand for it. I'm going to find out who the bastard is, and I'm going to bury them.

30

The sky outside the floor-to-ceiling windows is the hazy periwinkle color of pre-dawn. A ribbon of dark pink limns the horizon, hinting at the profusion of color to come when the sun paints the morning sky.

Words from the conversation I had with my mom the night before circle through my mind. She'd been surprised when I asked her about the internship with Daddy's office. Like she had no idea I was even interested in politics. Hadn't she noticed how informed I am? How at every event I bust my butt connecting with as many officials and dignitaries as I can, keeping myself informed of current events in other countries and how they pertain to politics here in the U.S.?

Apparently not.

When I asked her what my chances were of getting the internship, she'd laughed. Told me that I was welcome to apply, that the senator would award the internship to whichever student showed the most potential.

I'd been sorely tempted to hint that a little good old-fashioned nepotism wasn't such a bad thing, but I hadn't. It would be so easy to ask Daddy to simply give me the internship, but then I wouldn't appreciate it. Would resent it, in fact. Because then I wouldn't have earned it, wouldn't have proved myself worthwhile to him, and wasn't that the whole point? To prove to my stepfather that I'm worthy of his time investment, his backing in the political sphere? And maybe even outside it?

Guilt presses against my lower back, urging me to run faster. The soles of my athletic shoes slap against the treadmill in the otherwise silent fitness center.

I shouldn't have talked Ricardo out of going to Haiti with his mom. If he has the chance to rebuild his relationship with her, to start fresh… He should take it, regardless of what that means for us.

The weighty truth of it hits me in the gut, making my steps falter and the toe of my shoe skid on the treadmill. A tiny cry escapes my lips as my balance swings forward, pitching me face-first into the path of the conveyor beneath my feet. I catch the rim of the control panel at the last second, blinking, my heart throbbing. My feet take up the pace of the treadmill as I right my body. I was this close to giving myself the rug burn to end all rug burns.

And the night before a big campaign event too.

"Are you in need of assistance, Miss Cavendish-holt?"

"I'm fine, Steve. Thanks."

Slapping the off button, I climb down from the treadmill and wipe away the sweat that's beading on my temples. "I'm done for tonight. You ready?"

He nods, following me along the hallway, which is shrouded in soft, early morning light. The dormitory is quiet as I ascend the stairs, grateful that most of my classmates are late risers. These early morning hours when I'm up finishing my schoolwork or exercising are some of the only ones I get during which someone doesn't expect anything of me. Want anything from me. It's the only freedom I get, which is why I sacrifice that extra hour of sleep to the blasted beeping of my alarm clock.

I can't find my room key, so I have to get Ms. Poppin to

unlock it. I gather my toiletries before trudging down the hall to the bathroom. It, too, is empty.

The hot water pours down over my sweaty body, relaxing my muscles and flushing my skin pink. The steam fills and expands my chest. If only I could stay in here all day long.

Ricardo should go to Haiti with his mom. In my relaxed state, I don't push away the idea when it returns to the forefront of my thoughts.

How much longer is she going to stick around, teaching classes for Professor Rook and popping into the eatery on an almost daily basis in the hopes that her son will break his wall of silence and talk to her?

If it were me, I'd have written him off by now. I don't have time to chase after people who aren't into me. So why did I waste so much time trying to make Kenneth jealous by fake dating Ricardo?

My gut clenches. It was such a waste of time.

Kenneth was never truly interested in me. Adrienne and Genevieve were right about that. Plus, now that I'm with Ricardo, I know what real care and attention are like. Sure, he's a giant flirt, but there's a whiff of honesty beneath his silliness that hits me right in the feels every single time.

It's terrifying.

Half of me wants to run headlong into this, whatever it is, with everything I've got. Just like I do with tennis, my classes, preparing for Daddy's campaign events, shopping. But the other half? The dark, shadowy corners that I pretend not to see? Those parts want to shove Ricardo out of the metaphorical door to my heart and lock it tight behind him.

Being with Ricardo leaves me vulnerable and exposed. Emotions I am not used to and don't enjoy at all. It reminds me of the first time I went sailing alone. My brain knew everything I needed to command my craft over the smooth, glassy water. But my heart? It locked up in fear, and I almost ended up calling it quits before I even got started.

Fear of failure. That's what this is.

The thing I'm realizing about myself is this: if I'm not one hundred percent sure I'll succeed, I don't always even try at all. Because flopping at something publicly is much worse than the regrets I carry about not even trying. It's one of the main reasons I started buying uppers from Professor Rook last year. They gave me an extra edge I needed to remain at the top of my classes.

But do I want Ricardo to be one of my regrets?

No, but I also don't want him to come to resent me for not insisting he go to Haiti, either. Because if he stays with me and risks his final tie to his mom, it would poison our relationship eventually. The what-ifs would consume him from the inside out. I can't let that happen, no matter how much pain it causes me to let him go. Even though it'll be more harmful to my heart than I dare to admit.

Once I'm dressed, I slide into my desk chair and open my tablet to the chart I've made with all of my findings regarding Professor Rook's death. There are still so many loose ends. The driver. My attacker. The threat and attack on Gul. Kenneth's presence on campus that night and his flimsy excuse.

I've been keeping tabs on the news coverage of the event, which has petered off considerably in the weeks since it happened. I hardly get any alerts on my phone anymore.

As I read over my notes, I chew on the inside of my cheek. I have to do something. Push someone's buttons. See what shakes out.

Starting with Kenneth.

It's still early, so I have time before class.

He's behind the desk when I walk through the frosted glass door into the health center.

Stepping up to the desk, I lower my voice. "Can I talk to you for a sec?"

Kenneth's face registers surprise, and then he glances around. He speaks loud enough to be heard by anyone else who might be in the vicinity. "Do you have an appointment?"

"Sorry, no. I just have a couple of medical questions."

He pushes back from the desk, eyeing Bodyguard Steve. "Follow me to one of the exam rooms. Right this way."

Gesturing for the older man to remain where he is just inside the door, I follow Kenneth down the clean, pale green hall and into one of the vacant rooms. He closes the door and leans against it with crossed arms.

There are jars of implements on the sideboard. Cotton balls. Swabs. Gauze. Condoms. Something about it strikes me as funny as I pull myself up onto the exam table and cross my ankles.

"You had medical questions?" He uses finger quotes, his eyes never leaving my face.

I shrug casually. "You never told me the real reason you were on campus the night Professor Rook was killed. I don't believe that nonsense about turning in forms. At midnight? Come on. What's the truth?"

Kenneth shakes his head, uncrosses his arms. One hand clamps around the doorknob. "It's none of your business, Char."

Swallowing, I infuse my eyes with as much steel as I can muster. "If you don't tell me why you were here, I'm going to submit the video of you on campus to the police. They'll be able to figure out whatever it is you're hiding."

A muscle quirks in his jaw. "You wouldn't."

My chin lifts in a clear challenge. *Try me, Ken Doll.* I've had about enough of the shenanigans that have been occurring on this campus since September. Far too many people I care about have been hurt, almost killed. It's got to stop. I'm pretty sure Kenneth didn't kill Professor Rook, but something about the last time we spoke has been bugging me. He knew the professor's first name, almost blurted it out when I questioned him. And I'm positive I never told him about any of my professors. So how would Kenneth know the man's first name?

I lean forward, fastening my eyes on his face. "I would. I don't know what motive you would have to hurt the professor, but you were nearby for all of the other incidents. The health center is right around the corner from the vending machines where I was attacked, and it's close by the surveillance office too. And you were at my birthday party when Gul was poisoned. That's plenty of opportunity. I have a hunch the police will be able to find a motive." My phone vibrates in my bag, but I ignore it. Probably a text alert for my news app.

The air in the room is charged with angry heat, but I don't back down. Don't show any weakness. It's something I've noticed Daddy does, even in the most frustrating of debates. His stony demeanor ruffles his opponents into saying something stupid they can't walk back. I'm hoping it'll do the same to Kenneth.

What I don't count on is him advancing slowly toward me, an angry set to his shoulders.

Before it occurred to me that he could be behind the attacks, I never sensed that he would try to physically hurt me, but as more time has passed since our relationship, clarity has descended. There is so much about Kenneth that I don't know. Including what he's capable of if backed into a corner.

I put a hand up. "Wait."

He takes another step toward me, and the arms that I once thought were beautiful and lean now look menacing and brutal. Strong enough to choke the life out of me.

The air in the room presses closer, hot against my face, threatening to suffocate me even before Kenneth's outstretched hands wrap around my throat. My eyes skim the desk for something with which to defend myself. A stack of files. A pen. Tablet and stylus. Nothing with much potential. Which is why I brought the taser I bought after my attack.

Zing! The device trills as I pull it out of my backpack and level it at Kenneth's chest. "Don't take another step."

Kenneth freezes, eyes sizzling. His stance is fluid, like an animal hunter poised to spring on its prey unaware. "You can't be serious. You think I'd hurt you, after everything?"

My mouth goes dry as I realize the look in his eyes is fury, and I'm his prey. "I don't know what to think anymore, Kenneth." But my hand wavers. Can I really tase him? Do I have what it takes?

His cruel mouth tilts upward as Kenneth takes another step closer, daring me to do it. Doubt is written in the smile lines around his mouth. He doesn't think I will do it.

Swish. The sharp darts of the device shoot forward and embed themselves in the front of his shirt. His body seizes as a low crackle fills the air.

I do have what it takes.

My hair stands on end as Kenneth topples to the floor and doesn't move even after the device stops firing. Speechless, I gape down at his rigid body sprawled over the tile floor. Even though I felt no effects of the taser's zap, my muscles have locked in place.

Kenneth groans. Tries to sit up.

Bending down, I pry the barbs out of his skin, making him

growl.

My eyes widen in shock. That tone. I recognize it.

Stop looking into Rook's death, or I'll kill you.

"That was… uncalled for," he rasps, lurching upward.

My hands are shaking as I reload the taser. "It was you. You attacked me in the hallway. You almost broke my nose! Why?"

He eyes my trigger hand warily, not wanting another round of the high-voltage shock. "I couldn't have you looking into Rook farther, wondering where he got his supply. You know how expensive medical school is?"

"So you're paying for it by dealing drugs?" My words rise, unbidden, until I'm shouting. In my surprise, I've dropped my weapon hand.

Kenneth lunges.

With a cry, I leap over him and scramble against the door. The knob won't turn. He's locked it without me noticing. Kenneth pushes to his knees, regains his feet. The taser clicks in my hand, but doesn't fire. I must not have gotten the new cartridge in correctly. A roar in my ears obscures my hearing as my eyes scrabble over the back of the door for a weapon, anything. Heart pumping hot frenzied blood through my veins, I yank a clipboard out of its slot on the wall and hit Kenneth over the head with it as hard as I can. I am no Anne Shirley.

He yowls, rubbing at a bleeding gash under his hair.

I twist the tab to unlock the door and fling it open before Kenneth has a chance to hoist himself off the floor. Frantically, I shove my taser into my backpack, not bothering to watch where I'm going.

Bodyguard Steve leaps away from the wall as I barrel out of the hallway. "Miss, are you all right?"

The door of the health center slams against the wall as I

fling it open. It makes a hammering thud against the wood paneling, but I don't stop. I have to put distance between myself and Kenneth.

Several of the uniform-clad students in the hall swivel to look at me before resuming their walk toward the eatery. I'm thankful I don't seem to warrant their scrutiny as I scrub a hand down my arm.

Good lord, Kenneth just tried to hurt me. Didn't he?

I'm not thinking straight as I jog down the hallway, my chest heaving at the adrenaline shot that's working my muscles in overtime. Which is why I run headlong into Grady outside the eatery.

"Sorry, sorry," he says. "You all right?"

"My fault. Sorry." I weave past him, but a hand shoots out and taps my arm.

"Wait."

My guard glares at him, making Grady withdraw his hand.

Panting, I wave the older man away. Take a deep breath. "Thanks, Steve. I'm okay. Really."

He doesn't move, the set of his face somber. I doubt he believes me, since I was just fleeing from the health center like a bat out of hell.

"I'm glad I ran into you." Grady's hushed whisper pulls me up short. Turning toward him, I study his face. Grady tugs his gaze up to meet mine.

"Why were you looking for me?" I sound like I've just run a marathon.

Glancing around at the press of scarlet and navy bodies around us, he scoots toward the wall.

I follow him, avoiding bumping into my classmates as they stream along the hall and into the eatery for breakfast. The scent of sizzling bacon makes my mouth water, but I wait.

Grady and I don't usually talk much, and the fact that he was looking for me has my interest. "What's up?"

He takes a deep breath. "You used to date the health center intern, right?"

I nod slowly, my pulse jumping at the memory of Kenneth stalking toward me moments ago. "I did. Not anymore. Why?" The words come out sharper than I intend, but I don't retract them. Girls are so focused on being polite sometimes that it's a stumbling block to getting stuff done. Not me. "Results now, apologies later" should be my motto.

Grady hesitates. "Have you seen this?" Taking out his phone, he calls up a video.

It takes me a second to take in the massage tables and exercise equipment shown in the opening shot. It's a chiropractor or physical therapy office. People are giving and receiving treatment in the well lit room. In the far ground, two men are hunched together. One in casual athletic wear and the other in a doctor's coat. Athletic guy jabs White Coat in the chest. Their voices rise.

"I'll end you," athletic guy yells.

"This is not the place," the other shoots back.

Athletic guy pushes the other man into the glass. The rattling reverberates through the room, attracting the attention of everyone there.

Athletic guy throws up a hand to wave off the therapist approaching him and walks out of frame.

My jaw drops.

The guy in the white coat? It's Kenneth.

And athletic wear guy?

Professor Rook.

My head spins. Kenneth and the professor fought months ago, in full view of a bunch of people in this chiro/therapy office. What were they arguing about?

I shake my head. It doesn't matter. The police will likely see it as a motive for Professor Rook's death. "How did you find this?"

Grady points at the top of the screen. There's a news headline there. *Murdered Professor in Fight with Med Student.*

Chattering fills the eatery, not masking the sound of the video as it spools out of someone's phone. Loud and commanding attention.

Dread fills me as I peek around the corner into the large room. Groups of students are hunched over their phones. Showing their neighbors. The video spreads like wildfire through the student population here at the academy. Several heads rise to look my way.

Bolting behind the pillar to rejoin Grady, I scan the article, praying I'm not mentioned. My shoulders sag in relief as I reach the end of the short column. There's no hint that Kenneth was involved with a student here. Thank goodness. Daddy would have a conniption if I was linked to this mess any further.

Apparently, the fight between Kenneth and Professor Rook occurred last October, two and a half months before the hit-and-run that killed the professor. The scant information about Kenneth in the article leads me to believe they didn't approach him prior to publication, or he refused to comment.

Smart move, but it won't matter now.

Grady's quick intake of breath makes me look up. He points toward the dormitory entrance, where one of the security guards is escorting two people I recognize down the hall toward us. Detectives Cahill and Gupta. I'm glad to see them, despite the hell they gave my sister about Na's murder last semester. They were only doing their job. Now their job is leading them to Kenneth.

Behind me, the door to the health center opens. Kenneth peers out, face pale and sweaty. "Char, you have to help me," he rasps. "I think the police are coming for me."

"Correction. They've come." I point down the hall.

Kenneth groans as he rakes a hand through his hair. "You have to help me, Char. I didn't kill him, I swear."

My eyebrows rise. There's no way I'm helping him after what just happened. What I discovered. "How can I trust anything you say?"

He rears back as if I've slapped him. Swearing under his breath, Kenneth closes the health center door without another look my way.

I whip around to watch the detectives as they draw closer, leaning to whisper to Grady. He's gone. I don't know where he went. Chicken.

The detectives and security guard draw even with me. One asks me if I've seen Kenneth Alderman.

I nod, pointing to the glass door to the health center. "In there."

Thanking me, they open the door and go inside.

Reeling, I lean back against the wall. It's over.

Although I don't understand why he would have done it, I'm ninety-nine percent sure Kenneth killed Professor Rook. Which means I was dating a man capable of murder. A man who physically attacked me to protect himself. My legs wobble under this revelation. Shaken to the core, I clamp my eyes closed. Trembling hands support me against the wood paneling.

Grunts from inside the health center cut through my swirling thoughts. I peek one eye open, but can't see anything through the frosted glass beyond shadows and flashes of movement.

After a moment, the health center door swings outward, revealing Detectives Cahill and Gupta pushing Kenneth along in front of them. He's handcuffed, the expression in his ice blue eyes primal. Animalistic. Desperate. "Char, you have to help me. I didn't kill him. Please."

Detective Cahill turns to me. "We're going to need to speak to you, Miss Cavendish-Holt. Can you come down to the station after classes today?"

Resolve hardens in the pit of my stomach. It's time to come clean. Tell them anything they want to know. I nod in assent. "See you this afternoon."

"Charlotte. Please! I didn't do it." Kenneth's voice sounds guttural and thready now, as if extracted from him unwillingly.

I watch with a cold expression as the detectives take him away.

31

By the time I'm done talking to the police at the station, I'm exhausted. Wrung out, as if all of the energy has been wrenched from my body. I'd much rather remain here, in this squeaky aluminum chair beside Detective Gupta's desk, but I can't. Despite the bone-deep fatigue I'm feeling, I still have to face the press that are crowded onto the sidewalk outside. A politician's work is never done.

Our family lawyer, Ms. Cain, prepared a statement for me to read that implies my involvement with the investigation without explaining that I was secretly dating the suspect up until a couple of months ago. *Best not to add personal entanglements to the public arena*, Daddy said.

I glance over to where he's standing near the station door, conferring with Ms. Cain in low tones. When he catches my eye, his face changes to a gentle smile. I smile back.

I happen to agree with Daddy about keeping my involvement with Kenneth private, but for other reasons. Daddy's worried about his image in light of his spot on the party's presidential campaign ticket. I'm worried about my dirty laundry being aired in front of the entire world. Everyone knowing I'd been dumped. Whatever. It's not going to get out, so who cares? It's old news. It doesn't sting anymore. Mostly.

"Are you ready, Charlotte?" Daddy's hand is heavy on my shoulder.

Meeting his piercing green eyes, I nod. "I was born ready."

To my surprise, he squeezes my shoulder before letting go. It's nice.

I stand up, fastening the buttons on my wool coat. No faux fur in front of the cameras, because no matter how much I insist it's faux, not everyone believes me. And I do not want to end up splattered with crimson paint by an animal rights fanatic.

Bodyguard Steve pushes open the glass door and the four of us step outside into the blustery, cloudy day.

The press swarm on the sidewalk but don't enter the parking lot, as if they're dogs wearing high frequency collars that prevent them from setting foot on the premises. The frenzy of shouted questions and flashing cameras reminds me more of a pack of dogs salivating over a juicy, meaty bone than it does of the journalists they really are. I shiver, pulling my jacket collar tighter around my neck. Can't leave my jugular exposed when working with the feral creatures.

Working to keep my expression serene, I approach, stopping at a careful distance.

"Miss Cavendish-Holt will take three questions," Ms. Cain says, pointing to one of the journalists. Predicting the questions they would ask was tricky, but together we worked on some responses that should give the media something to analyze to death for the next few hours. Hopefully something more interesting happens before too long, though.

"What is your relationship with Kenneth Alderman?" A woman holds her microphone out toward me to catch my answer.

"I was acquainted with Mr. Alderman this semester when he began working as a medical intern at the health center at school." According to Ms. Cain, Headmistress Morgan insisted we avoid mentioning Brat Academy by name, as if that will prevent any more bad press. Like that'll help. Since the murder last semester, a fair few articles have been written about the safety of our school. In fact, I'm surprised so few students have withdrawn after the months we've had.

"Were you close with Professor Rook? How has his death affected you?" The man who asks shoves his glasses up his nose with one hand before poising his fingers over his phone.

"Professor Rook was a good teacher who didn't deserve to be killed in this manner. I wish his family comfort and support during this time of grieving." Thanks again to my lawyer, I know that the professor is survived by his parents and two older sisters. And although I wasn't a fan of his, I've come to believe that being killed by a car wasn't justice, but the result of pure hatred. Why Kenneth thought he could solve his problems by running the man down, I'll probably never know. I considered asking if I could speak to him, but Ms. Cain preempted my request by stating in no uncertain terms was I to interact with him at all. Ever. She's probably right.

"Last question. Yes, sir," Ms. Cain points to a journalist standing in the back of the pack. He steps forward, greedy eyes fixed on me.

My stomach churns, hoping to get this question over quickly so I can get back to the privacy of school. After the day I've had, there's no way Adrienne can deny me some raspberry cheesecake macarons. Taking a deep, calming breath, I focus on him.

"There are rumors that Professor Rook was selling drugs to students on campus. Is it true that you were a customer of his?"

The resulting clamor from every person on this sidewalk is the stuff of nightmares. Specifically, mine.

No, no, no, no, no. My heart jumps into my throat as I

struggle to keep my composure. God help me, my mouth almost drops open. It's only by the grace of the hundreds of hours I've spent perfecting my politician's smile that I control my features.

Daddy's nostrils flare. His only tell.

Ms. Cain immediately steps forward, holding up a hand. "No comment. No more questions, please. Good day, everyone." She's kind but firm. Exactly what we need right now.

"So this isn't your mint tin with amphetamines inside?" The journalist holds up a photo of a breath mint tin containing three tiny white pills.

My hand rises unbidden toward the photo before I jerk it back.

Daddy flinches. Actually flinches.

Ms. Cain shuts the journalist down with a quick, "No comment," but it doesn't matter.

My mind is racing. The tin in the photo looked just like mine. How did that journalist get that photo? I bite the inside of my cheek to keep from cursing. I should have thrown those stupid pills out when I had the chance. Now those three tiny discs might be enough to end me.

Bodyguard Steve ushers the three of us to the car as the rapid-fire questions of the rabid rabble rise in the air like smoke, choking out all other noise. Pointed, jagged questions prick at my skin, making tiny holes in my armor that threaten to expand. Expose the soft belly of my reputation to the killers behind us.

It doesn't matter that I didn't answer that final, fateful question. The story will be out in a matter of minutes, my hesitation the only corroboration the journalist needs to smear my name to high heaven.

Daddy turns to me as soon as the car turns the first corner. "Drugs? Is that true, Charlotte?"

I squirm under his intense gaze, wishing there was any answer I could give besides the one I'm about to utter. But lying would be fruitless. The confirmation of my unworthiness has already been planted in his mind.

"Yes, it's true. But before you yell at me, please let me explain."

My stepfather's mouth snaps shut as his nostrils flare.

I close my eyes and take a moment to corral my spiderwebbing thoughts. When I open them, I speak. "It's true that I purchased small amounts of amphetamines from Professor Rook, beginning last spring and through last semester. You have to understand, the pressure on me at school to do well in my classes is colossal. As is the pressure I'm under as your daughter to cultivate a certain public image. I'm not trying to blame you. I take full responsibility. But sometimes, I just needed a little boost of energy to get my work done. That's all. I'm not addicted to them or anything. I haven't actually taken any of the pills since early last semester."

In the front seat, Ms. Cain is taking notes in her phone.

Daddy exhales through his nose. "Then why did you still have them in your possession?"

Heat fills my cheeks. "I kept them just in case. Kind of like a safety net, even though I knew I'd never use them. I thought they were still in my desk drawer. I don't know how that journalist got that photo."

"Check your desk as soon as we arrive at the academy. If the tin is still there, dispose of it immediately." Ms. Cain waits for me to meet her gaze before nodding decisively.

"Yes, ma'am."

Daddy turns toward the window, muttering to himself.

Something about "trouble" and "Cal."

Hard rocks form in my gut. Probably he's comparing me to my squeaky clean brother, whose only crime thus far is sneaking off campus for art classes. And possibly a morbid taste in subjects, if the piece he did of his ex-girlfriend as a bleeding vampire is any indication.

A warm hand settles over where mine are clenched in my lap, startling me. "Should I take you to an addiction specialist? Do you need medical treatment?" The softness of Daddy's voice colors the inadequacy churning through my veins and dyes it a deep, bloody red. The color of guilt.

I shake my head. "No, I'm fine. Really."

He nods, squeezing my hands lightly before turning his attention to his phone.

My eyes find the window, watching as leaves are carried away by the wind, forming miniature tornadoes along the curb. They're an adequate picture of the chaos that is my life.

As the car's tires consume the street, taking us ever closer to the academy, my resolve crystallizes. Somehow I will weather this unfortunate situation. I'll win the internship Daddy is offering, and I'll prove my worth. Once and for all.

<h1 style="text-align:center">32</h1>

I stand in the doorway watching as the black luxury sedan pulls away from the curb with my sister and brother inside, accompanying my parents to their black tie fundraiser this evening. Adrienne looked fantastic in the dress she borrowed from Gul, and thanks to me her makeup was perfectly elegant. Cal looked suitably miserable at being required to attend Daddy's event, as usual. But the dull, jabbing pain behind my sternum won't abate. As the distance grows between us, it sharpens, as if a large-gauge needle were being pushed into my chest cavity.

I know the reason I'm being excluded from tonight's event. After everything that happened yesterday at the station, and today, my evisceration via one journalist's questions, I'm being benched. Daddy doesn't want me standing next to him as he schmoozes potential donors to his campaign. For the first time, I'm a liability. My appetite, which before was roaring to be sated, has been sufficiently murdered by my stepfather's tactful dismissal. *I thought you'd want a night to rest,* he'd said. If only that were the real reason I was being left here alone.

The politician in me understands this move. It's not personal; it's politics. Distance between us prevents his clean hands from being stained by his "wild" daughter's apparent drug use. It was my choice to purchase and ingest those tiny white pills, after all. I knew the potential consequences, but I did it anyway.

The daughter in me? She's a wailing little girl, curled into the fetal position as wrenching sobs convulse her body. Tears threaten, but I refuse to succumb in the middle of the dormitory doorway, where anyone could see me. Pinching the bridge of my nose to stem the rising tide, I trudge up the stairs to my room. At least I'll have a few hours alone to lick my wounds.

But no.

Ricardo is waiting outside my door when I get to my dorm room. At the sight of me coming up the stairs carrying my killer heels in one hand, he pushes off the wall and wraps me in his arms. When I stiffen, he pulls away, running his fingers down my sides, looking me over. "Are you okay? Why haven't you left yet?" I know what I have to do, but the unconcealed worry in his eyes is going to make this a lot harder.

Gently, I brush his hands away. "I'm fine. Daddy wasn't pleased, so he made me stay here. But he'll get over it as soon as I win that internship." I hope. I can't entertain any other outcomes, or I might unravel completely. Getting my brand new room key out of my purse, I unlock my door and step inside. I never found my old one, which makes sense. Kenneth probably stole it and broke into my room, stumbling on the tin of pills. He'd know immediately what they were. And at the first chance he got, he probably sold a photo to that journalist.

Maybe it was better Ms. Cain didn't let me talk to my ex. I might have throttled him.

I step into my room, waiting for the Tiffany blue walls and creamy accents to sooth my fraying composure, but there's no serenity awaiting me. Not yet.

Ricardo follows me inside. "You assume you'll win, even though you're up against me? Mon coeur, have some modesty." Tone light, he slings an arm around my shoulders and attempts to pull me into his side.

I evade him. Pull together the scales of my armor so there aren't any gaps. Prepare myself for the coming onslaught.

Ricardo's eyes flash with hurt at my rebuff, but he doesn't move to touch me again. Probably for the best. "What's wrong?"

"Nothing. And you won't be here. You'll be in Haiti with your mom."

He shakes his head. "I'll be… What? I will not. I told my mom yesterday that I'm not going."

So that's where he was when I tried to call him from the car on the way to the police station. Well, good for him.

"Why not? You should." My tone is cold, detached. But inside I'm a flame, razing the foundation of our relationship until it's nothing but charred ash and dying embers. If I'm going to focus on repairing my reputation, the way Daddy sees me, it has to be this way. No distractions, even ones I desperately want to indulge in.

Ricardo runs a hand through those downy curls. "No, I shouldn't. I don't know why you're saying this, but you don't mean it. You trust me." The question is clear.

Do I trust him, really? *Yes.* After everything that has happened to Ricardo and me this semester, I know deep down that he'll always have my back. Won't betray me. Unlike most everyone around me, Ricardo sees me. A high-strung, control freak, perfectionist who never lets her hair down unless she's dared to do it. A girl who works furiously and loves deeply, despite my aloof manner. He sees me, and cares for me.

And yet…

"No, I don't. Not really. How can I? Freshman year, you let me kiss you, and then you didn't talk to me again. You'd already gotten what you wanted."

Ricardo blanches. "Is that what you think? That after *you kissed me*, I—look, that first day, when you kissed me, I was ecstatic. I thought the most beautiful girl at the academy was choosing me, out of all the spoiled peacocks that strut around this school. Then I find out that you're Senator Holt's daughter. The guy who's made his career on immigration reform. You're telling me you didn't kiss me because it was exciting? The idea of being with someone who wasn't an American?"

My expression hardens. He has no idea what he's talking about. There was not an iota of allure in kissing him because he was from a different country. It was because the moment I saw him, I knew. I knew we would be great together. But I can't dwell on that now. "Last year, you toyed with Genevieve for much longer, and look how that turned out?"

Ricardo startles, anger flashing in his eyes. "Are you serious? This is what you're using to break up with me? After everything? I lied to the police for you, Charlotte. I tampered with the security footage. No matter that you're innocent. You know what would happen to me if anyone found out what I've done? And still you don't trust me? I don't believe this. I was knocked unconscious by your ex-boyfriend, for crying out loud. What kind of player would stick with a girl after something like that, unless he..." He breaks off, scrubbing a hand over his face. "Mon dieu, Charlotte. Can't you see it? I love you."

My entire body goes up in searing flames. He *loves* me?

Everything in me aches to run to him and throw my arms around him. Let the soothing balm of his kiss quench the flames licking at my heart. Let him know that not only do I trust him, he makes me happy. I want to make him happy too. But one more time I deny myself. I can't do this right now. I can't afford to be preoccupied, not when my relationship with

Daddy is in jeopardy. My plans for my future as president of the United States.

I don't know when I began, but I'm shaking my head. Holding back a torrent of tears, which I will never let him see. Never tell. Instead, I let my silence speak for me. Ricardo can make whatever assumptions he needs to leave me.

A hush settles between us as our harsh words sink to the floor like jagged shards of broken glass. Glittering in their dark capacity to lacerate vulnerable hearts. The crackle of energy is doused, leaving me chilled to the bone.

Ricardo's chin comes up. "If you're going to be that way, maybe you're right. Maybe I will go to Haiti with my mom. She at least will look past my crap to see who I've become. She doesn't have a choice, since she missed most of it."

I see you, my heart whispers. His cocky facade for what it is, a shield he uses to keep people at bay. Because deep down, just like me, the question his soul asks is, *am I enough*? But I can't answer that question for him.

I don't move.

Ricardo brushes past, refusing to look at me. Then he's gone, footsteps stomping up the stairs to the boys' floor.

I slam the door shut and bolt it before I change my mind and go careening after him. The silence in my room feels raw and unwelcoming.

A knock on my door makes me jump.

I spin toward it, unable to keep the hope from seeping into my eyes. It's Ricardo, back after our fight to patch things up.

But it's not Ricardo standing in the hallway when I fling the door open—it's Gul.

"What do you want?" I snap, not bothering to tamp down the voltage in my words.

Gul glares at me. "This again? Really? I thought we were becoming…"

"Friends?" I scoff, regretting it immediately. After hearing how lonely Gul is at school, the reason she leaves the dorm to call her mom, how can I be so cruel?

The girl's eyes blink closed, and when she opens them, her composure is set. "Never mind. Let me know when you're done with your Na impression, so we can talk."

It's like she sucker punched me in the mouth. Am I really as mean as the girl who was murdered last semester?

Gul stalks down the hall, not looking back.

After a beat of stunned immobility, I jog after her. "Gul, wait!"

She stops, turns, frowns. "Yes?" she asks through gritted teeth.

I yank my headband out of my perfectly coiffed hair, straightening it. "I'm sorry. That was uncalled for. It's been a long day." Reaching up, I pull the pins out of my blond tresses and shake them out. My scalp tingles at being freed from the chic updo that I slaved over this afternoon. Wasted energy, since I'm here instead of at Daddy's dinner.

Gul's features soften, but only just. "That's no reason to treat me like crap."

My hands drop to my sides, clutching the hair pins. "You're right. And if you still want, I'd like to be friends."

This earns me a tentative smile. "Okay."

Hooking my arm through hers, I draw her back to my room and close the door. "What do you need?"

Her dark lashes fan over her cheeks as she settles herself in the center of the white velvet bench at the foot of my bed. "I was hoping you'd tell me what was going on with Kenneth? Did he kill Professor Rook? Did he attack you and Ricardo and me? If he did, did he say why? I haven't done anything to him."

I open my mouth to speak, then close it. I have no idea why Kenneth would try to poison Gul. Now that I think about it, the knot that formed in my stomach when I confronted Kenneth hasn't loosened. Kenneth is behind bars, unable to hurt anyone else. So why do I still feel so uneasy? "I honestly don't know. Maybe he wanted to frame me for it? I don't know—"

Gul's hair falls forward over her shoulders as she pulls at a string at the hem of her blouse.

The sympathy in her gaze convinces me that she understands. The pressures we're under as the daughters of high-profile politicians. Hell, she lies to her mom every time they talk for that very reason. It never occurred to me before, but Gul might be a kindred spirit. Like Genevieve. Adrienne. Ricardo.

A knife twists in my stomach.

I punt the welling hurt away and focus on my new friend. "I don't know why he did it, but you don't have to worry about him anymore. Between the information I gave the police about Kenneth today and everything they'd already gathered, he won't be bothering anyone for a long time. Let's put it behind us, okay?"

Her smile widens. "I can do that." She stands and wanders toward my door before looking back at me. "Want to play another game of truth or dare? I bet I could round up some people to make it interesting."

My fingers tap on my knees. "Tempting, but I need some alone time. Rain check?"

With a nod, she leaves me alone.

As soon as my door latches, I fling myself on my bed to go over today. And maybe to mope, just a little bit.

My boyfriend said he *loves* me, and I pushed him away. Essentially broke up with him. More than anything I wish I could have answered Ricardo. Told him how I feel in return. Even though I've never said those words to a boy before.

And with my track record, it makes sense.

My one serious ex-boyfriend is a murderer.

Gul's questions churn in my thoughts. Why did Kenneth attack her? The idea that he was trying to frame me isn't sitting right. He has no motive, really, because at that point there wasn't any heat on him. The spotlight came later.

There's something niggling at my consciousness, something I'm missing, but I can't grasp it. Every time I think I get close, it dissolves into thin air.

The decor around my room is only a distraction. Framed photos of my family and friends smile at me from my desk and dresser. Make my thoughts jump ad nauseam from Kenneth to Ricardo to Daddy's dinner tonight.

I can't focus here. I need a change of scenery.

Maybe then the sheer weight of the knots in my stomach will lighten.

33

The view from the roof is unobscured. Violet streaks slash over the darkening expanse as the sun retreats behind the horizon. Frigid air rakes over me, cutting through the flimsy fabric of my blouse, making me wish I'd brought my jacket. Bracing my arms around my torso, I step out onto the roof and move briskly toward the darkened greenhouse. Soon the day's light will give way to a milky purple over the academy.

It was sheer luck that someone called my bodygyard a minute ago, distracting him so I could slip away. I need a few minutes alone.

Relieved that the glass structure is unoccupied, I step inside. My chaotic mind craves the quiet of the greenhouse. The earthy scent of moist potting soil. Greenery brushing against my arms. Turning on the interior lights reveals the metal frame in stark angles.

Warm, humid air wraps around me, cutting off the chill that moments ago caressed my skin. Despite the warmth, my arms are pebbled with goosebumps. The unsettled feeling in my belly simply won't go away. I thought leaving the confines of my room would help, but it hasn't.

Walking slowly down the rows of plants, I stop to study the various growing projects in progress. Botany never really interested me, but I need something to occupy my mind, or I'll spend all night beating myself up for not realizing Kenneth was a psycho.

If he did any poking around the student files in the health center, he would know about Gul's allergy to peanuts. It would be easy to get ahold of a small amount of peanut oil and put it in her food. He stood next to her in the buffet line at my birthday party, and she was busy whispering with Grady as they got their food. Probably about what a loser I was for inviting my ex-boyfriend to my party.

It was stupid. It almost resulted in another death. When will my actions stop causing hurt to everyone around me?

Moving to the next project, I study the glass cloches covering each of the small plants. Each one is surrounded by a ring of a different substance. Fertilizers. Coffee grounds. Ice.

"Didn't think I'd find you here." Grady's voice makes me jump and spin around to face him. A hint of amusement lifts his lips. He picks his way toward me, careful not to upset any of the plants whose leaves hang over the edges of the long, weathered wood benches.

I take an uneven breath, trying to present a calm demeanor. "I needed a change of scenery. You know?"

Grady's head bobs. "How're you doing? With Kenneth being arrested?"

"It's hard to believe, actually, but I'll be okay."

"You always seem to have everything under control." His eyes dart up to mine before moving away.

Surprised, a loud laugh bursts from my throat. "You don't know what you're talking about. I'm barely hanging on. My Daddy is disappointed with me, Ricardo is leaving for Haiti, and Adrienne and Genevieve are busy with their boyfriends. I'm afraid all you see is a carefully constructed mask. Underneath, I'm just a girl."

"You are definitely not just a girl." The faint snarl on the last word catches my ear. My eyes turn to his. They're dark.

Inscrutable.

The hairs on my arms stand up, but when he speaks again, his voice is even, calm. I must have imagined the flash of anger I heard in his words.

Grady's attention shifts to the covered plants in front of us. "Looking at my project?"

Rolling my shoulders back to soothe myself, I put a hand on the nearest cloche. "This one's yours? What are the coffee grounds for?"

"Studying the effects different substances have on plant growth. Pretty basic, but still interesting." He runs his fingers over the glass domes, eyes locked on his plants. Then he looks at me.

I avoid his gaze, unsure what to do with the knot of unease tightening in my chest. "What's the ice for? Watering as it melts?"

"Does it look like regular ice to you?" He points.

Now that he's pointed it out, the ice doesn't look normal. White vapor rises from it, swirling in the cloche. It almost looks like…

A balled up plastic bag pokes up from behind the bench. Leaning forward, I try to read the label. It's dry ice.

Wait.

My mind flashes back to Ricardo unconscious on the floor. Eyes shut. Lips turning blue. Bodyguard Steve found a bag of dry ice in the AC vent that night. Bile rises in my throat.

Grady leans a hand on the edge of the wood bench, effectively barring me from the exit.

A chill slides down my spine. Did he do that on purpose? "Grady…"

"Yeah?" He leans forward, crowding his lithe frame into my personal space.

I take a step back.

He doesn't move.

"When you said I wasn't just a girl, what did you—?" My throat dries at the black look in his eyes. I never knew blue eyes could be so cold. Cruel. Shut off.

"I think you know, Charlotte." He advances toward me.

In a flash, everything clicks. This entire thing wasn't about Professor Rook. It was about Rhiannon. Grady's ex-girlfriend.

Grady's expression is ominous. Shoulders hunched. Jaw squared in determination. "Professor Rook sold her the drugs. So I ended him."

"But… You weren't even back from Austin yet." As slowly as I can, I skim my hand along the bench behind me, grasping for anything to use as a weapon. My fingers come away empty, dusted with potting soil.

Grady's hair brushes his brow as he shakes his head. "Come on, blondie. Ever heard of a private jet?"

My chest constricts. I have, actually, but Daddy doesn't use them because of his "of the people" persona. No. When we fly somewhere we fly business class. I kind of admire him for it, and also find it irksome. I've seen those coach seats, and they look *nice*. But now is not the time to dwell on that.

Grady's eyes slice through me like a hot scoop through cold ice cream. "Once I had Rook out of the way, I focused on the next target—Gul. I figured she spread those rumors about Rhiannon that got back to her folks. They didn't let her come back to school this year. And then there's you."

Me? I'm the one who told Rhiannon to go to the professor in the first place. I was right to blame myself. And from the menacing look on Grady's face, he does too. I lick my lips. I have to stall. Or I'll be victim number three. "Did you see Gul on your way out here? She was supposed to meet me."

Grady's smile curls further into a sneer. Dark pools shade his deep set eyes. When he speaks, his voice is transformed. Infused with venom. "You're such a liar. She's not coming. I already took care of that loose-lipped cow."

The anxiety that had lit in my belly grows into full-blown panic. Cold sweat makes my palms go clammy. "What did you do to her?"

Without taking his eyes off me, Grady reaches across the wooden bench and tugs at the plastic dry ice bag. It drags against the back edge of the bench as it comes free. "Doesn't take long to suffocate someone. Had to do it to my hamster once, after it had a stroke. Turns out, people look a lot like that when they die. Bulging eyes. Clawing breaths."

My eyes run over his arms, looking for signs of a fight. There's nothing.

Grady's got a long-sleeve black shirt on under his Dallas jersey. A white star against a silver background. The star snags at something in my memory, bringing it to the surface. A white star reflected in a pane of glass. "The video of Kenneth and Professor Rook. You took it, didn't you?"

He taps a finger to his temple. Brandishes the bag with the other. "Two down, one to go."

Professor Rook and Gul. Dead. I'm next.

Gulp.

"You don't have to do this. I won't tell anyone what you did. Kenneth will go down for it. All of it."

Grady rolls his eyes. "This ain't about justice."

"So he's innocent, then?" Despite the peril of my situation, I have to know. Was my gut completely wrong about Kenneth? Or just a little off?

The boy eyes me. "Don't know. Wasn't me who gave you those shiners that time, though. Wanted to thank whoever it was, but didn't get the chance."

So it *was* Kenneth who attacked me earlier this semester. Everything else? The perpetrator is glaring right at me. "This is wrong. It isn't justice."

Grady's laugh is short, harsh. "It's revenge. Rhiannon didn't deserve what y'all did to her. She never would've taken pills if you hadn't given her a shove." He looms toward me. Calculating fingers grazing the bench edges as he comes.

I scuttle backward, eyes scanning for a way out. If I can just reach the end of the aisle, then maybe I can bolt down the next one.

Grady charges, lowering his shoulder to plow through me.

My heart skitters. Tripping over a watering line, I tumble butt first toward the gravel floor. My fingernails scrape the table edge. Splinters bite into my fingertips. I land in moist, heady earth. Clenching my fists, I fling the dirt into Grady's eyes.

"Argh!" He rears back, pawing at his eyes. "You bitch."

I don't give him another shot at ending me. I'm up in a single second. Rounding the center bench and powering up the other aisle. Eyes locked on the exit door. Hands outstretched.

A bellow cuts through the air as something heavy smashing into the side of my head. Dirt rains down the front of my dress. Stars cloud my vision as the pain radiates through my skull and down my neck. I have to… I'm so close… But I can't focus on anything but the waves pummeling my brain.

Rough arms grab me from behind, locking around my waist and cutting off my air. "Got you." Grady's hot breath rushes over my neck, making my stomach lurch.

I try to focus on the self-defense training I got, but it flies out of my head when the dry ice bag is thrust down over my head. I can't smell it, but I know there's CO2 in the bag.

Enough to kill me?

I thrash. Kick. Elbow. Fight with everything I've got.

It's not enough.

The bag tightens around my neck, cutting into the skin below my jaw. "No!" The scream rings in my ears as I claw at the heavy-duty plastic. Trying to make holes so I can breathe.

My lungs keep fighting. Rise. Fall. Burn. I'm running out of oxygen.

34

A cold wind slaps my calves, jerking me awake. My eyes focus, and immediately snap shut again. I'm staring five storeys down to the brown, withered grass of the shadowed academy courtyard. The trees lash back and forth in the wind. The few remaining leaves are flung mercilessly, their brittle edges scraping the ground. Not a single person is down there to see me. To call for help.

Grady is holding me over the edge of the building. His biting hands clutch my waist. Fingertips dig into my skin. The scrolled lip of the roofline cuts into my stomach. My skin scrapes until it's raw. The icy current lashes my skirt against my legs. Goosebumps line my flesh.

The bag is still over my head, but Grady's fingers are no longer choking off my air supply. I take in a gulp of air. Flimsy plastic sucks inward toward my mouth. I stop it with one hand. Fight down the panic. The flailing makes my torso wobble over the concrete edge. I scramble with both hands, searching for something to grip. Anything.

"Awake, eh? Ready for your last flight?"

"Grady, don't do this." My mouth is muffled by the bag. My feet scramble over the flat roof, my steps uneven. I've lost one of my shoes. Rough tar digs into tender skin of my toes.

"Have to. I'm fixing to finish what I started. Rhiannon deserves justice, and I'm gonna give it to her."

My fingers wrap around a piece of decorative trim. A

handhold. I push up with all my might. Arms straining against gravity. A powerful groan cuts through the quiet. My heart leaps before I realize the soul-shaking sound came from me.

Grady slams my abdomen down over the decorative stone, forcing the breath from my chest.

My lungs work feverishly to puff out my chest in an even rhythm. I can't stop gasping. My eyes lock on the ground five storeys below. Gentle hills covered in dead, beige grass and dotted with naked, spooky trees. A worn cobblestone walkway. If I fall from this far up, what are the odds I'll survive? My stomach clenches as fear flows from my core through my entire being. My heart skitters around my rib cage, making my thoughts fuzzy.

"Charlotte?"

The familiar voice is like a light in the darkness. Relief floods me. But only for a moment.

Grady stills at Ricardo's call. Leaning forward, he hauls me a few inches farther over the edge. "Stay quiet, or I'll make this slow and painful."

It's already too slow and too painful.

Footsteps approach, and the greenhouse door opens.

Frozen in place, I weigh my options. Stay still and hope I can overcome Grady on my own. Fight and scream and hope Ricardo gets here before Grady can finish pitching me over the edge.

Rearing up again, I twist in an attempt to see where Ricardo is. I can't see anything on the roof because of the angle Grady's forcing my body into, but the greenhouse must be blocking Ricardo's view of us. Otherwise he'd already have Grady on the ground. I know it with everything in me.

Grady stops my backward arching, shoving me down once more with a forearm across my back. His scorching, rank breath hits my skin, making revulsion roil in my throat.

The greenhouse light flicks on. Grady must have turned it off after he knocked me out.

"Char? I found your shoe. I know you're up here somewhere. Gul told me where you were heading. Please talk to me."

Surprise and relief hit me at once. Gul's still alive!

Grady curses low. Harsh fingers dimple my flesh. Leaving marks of his anger on my skin.

Adrenaline shoots through my veins as I struggle against my attacker. Kick my legs. Pinwheel my arms. With renewed energy, I scream. "Ricardo! Help!"

Grady's blunt arms wrap around my waist. With a heave, he lifts me up, suspending me over the edge of the building. His long arms are surprisingly strong, but I'm already slipping through his grasp. He won't be able to keep this hold on me for more than a few seconds.

My arms hang below me, fingers splayed. If I fall now, it's over. Everything I worked for will be erased. I'll be just one more fatality at the academy. Notable only in my death.

An image of myself lying still on the pavement below flashes through my mind's eye like a premonition. This is it. I'm going to die.

With the realization comes a moment of clarity. I'm not going down without a hell of a fight. Bellowing, I kick out my legs. Reach.

Just as Grady lets go, I lock my legs around his waist. He yells in fear as his added weight propels us over the side of the academy.

"No!" Ricardo shouts from a few feet away.

Grady and I fall. Spin through the air as we both scramble. Try to grab onto the side of the building. But we're too far from the intricate facade to grasp it. Darkened windows gape as we plummet toward the ground and almost certain death.

Blood rushes through my ears, blocking out all other noise.

Grady slips from between my ankles, screaming. His face distorted in terror.

With immense effort, I reach out and take hold of the front of Grady's shirt.

We crash through the naked boughs of the nearest tree, its brittle limbs tugging at my clothes and scraping red traces into my skin. My wrist slams against a thicker branch with a crack, and pain shoots along my arm.

The hard, frozen ground meets us with a crunch as we smash into one of the bushes. Twigs snap and scratch over me like needle-sharp claws, igniting my skin with a dull burn.

My attacker lies underneath me, splayed out over the flattened center of the shrubbery. His eyes are shut and one of his legs is bent at a sickening angle, but he's still breathing.

Gasping, I try to catch a breath, but all of the air has whooshed out of my chest. It's as if a weight is compressing my chest, rendering my lungs unable to expand.

As soon as I get a gulp of air, I recoil. Scrambling off him and away, afraid he'll lunge at me like the villain in a horror movie. My heart batters my ribs, but I can't peel my eyes off the unmoving form sprawled over the ground. Pain lances up my arm. One of my wrists feels like it's been shot through with a nail gun, but my legs feel okay.

My chest heaves a sob. It's over. It takes every ounce of strength I have left not to keel over into the grass.

"Charlotte!" Ricardo's yell from above makes me jump and swivel around to look upward. I drag an arm across my eyes.

He's there, leaning over the side of the building. A familiar shape in the dark. "Are you okay? How about Grady?" The questions come out strangled.

"I think I'm okay." My voice cracks. I prod at Grady with one foot, but he doesn't so much as flinch. Wincing, I crab-walk further away and collapse on the shards of dormant grass. My entire body is heaving with the force of what's just happened, and my mind is whirling so fast it's being scrambled.

"I'm coming," Ricardo calls. "Don't move." A door slams shut.

Little chance of me going anywhere. I don't think I could get up even if I wanted to. Instead, I stay there: arms around my knees. I'm shaking so bad my bones are chattering. The neat twist I'd put my hair in earlier hangs sloppily off to one side of my head. It's a tangled mess of pins.

Nearby, sirens slash through the silent winter night. Please, please let them be coming for me.

Grady's still form draws my gaze like a magnet. The wind catches his hair and it floats above his head like seaweed in the deep. His chest continues to rise and fall in jagged, uneven pants.

I exhale loudly and watch as my breath wafts upward in a puff of swirling steam.

The door to the courtyard is flung open with a slam, and Ricardo sprints toward me over the grass. Collapsing on his knees he enfolds me in his arms. His heart beats a frenzied, uneven rhythm into my back. Shuffling around on his hands, he pulls on my arm, encouraging me to unfold from my little ball. I comply, and he looks me over from head to toe, his hands gentle on my elbows and knees. "Charlotte, mon coeur. Are you hurt? Anything broken?"

"I think my wrist is broken." I hold out the arm that is

radiating pain.

Taking a gentle hold of my forearm, he presses a kiss to the back of my hand, like my mother used to do when I got cuts and scrapes as a little kid. My heart squeezes, not unpleasantly this time.

Ricardo glances over my shoulder at Grady, and then his eyes fix on me. "My heart stopped when I saw you fall off that roof. I thought…" The devastation in his face does things to me. I put up a valiant fight, biting my tongue to keep from crying, but the tide won't ebb. The boy looking at me won't think less of me if he sees me crying. No, instead I have a sneaking suspicion it will make him like me even more. But the simple truth is I can't hold it in anymore. Not sure I even want to. With a shudder, I let go. "Grady killed Professor Rook. And tried to kill you and Gul," I whisper through my tears.

Understanding lights his eyes. "For Rhiannon."

I nod, unable to speak.

"It's over now," he whispers, dragging me into his lap until my side is pressed against his chest. His arms tighten around me as I bury my face in the front of his shirt. There's a gentle press of a kiss on the top of my head. Faint words carry on the breeze. "Je t'aime, mon coeur."

Sniffing, I look up into his eyes, not sure I heard what he just said correctly.

"You still…?" I whisper, hardly believing it.

Tightening his arms around me, he nods. "Je t'aime, Charlotte."

I have to give him something in return. Not because he expects it, but because I'm beginning to see that that's what love is. A give and take between two people who care about each other so much it drives them to study each other, serve each other. Make each other happy in a bunch of little ways.

Big ones too. "You asked me why I kissed you, our first day of school?"

He nods, staring into my eyes.

"It was… I wanted to… You were the most beautiful boy I'd ever seen, and you had this aura about you. You were so enthusiastic about being at the academy. So earnest. And I knew that we could be great together, if I just let you in. I wanted to see what it would be like."

"So you kissed me."

I bite my lip. "Was that wrong?"

His face splits in a devastating smile. "You can kiss me anytime you want, mon coeur."

"Ricardo?"

He inclines his head. "You're in love with me too? It's about time you admitted it, woman."

"Shut up. And yes."

"Yes, what?" Ricardo's eyes glint as he teases me.

Taking a deep breath, I wrap my arms around his torso and press my face into the folds of his shirt. "I love you too."

A quiver runs through his body. A sigh. A breath he was holding in, waiting for my response. Pressing my cheek against his chest, I exhale as his warmth washes through me.

"Just try not to fall off any more roofs, okay?" He breathes into my hair.

"I did not fall! I was pushed. There's a difference."

"All the same… Now that you've solved Professor Rook's murder, maybe you should turn your attention to something else you're passionate about. Something preferably much safer."

"Politics?"

His warm laugh rumbles across the silent courtyard. And then he's singing. It's a low, quiet sound. One of my favorite songs. Singing for me. Just like I always dreamed someone would. Peace ripples through me as Ricardo's voice fills the quiet.

Neither of us moves until the firefighters come rushing into the courtyard.

35

I'm sitting in the ambulance being checked over when my parents' sedan pulls into the parking lot. Daddy doesn't even bother to park properly before he and my mom fly out of the vehicle and dash toward us, faces drawn in worry. Blowing past Cal, Adrienne, Mikhail, Genevieve, and Ricardo, they reach the ambulance.

Brushing off the EMT's hand on my shoulder, I stand. "I'm okay, really. I just—"

Cutting off my explanation, they pull me into a hug so tight I can barely move. It's heaven.

Over my head, Daddy asks a question. "She fell off the roof? How is that even possible?"

"Ask questions later, Terrance. Let's let the nice man finish looking her over first." Mom reluctantly lets go of me, but I don't submit to the EMT's gesture to retake my seat.

Instead, I look up at Daddy. "I have to say something first."

He's never looked so scared as he does in this moment, standing in front of me in a rumpled t-shirt, sweats, and his house slippers. "Go ahead, princess."

The nickname catches me off guard. He hasn't called me that in years. Its use dredges up old frustrations. The hairs on my arms bristle. "Okay, first, please don't call me that. I am not a princess. And second, I resent the fact that you've been grooming Cal as your successor when it's me who wants to be a politician. Let Cal go do art, and train me instead. I know everything about the party platform, government, our constituents. Quiz me and I'll prove it. I'm ready."

Daddy gapes at me, clearly at a loss for what to say.

Clearing his throat, Cal steps forward. "She's right, Dad. The truth is, I hate politics. I'll stand up there and wave when you need the family during your campaign, but all the making contacts and rubbing elbows and crap? No, thanks."

"Oh, thank goodness," Mom says, lowering herself onto the back edge of the ambulance.

It's my turn to stare. "You knew?"

"Of course. I was waiting for you to stand up for yourself. I don't want you to think you have to let me do your fighting for you, Charlotte. You've got enough strength to do it all by yourself."

I wrap my arms around her. "I'll always need you, just not in the same way."

She smiles into my hair as her gentle hands rub over my spine.

Daddy finally finds his voice. Clearing his throat, he puts a hand on my shoulder. "You're telling me you want to follow me into politics? And Cal doesn't?" He blinks as he looks between my brother and me.

I give an emphatic nod while Cal shrugs.

He blinks. "Wow. I had no idea. I wish you'd told me sooner."

"Come on, Daddy. I did everything I could to let you know. I'm constantly asking you questions about the party and your campaign and everything. I'm surprised you didn't get it."

"But you never said."

My eyes widen. He's right. I did everything but verbally tell him I wanted to be a politician. How can I be surprised he didn't know? He's not a mind reader. My lips purse together. "Are you saying that if I told you sooner I wanted to be a politician, you'd have supported me?"

Daddy shakes his head in disbelief. "I'll support you in whatever you want to do, even if I'm dubious as to its efficacy as a career path." It's obviously a reference to Cal's art, and my brother grumbles under his breath.

"I want to be a chef!" Adrienne chimes in, making me laugh.

"Thank you, Captain Obvious," Cal says with half a smile.

"I just want you to be proud of me," I say in a low voice, studying Daddy's face.

His mouth curves up in a smile. "I'm proud of all three of my children. An artist, a chef, and a politician. I've got a designer, caterer, and speech editor built into my little family. What more could I ask for?"

All three of us groan good-naturedly at his feeble joke.

The laugh lines around Daddy's mouth tighten. "But about that tin of drugs…"

I swallow, not sure what he's going to say. "Actually," I interrupt. "I have an idea about how to handle that."

We're gathered in the foyer of the academy. Adrienne, Cal, Ricardo, Genevieve, and Gul. Mikhail stands a few feet away, ready to step outside when we give the signal. Daddy fired Bodyguard Steve for leaving me unattended long enough to be pushed off the academy roof, and is already looking for a replacement.

Through the heavy wooden doors comes the low murmur of the press setting up cameras and microphones. Warming up their voices. Practicing the phrasing of the questions they'll inevitably lob in my direction once Ms. Cain opens the floor for questions.

Gul meets my look, her expression guarded. Grady never woke up after our fall, and it's been hard for her, knowing that he tried to kill her while simultaneously dating her. The wary expression she turns toward Ricardo and Mikhail when they're being sweet to Adrienne and me inclines me to believe that it'll be a while before she trusts another guy. Hopefully she'll speak up if she needs help.

Closing my eyes, I go over what I'm going to say one more time, followed by the responses Ms. Cain and I worked on for the few questions we'll take afterward. None of the journalists outside will catch me off guard this time. Not after Headmistress Morgan found the tin of drugs in Grady's room and confiscated them. I wanted to watch, to make sure the last vestiges of Professor Rook's influence on me were destroyed, but of course the headmistress refused. I should have had Adrienne ask her for me. Then maybe she would've consented.

My mom wraps me in at least the third or fourth tight hug she's given me this morning. Relief shines in her blue eyes. "Sorry. I don't want to wrinkle you, but I can't seem to help myself."

I laugh, thankful she's here with me. Daddy too. He puts a hand on my shoulder, drawing my attention up to his face. "I'm so proud of you, Charlotte. That's one heck of a speech you wrote."

I grin. I'm pretty proud of it too.

Mrs. LaGuerre comes in, and Ricardo winks at me before turning to his mom. They talk in low voices, smiling. At my urging, he's going home to Haiti this summer to spend time with her. I'll miss him, but we've already arranged for my siblings and I to fly down for a visit midway through the break. It's going to be awesome.

A tap on my shoulder draws me around to face Ricardo. "You ready?" He grins down at me.

"If Robbie Duncan Jr. can come back from his stint in jail to become a worldwide star, I can overcome poor-quality photo of alleged drugs."

"I don't think that's his name, but I know what you mean. You're going to be great." With a glance over my shoulder at my parents, he tugs on my hand to pull me into him.

I go willingly, wrapping my arms around his neck.

Inhaling deeply as if breathing me in, he drops his face toward mine. Fingers wrap in my ponytail and give the smallest of tugs. Warmth pools in my chest. "Ricardo," I warn, low enough that no one can hear me.

"Just one tiny kiss? For luck?"

The corner of my mouth lifts. "Just one. And it had better be good."

That's all the encouragement he needs to press his mouth to mine. Sparks shoot through my veins as he kisses me. It's the slow, assured brush of someone who knows where he stands. I love it. Kissing Ricardo is like what I imagine flying to feel like. Soaring high over the pink-streaked sky as my fingers skim cotton candy clouds.

"Char," Adrienne taps on my arm, making me pull away from Ricardo.

Daddy's got an eyebrow raised at my unabashed display.

"What? I needed a good luck kiss, didn't I?"

Daddy shakes his head, but there's a trace of amusement in his eyes.

Ricardo beams as he snakes an arm around my waist. After a quick peck on my temple, he withdraws. "I'll be right here, mon coeur. Maybe we can go get some ice cream after."

"It's way too cold for ice cream," I protest, but

halfheartedly. I'd eat ice cream with Ricardo any time and in any weather. He'll be happy to warm me up afterward.

Ms. Cain peeks out the front door before nodding to us. It's time.

Straightening my shoulders, I walk toward her, grateful to have my loved ones at my back. In a few minutes, I'll have delivered my speech. Admitted to a youthful indiscretion. Asked for forgiveness. And plugged Daddy's candidacy too.

My skin stretches and pulls as I move, sore from my ordeal last night. The bruises reminders of everything I've been through over the past eight months. All of it was in preparation for today. My first morning in the light. Because once I deliver this speech, I won't just be a high school girl who solved a murder. I'll be Charlotte Cavendish-Holt, future politician. Maybe even future president.

Acknowledgments

As with every book I write (I can't believe this is my tenth!), there are many people to thank. Many minds go into the completion of each book.

First, to Madeline Dyer, Suzanne Lazear, Mocha Von Bee, and Carmen Norris for reading various drafts of this story and giving insight that helped me make it the best I can: thank you. Your contributions are invaluable.

Thanks go to Christina Kobel, the best plot hole sounding board and hyphen expert a writer could ask for.

To the Write Bitches, who give the encouragement I need to keep writing, even on the days when all I want to do is bake something, you ladies rock!

Lastly, to my husband, Adam, and my two girls. I could not do this without all of your love and support. Thank you for giving me the space I needed to write a book while holed up in the office. Thank you for celebrating my successes and joining me to mourn my failures. I think I probably owe you a delicious dessert right about now.

About the Author

Emily lives in sunny Southern California with her husband and daughters. She started writing in elementary school and continued writing in college, where she earned a degree in creative writing. She often gets ideas for stories from the lives of her friends and family. When she's not writing, she enjoys cuddling with her two dachshunds Nestlé and Kiefer, crocheting, watching television, and enjoying the sunshine with her daughters and their flock of backyard chickens.

To learn more about Emily, visit her website: www.emilykazmierski.com